EVERYONE PAYS

ALSO BY SETH HARWOOD

Jess Harding

In Broad Daylight

Jack Palms

Jack Wakes Up

This Is Life

Young Junius

Triad Death Match

Stories

A Long Way from Disney

Fisher Cat & Other Stories

EVERYONE PAYS

SETH HARWOOD

THOMAS & MERCER

This is a work of fiction. Names, characters, organizations, places, events, and incidents are either products of the author's imagination or are used fictitiously.

Text copyright © 2016 by Seth Harwood
All rights reserved.

No part of this book may be reproduced, or stored in a retrieval system, or transmitted in any form or by any means, electronic, mechanical, photocopying, recording, or otherwise, without express written permission of the publisher.

Published by Thomas & Mercer, Seattle

www.apub.com

Amazon, the Amazon logo, and Thomas & Mercer are trademarks of Amazon.com, Inc., or its affiliates.

ISBN-13: 9781503935143
ISBN-10: 1503935140

Cover design by Christian Fuenfhausen Design.

Printed in the United States of America

For Kelly

"Wash me throughly from my wickedness and cleanse me from my sin. For I acknowledge my faults and my sin is ever before me."

—Psalm 51, *Book of Common Prayer*

john (noun): "A prostitute's client. Origin early 20th century . . . from the given name John, used from late Middle English as a form of address to a man, or to denote various occupations, including that of priest (late Middle English) and policeman (mid 17th century)."

—*New Oxford American Dictionary*

PROLOGUE

It wasn't enough that she was with me. What woke me at three in the morning were her sins. Original and then some.

She had been with men. Her secrets—what they did to her, the things she had endured—I knew they were hidden. The scars I could see. The secrets I couldn't.

What they did to her body.

I listened to her breathe as she slept, the subtle wheeze of her rest, until I couldn't stand it any longer. I got up, felt the cold stone floor under my feet, poured water for coffee.

The window let in a damp breeze from the rain, so I tucked her in tight.

Outside, all was dark. The street above our basement room was quiet, for the time being.

During the day I hear confessions, save souls.

But I did things in my past that would shame a heathen. All the atoning in the world wouldn't save me.

Then she came to me, the innocent I might still save.

I saved her body, not her soul. Treated her and nursed her back to health. Protected her.

But her soul wasn't clean yet, wasn't ready to greet Him. Not yet. All she had done needed cleansing. Erasing. The things she did. The men who did them to her. I would work back through these sins, start where they began.

These men needed to be brought to Him. To judgment. Only in this way could she be absolved.

First, the men.

I started with two names.

PART ONE
SUNDAY TO TUESDAY

CHAPTER ONE
DONNER

Our first call of the week took us to a man's apartment in the Marina—not the nicest place on the block, even a little on the small side, but that had no bearing on the extent of what we found.

The building was a four-story walk-up with the victim's place on the third. Small black-and-white squares tiled the downstairs hall, reminding me of the floors in lower Manhattan buildings where I'd grown up.

I climbed the stairs with Hendricks behind me, neither of us dragging. It was only our first day on call.

When we arrived at the apartment, uniformed officers in blue stepped aside to clear our path. I could see by their eyes that they were ready to turn this one over, get as far away from the scene as they could. A rookie I didn't recognize gave me a double take, confused about a woman working homicide, thinking I shouldn't walk into this kind of mess.

Or maybe he could tell I didn't mind and that's what caused his confusion.

And I didn't mind. It was my job.

I was a homicide investigator like my father before me. Just on the other coast. It would have driven him mad to see a woman working these cases, and maybe that's why I got involved. At first.

Now I wouldn't give this up for the world.

As we walked in, my favorite medical examiner met us in the hallway: Dr. Marlene Ibaka, who always wore a smile, even in the worst situations. This was that rare occasion when she didn't.

We all have our weaknesses, the things that get to us.

God knows I have mine.

"Guy has his own dungeon in here, Donner. A real sleazebag." She pointed at a bookcase just inside the entry. "You'll want to check out this vic's pics."

I found myself facing a shelf of Polaroids featuring skinny young blondes tied up and mostly nude or in various states of undress. A few had fresh cuts, blood dripping.

Bondage, S&M, torture: these could be bought in San Francisco like bread and milk. The Rice-A-Roni of the streets.

Hendricks leaned in over my shoulder. "Lovely citizen we got here, Donner. The kind of turd you like to bag and tag."

"Careful," I said.

He was right: the guy who lived here, our victim in this case, was the kind of perp I loved to take down during my four years on vice. Now homicide put me on the other side of the line, investigating his killer, walking into a job I might have fantasized about doing myself. But I couldn't talk about that here, not even as a joke.

"One pic is missing," I said. There was a gap in the middle of the shelf, just the right size for another photo.

"Already in my notes," Ibaka said. "Come on. You got to see this."

She led us off the hall into a side office that had been fitted with pads covering the walls and floor. A padded cell, his dungeon. No windows. One wall had handcuffs mounted high, medium, and low. The high ones had held the wrists of the women in his photos. With their arms raised, they'd have barely toed the floor.

Thick black blood pooled in a corner.

"That his?"

"Your lucky day." Ibaka pointed at more of the mess. "All this came from the owner of this nice little enclave."

I clapped my hands. "Well, I'm done here. Hendricks?"

He laughed his fake laugh. "Ha-ha. Now we work this."

"You bet." I hit him on the shoulder.

"How old is the blood?"

"We put the body at eight hours." Ibaka tilted her head toward the back of the apartment. "Perp left him in back, on his bed, but it looks like he did the business of it in here."

I wanted to spit, get the stench and taste of the place out of my mouth, but couldn't contaminate the scene. The last thing I wanted was some tech picking up my DNA and submitting it, throwing a lawyer grounds for dismissal if we ever got into court. That, and the jokes I'd hear about being one of this idiot's tricks.

Instead, I hawked a greener into a coffee napkin from my pocket. That cleared the taste but not the smell.

Hendricks started back over the particulars. I'd read them out loud in the car, but sometimes going over them again at a crime scene helped us develop our process.

"Victim is a white male. Last of Piper, first of Jay. Thirty-four. Lived alone. No criminal record. Employed by tech firm downtown. Never married, no kids, blah, blah, blah." He scanned the notes.

"Upstairs tenant comes home, sees the vic's door open, pokes his head in to make sure everything's okay. It isn't. He finds the blood in here, gets upset, runs home, and calls the Northern. When they get on scene, they find the body and call us."

"Neighbor didn't stick around to see the body?"

"Apparently not."

Ibaka and I shook our heads. Our kind of curiosity was definitely not universal.

Hendricks said, "Did I miss anything?"

"That." I pointed to the floor beneath the cuffs.

"What is it?"

Ibaka and I answered at the same time. It was one of the vic's little toes.

"Jesus," Hendricks said. Then he crossed himself in apology. As a recovering alcoholic, he had only recently come to find religion.

"Looks like a left toe, if I had to guess."

Ibaka said, "I was going to bag it but figured you'd want to see the placement, get a sense for where it fell. You know the pictures don't do these details justice."

I winked at her. "I know. Live in the flesh."

We smiled at one another: two women on a job we loved, in departments that grudgingly acknowledged our existence. We had each other though, which was nice.

I crouched to get a better look. "Clean cut."

Hendricks said, "Maybe our perp's a butcher."

"Not for this much meat," I said. "Throw it on rice, this'd barely qualify as a nigiri."

Ibaka said, "Maybe a maki roll. One piece." She laughed, then went on. "More of a torture sadist is my thinking. Likes turning the tables on his vic."

She knelt down by the wall, shining her flashlight on something small and pink. "Check this out."

I came over, saw what looked like a piece of a tongue.

"Took him apart in pieces," I said. "Bloody lovely."

"That's nasty," Hendricks said. "What is it?"

I pointed. "See the taste buds there?"

"Butcher."

I looked up at him, shrugged. "It's a theory."

Around the tongue was more blood, by now half dried.

"This guy's trying to do something else with his cuts. He likes it. This is personal."

Hendricks followed me around the room, taking notes as I ticked off what I saw: blood spatters; footprints in socks, a lot of them from the same feet; the lack of a scuffle; blood and skin fragments left on the highest handcuffs; several kinds of whips and ticklers, unused, along with a series of gags in varying sizes and shapes in a corner; as well as a few pairs of extra handcuffs and some thick rope.

Ibaka gestured toward the hall. "Ready for the body?"

"Most definitely."

She led us to the back and inside Piper's bedroom. Three young male techs stood around our victim, who was laid out like he'd been taking a nap—except his throat was cut. The techs huddled over his face, shining little flashlights into his mouth. Something human stuck out of it.

One said, "Looks like tendon." He held a forceps *and* a flashlight, leaned in even more over Piper. "I got twenty says it's from an Achilles."

Just hearing that word turned my blood cold. I felt my palms tingle as I remembered the pain and weakness I'd felt when my own Achilles had snapped in the state basketball finals against Chabot College. All I did was plant my right foot, then I heard a pop! I was never the same player again. Next thing, I was transferring from City College to Berkeley on the strength of my academics, *not* my jumper.

The second tech said, "You're on." They bumped fists, and I wanted to strangle each of them.

From where I stood, all I could see was about an inch of flesh sticking out of Piper's mouth.

Ibaka stepped in. "How about a little respect for the deceased."

They laughed. "Right on. We got you."

To them we were just old-school. Just dinosaurs following rules that no longer existed.

Hendricks stepped up to see what the techs had going. I could tell he still wanted to develop his butcher theory.

With the forceps, the first tech removed the meat. By its length and thickness, I could see it was an Achilles. He'd been right, and I hadn't taken anatomy for nothing.

The other tech held up his twenty. "Double or nothing it's his."

"*Who else* would it belong to?"

"Fine."

They exchanged the bill. Ibaka frowned.

"Where do you find these kids?" I asked.

She shrugged. "You know how this is. They all think they're on an episode of *CSI*."

As the tech slid his finding into an evidence bag, I saw the bite marks on it that struck me cold. Our guy had done this when Piper was *alive*.

"You okay?" Hendricks asked.

I nodded, never wanting to show weakness. But he was barely aware of me. He stood transfixed by what he was seeing. "Someone wanted this pervert to bleed. Bad." He coughed into his hand, and I could see him getting a little squinty around *his* eyes. I hadn't seen him like this in years. Not since the birth of his daughter.

CHAPTER TWO

When we finished examining the bed, we rolled Piper over and found his right leg cut from calf to foot, his jeans a mess of blood. The Achilles had been ripped out in a mess of a job. I didn't want to guess at the tools used.

"Off the bone," I said.

"Left foot." Ibaka pointed to where the little toe was missing.

Other than what had pooled in the bed underneath Piper's foot and neck, the bedroom was surprisingly free of blood. All the cutting had happened in his torture room, just like this victim had liked it. I could almost admire the logic.

Hendricks said, "Even with all he did on his own pain trips, what all he did to those women in the pics? I almost feel sorry for this guy."

"Can't say I do. Slug like this? Dime a dozen in vice. You saw those girls. How many of them had cuts?"

"Not like this. Nothing deserves *this*."

I turned on Hendricks faster than he was ready for. He stepped back. Big as he was, I didn't worry about scaring him.

"You sure? You ever been tied up and tortured?"

Hendricks stepped around me to the bed. "This guy had a family somewhere. Think about that."

I did. But I also thought about how I'd have done it to Piper: I'd have made a few changes. Nothing as dramatic. More with his gags and whips, perhaps, unless he liked that. Wouldn't want that.

Imagining what I'd do to the bad guys was a little game I liked to play in my head, but I was never serious. This was what I always told myself.

"I got a ball gag here." Hendricks bent over to pick something up. I could almost see it before he showed us: a black leather strap and a standard hard rubber ball. Just like the others in his dungeon.

Then he lifted it up, and there it was, hanging limp on the end of his pencil. It had teeth marks deep into the rubber. Multiple sets. And blood.

Hendricks said, "I'm gonna need a bag for this."

Ibaka handed him a large.

CHAPTER THREE

That night I had to blow off steam, so I went to the Potrero Rec Center, a gym near my condo in Potrero Hill that had open court four nights a week. Basketball for the guys, mostly, but on plenty of occasions, I brought the discomfort of having a girl in the mix.

Ever since junior high, basketball had been my release valve, my way away from whatever troubled me. Now I played to get away from the visions of bodies, the thoughts of pain, memories of my Achilles tear that had come up at Piper's. I shot by myself on a corner basket while a three-on-three went on at the other end.

Hooking in layups from both sides—my own Mikan Drill—not only built up a good sweat, but also helped with everything going on in my head. Almost everything, that is. Even shooting around can't take away *some* things, like what it was like being single at my age, watching all your friends first get married and then start having kids. Now I was old enough that they were starting rounds of divorce, definitely not something I minded missing out on, especially with kids in tow.

As the daughter of a single-parent father, I knew all about what it was like growing up in a broken home. Not that my dad hadn't done everything he could, anything possible to give me a leg up in the world. But like I was relearning in my own life, the days, nights, and long hours of a homicide investigator didn't leave room for much else.

On a break from shooting, I watched the guys play three-on-three on the other court. They were into their second game, all of them sweating and holding their knees at any opportunity. They were tired and out of shape, which was true for most of the guys my age or older who still played.

Usually I waited until they were winded before I asked into the game. Tonight none of the regulars who knew me were around though, so I had to give "the guy thing" its wide berth. Some didn't like to play with a girl. A woman, sergeant, investigator, hot chick, whatever they called me in life or out on the street, even if they called me for a date—here on the court I was always "a girl."

And that suited me fine. They were guys; I was a girl. And if I could come in and show a few of them I could play, even drop a few outside shots on their heads and get them to play real defense, I was winning a personal battle all my own.

I dribbled in zigzags with my left hand, still watching their game, waiting for my chance. One guy was good: an Asian kid in his late twenties with a nice body and a full head of hair. He faked, then drove by his man after a quick crossover and laid it in. His teammates gave him high fives, but the one guarding him was pissed.

I had to laugh. It really was a nice move.

I started flipping the ball out to myself with backspin, gathering it, then popping jumpers from the elbows. Shoot, rebound, dribble to the other side, flip it out, catch, turn, and shoot. All in rhythm. It felt good, the back and forth, images from Piper's and thoughts of my Achilles tear nearly forgotten.

"Hey, you want to play?"

I turned toward the game. One of the older players had pulled up lame, something with his hamstring or quad, it looked like. Everyone else stood around, hands on hips. At this late hour, we were the only ones here. With no one else to ask, they all looked at me.

"What do you say?" the young Asian guy asked. This close up, I could see he was cute.

"I'll play." I bounced my ball into the bleachers and jogged over to their end, trying not to look like a happy puppy whose owner had just picked up the leash.

A bald guy, in good shape and with a handlebar mustache, passed me the ball on a bounce. He was shirtless, clearly confident in his frame. "Take a few shots. Get used to the weight."

I dribbled a little, then passed it right back to him. "I'm good."

"Ooh," his friends teased. Nobody wanted to be shown up by a girl, which was the main reason it was hard for me to play with them. Anyone guarding me was in a lose-lose situation. If I did well, they looked bad, but if they were actually trying, then they looked bad too. Maybe I liked making guys look bad.

Maybe I liked it a lot.

This guy was okay though. He smiled instead of getting upset.

"My bad," he said. "This girl knows her balls. What can I say?"

The others laughed; I had to smile. Call it an extension of the Hall of Justice, the locker room, or whatever, I just managed to gravitate to these situations.

Instead of explaining that I always shot with a guys' ball, I said, "Who's my team?"

The cute guy pointed to himself and a white guy my age wearing a swoosh T-shirt and SB Dunks. I was already unimpressed.

But I knew I had one good player to work with.

Turns out, the game was already half over: 13–11 with my guys up and the game to sixteen. For some reason, I have never liked playing to even numbers. No idea what it is, but back home we always played to fifteen or eleven, and that felt better. Never sixteen. Sometimes twenty-one, though that was a different game altogether.

"What's your name?"

I held out my hand. "Clara."

We shook hands. Too formal. "Alan."

"Or Claire is cool too."

On the court, little details like how to say my name didn't matter. I offered the option so people could choose what they thought was easiest. Honestly, I'd have been fine with just C.

SB Dunks was Edgar.

The oldest, shortest, slowest guy from the other team stepped up to guard me. He was in his late forties, I guessed. Bearded Caucasian male, 155 pounds. This would be fun.

Alan checked it up and passed off to me. I dribbled my guy around the circle, watching Alan to see what he would do. When he caught my eye and went backdoor, I scorched a pass in off the bounce, exactly where he wanted it. He laid it right up and in off the glass.

14–11.

"Nice." Edgar slapped my hand and then, when Alan ran by, patted his butt. I didn't need to be one of the guys like that. I could get posted up, guys would get a little touchy, but mostly I stayed away from hands on my ass.

I checked it and passed to Alan on the wing. He faked a drive, jab stepped, then faked a shot. His man bit, and Alan took two dribbles toward the middle, just enough to pull my man in, and then passed it to me on the opposite wing for a wide-open jumper.

I took the shot, hit it—*all net!*—and everyone stopped playing. It was only then that I realized they were playing ones and twos and that I'd lined up just outside the three-point line from force of habit. I'd ended the game without even knowing it.

"Good shot," Alan said. We touched hands.

Then the old guy with the hamstring problem jogged back onto the court, and Mustache passed him the ball.

"Run it back?" someone said, and just like that I was on the out-side again, heading over to my own hoop to shoot around by myself. I glanced over my shoulder, and Alan winked.

"That was a nice pass," he said. "Maybe I'll see you next time?"

"Yeah," I said. "Cool." I went over to retrieve my own ball and shot around for a few more minutes before I got bored. I decided to head home. Once I got the rush of a game, shooting around didn't cut it anymore.

CHAPTER FOUR

MICHAEL

The first name I had, Jay Piper, lived in the Marina. It was these types of guys—the ones who had cash and a need for what Emily provided—who lived there. They were who I'd find as I tracked back through her past.

I headed to his place on my night walk, cruised through North Beach, asking for him, but he hadn't been around. I saw fewer girls out this time of year. Maybe the January cold. Maybe someone had cleaned up the streets.

But not likely.

Used to be, the area near the strip clubs offered crowds and protection, the right kind of men: guys who liked women and girls. Every part of the city had something, whatever you wanted. You only had to know where to look.

I broke into his building, knocked on his apartment door. The light in the hallway, the speed of the dust in the air said he wasn't home.

Hadn't been in a while. I could wait out in the hall, hanging in the shadows until he came home, but that wouldn't be much fun.

Instead I broke his lock and let myself in. The first sight was a dark hall, its smell money and leather. There was another sensation, one that disgusted me. Partway down the hall I found a locked door, broke the handle, and opened it.

Inside, a small office had been converted into a padded cell: studded handcuffs fastened into walls, extra sets on the floor with shorter chains, whips and crops, nipple clamps, a few small knives. This was the first I must clean from His earth, absolve before Him to make Emily whole again.

This was more than I wanted to see, worse than I could have expected. Whether a hunch or my interpretation of Emily's breath when she slept, my study of her scars, I could not have guessed at these acts, this depth. That her past featured this kind of pain—that's what I was there to absolve.

At the end of the hall, his bedroom: normal looking, the kind of place he could bring any girl. In the dresser I found stacks of Polaroids. All of girls. They sickened me. I wanted to hurt him, make him bleed.

Emily's picture was among them.

I had to sit. I waited and counted to forty to catch my breath. Then fifty. Seventy.

At one hundred, I opened my eyes and could see without red. I stood, put the photos on a shelf in the front hall so he could see them first when he got home.

I wanted him to know exactly why I was there. Why he was getting what I had to give.

Back in his bedroom, I waited by the closet, the dresser beside me to support my weight.

CHAPTER FIVE

He came home after sunup.

Jay Piper.

If he were clearheaded, he might've noticed his pictures of the girls in the front hallway or seen me by the dresser near his bed. But he wasn't. Didn't. Light of day, and I was standing right there—him too drunk or too stupid to notice.

He threw his jacket on the chair, took his shirt off, and walked back out to the hall. I heard him piss for a long time, groaning, the bathroom door open. His jacket smelled of cigarettes.

I waited, counting breaths.

He came back and flopped onto the bed, yanked a pillow over his face to block out the sun. I stepped softly, even if he was too oblivious to hear, and leaned down with both hands and all my weight on the pillow.

He scratched at my hands, kicked his legs, tried to push himself up.

I bore down harder, holding his head in place until the kicking slowed. When I took the pillow off and rolled him over, he showed no signs of recognition, no respect for who I was. Of course he missed the presence of God.

I choked him out with my hands, then dragged him into the other room, his dungeon, where I bound him against the wall with his short-chained cuffs.

He was out when I started to work his ribs. I had my shoes off and bag gloves on. I started in with light jabs and straight rights, warming up, doing him like a heavy bag.

When I brought left and right hooks, I heard breaking: a few ribs.

He came to before I finished a round but by the end of the second three minutes was out again. I hadn't even started in on his face yet.

I took a break, hung my shirt on a hook in his bathroom, pissed in his tub, and wiped my face on a clean towel. At least he was good about laundry, his place far from a mess.

This was the kind of man to have a woman come in once a week to clean. Paid her cash under the table, didn't think twice about the world she lived in. Didn't care.

I did. I saw women like her in church every day.

When she came to clean, he would always keep the door to his dungeon closed and locked.

She would have no idea what was inside.

I threw his old coffee down the sink and filled the filter with the best stuff I could find: some Guatemalan single origin that probably cost thirty dollars a pound.

While it brewed, I took stock of his knives, deciding which one I liked most.

CHAPTER SIX
DONNER

Our week on call stretched from one Sunday midnight to the next, with Hendricks and me as the primaries and Investigators Jeff Lund and Andrew Peters as secondaries. Accordingly, the next call due to come in would be theirs.

On Monday, Hendricks and I worked Piper and our other cases hard, trying to get anything we could to move forward. I didn't get out of work early enough to hit the courts, though I thought about getting back and maybe seeing Alan, hoping we'd meet again. The best I could do for my sweat was a long run on a treadmill down at the Hall.

The next call, late Monday night, should have gone to Lund and Peters by all rights, but when they found a stack of pictures at the scene, ones of young girls in bondage situations—just like Piper's— they called us.

It was close to midnight when they did, and I was home watching *SportsCenter,* trying to drown out the images in my head with those of incredible athletes doing amazing things. These were far more appealing, and what's more, I could root for a team over the long term, even believe in it, but have no real consequences if they didn't win. Given that the closest basketball team was the Golden State Warriors, I was used to this brand of disappointment.

But maybe this year there was hope. Curry and Thompson, the Splash Brothers, were making me a believer. I knew Andre Iguodala would be big for them down the road.

On the flip side, my hometown Knicks were even worse—ruined by Carmelo Anthony and his shot-chucking ball-hoggery. They were on a straight shot to the bottom.

It had been six months since I broke up with my last boyfriend, Tim O'Malley, a good cop who wanted more than what was in my pants: a life together, a house in the suburbs, kids, everything. More than I could give.

We broke up.

What could I say? I wasn't ready to settle down, wasn't good at commitment.

Never had been. Except maybe to my job.

All this to say it wasn't a big deal when the call came. I was happy to get out and away from my life, to have something to focus on other than finding a way to sleep.

I was almost happy to hear about Doug Farrow, resident of the Tenderloin, murdered in his bathroom with a piece of his sink.

When they called, I went because I knew something serious was up, something I wanted in on.

Hendricks came along because that's what a good partner does.

He picked me up at my place, and we stopped at an all-night convenience store that would brew me a fresh pour-over. I let myself enjoy the smell of the coffee, knowing I was on the job and that my hours weren't my own for a while.

Hendricks bought a Monster, one of the new-breed energy drinks. Who knows what they'll realize these do to you in five years? He'll probably find himself sterile, which he might not even mind.

When we got on scene, both uniforms out front looked more peaked than they had at Piper's, like they wanted no part of what they'd seen inside. I recognized one of them as a friend of Tim's. He ducked my glance, something I was probably due. Because I didn't want to settle down, make nice, and play house, something was wrong with me. That was how Tim's friends saw it, anyway. Even though they could ride any tail they liked. Some of the old double standards never died.

Going up the stairs to Farrow's place, another walk-up, Hendricks asked how I was feeling about my love life.

"I feel just fine about it, thanks. And how about *you*? Judging by that slick tie, you're probably coming straight from a hot date."

"As a matter of fact, I . . ." I could hear the smile in his voice, didn't have to turn around to see him beaming. That I'd gone the whole ride without mentioning his sixty-dollar tie had likely been driving him nuts.

"Save it," I said. We were at the apartment, and I walked in.

Doug Farrow's studio was typical of the Tenderloin and its inhabitants: dirty and dark, drug paraphernalia tossed around, stains on the walls. All it missed from the street outside was a homeless guy in a wheelchair, begging for quarters, scooting himself in front of cars to collect pity or insurance claims—whichever paid out faster.

In a corner of the room was a mini fridge and a hot plate, barely enough of a setup to make a decent bowl of ramen. From the cotton balls, syringe, and burned spoon on the coffee table though, I could see all Farrow had been cooking lately was heroin.

He hadn't had any girls up here in a while. Getting hooked on smack can have that effect. Even the sex addictions fall away in deference to the bigger need. Farrow's pictures were strewn across his small desk in a mess. They were close enough to the ones we'd seen at Piper's, but all the same, Lund and Peters could have at least waited around for us to show before taking off.

I flipped through a few of the shots, planning to spend more time on them later, comparing the poses and kinds of knots, looking for the cuts and bruises to tell stories that made sense.

Patterns, predilections, profiles—that's what I wanted, what I hoped to find.

"We have any way of knowing if one of these went missing?"

No one answered me.

A thin mattress rested on the floor in one corner, a single grungy pillow and a fuzzy fleece blanket shoved out of the way. Someone had opened a window to let some of the stink out. This place was even mustier than Piper's.

"Don't these guys ever open windows?"

"Apparently not." Marlene Ibaka walked in from the small bathroom, smiling, enjoying a nasty late-night crime scene as much as I.

I raised my coffee to toast her. "Do you ever sleep?"

"Not at home," she said. "The husband and kids take care of that. So I just stay on. You know. Work, work, work."

"That's because you married the wrong Ibaka. If you'd gone with Serge instead of his distant cousin Stephon, you'd be made in the shade right now."

"Aye-aye, sir." She tipped an imaginary hat at me. Our joke that she could've married Serge Ibaka, the forward for Oklahoma City with an eight-figure salary, should have gotten old by now, but somehow it never did.

Hendricks cleared his throat. "You spinsters speak for yourselves. I had a hot date tonight. Dragged myself away from a *fine* woman to be up here!"

He puffed out his chest.

Ibaka flipped up his new tie. Its gold-and-blue diamonds were fancier than his usual; this one even had texture. "Must've been going well too," she said, "for it to go this late."

I said, "Rub it in, fine. But it's better if you give up some details for when we fantasize about it later." I raised my eyebrows, and he actually blushed.

Hendricks smiled. "*So* pretty, my dear."

Ibaka and I laughed. She offered me a knuckle bump, and I gave it.

He said, "We got a body here? Or what?"

"Oh, *now* he wants to get busy."

"Oh, we know he already did *that*."

We laughed again, but then calmed it down when we saw Hendricks's face. I almost felt bad for him; at the same time, if you couldn't laugh on this job, then what did you have left?

"In here." Ibaka stepped into the bathroom, a small enclosure that contained the place's lone sink, as well as a toilet and shower. Doug Farrow, the victim, was stark naked, his legs spread out in front of him. He sat in the sink, which had been knocked off the wall and was now on the floor. The pipes above his head were shut off now, but enough water had spewed to soak through his floor, through the apartment below, and to the shower stall of the apartment downstairs from that, where someone had reported the problem.

Other than his pale, water-soaked naked self, the most disgusting feature of Farrow's corpse was his face: I didn't need to see the faucet fixture to deduce what the perp had used to beat it in. What was left resembled slices of ham sandwich—flaps of white-bread skin so swollen they'd pass for Wonder and pink, shiny meat underneath. A complete mess.

"Lovely. Hendricks, snap a picture of *that* to bring back to your date. This'll get her going."

He pushed past me into the alcove, dutifully using his digital camera to get shots of the remains.

Then he stopped and whistled. "Look at the cock on this one, Donner. You see that?" He pointed. "Even pickled, it's got to be an eight incher."

I cringed and looked away from it, but he'd returned the favor: now I was uncomfortable.

"Always with the cock size, Hendricks. Still hoping to find someone smaller than yourself."

"Just the opposite. I mean—"

I cut him off with my hand. The idea of him talking about his junk was more than I could take. "Just take the pics, all right? You can compare measurements later."

He laughed as he got back to snapping.

The faucet fixture leaned against the base of the toilet. It had a flat base and jagged remnants of blood-caked caulk around its edge. The spout made a workable handle, but the uneven weight of the thing would make it difficult to swing with force. This was a crime of pure anger, unlike the calculated torture and patience we had seen at Piper's. This time our perp had barely thought about what to use. It all felt different, too dissimilar from the scene at Piper's.

"I think Lund and Peters may have roped us in on something," I said. "Other than the old pictures, this looks like a different MO."

"All comes out in the wash cycle, Donner. Calls all even out in the end." This—Hendricks's constant refrain for anything that seemed unfair—was the odd element of Zen dating back to before he started AA.

I thought about that sink, wondering what it would take to break the fixture off, guessing a guy would have to be pretty strong to do it, to kill a man that way.

Back in the apartment, I stepped toward the window and took a deep breath. The smell of sweat woke me back to the job. I slurped my coffee, wishing it were hotter, stronger, wanting more.

Then Ibaka was at my side, snapping off her plastic gloves. "Don't like that business about a dead man's penis, sister. Partner like Hendricks? You ever think about reporting his ass for harassment?"

I laughed. "*That*, that would be funny."

She shook her head, realizing the absurdity of the concept in our work environment. Any report would be a joke. Not only would it go nowhere, but it would be worse for *my* career than for *his*.

"Come on," I said. "It's all for show, to impress you. He's actually a really sweet guy."

"Sure he is. Sweet on you."

I gave her a wry smile. "We might have had it coming."

Then we both laughed, the best medicine of all.

"You want to look at the pictures?" She pointed to the desk.

"I guess it's that time."

CHAPTER SEVEN

I walked across the room in two steps and gave my full attention to what lay on the desk. There were more pictures here than at Piper's, and they were your standard pharmacy prints, not Polaroids. I saw some of the same faces. Not just the same look, but the same girls. Small blondes, young, but with a look like they'd been here before and knew exactly what they were willing to do for the money.

They were young, their legs thin enough to bulge at the knees. Some wore heels and held their legs together, but most had bare feet, their legs at odd angles to support the strange positions they attempted to hold. Smeared makeup, runny mascara, small breasts with pert nipples, just the smallest pooch around the navel. Too many had track marks on their arms from drug use, a far-gone look in their eyes that came with any consistent use of meth. They were only young enough to have desirable bodies for a little longer, already had started the slide into selling their pain.

In a few more months, the nights and drugs would take more of a toll: they'd put on weight, lose the last veneers of youth, the remaining light in their eyes. Catching tricks would get even harder; they'd have to resort to even more desperate means to score.

During my time on sex crimes, I'd seen the story play out too often and with too many girls, barely women. Many had families somewhere, people who would want them to come home if they knew.

I looked at one picture, a girl with a tattoo on her neck, her nose pierced. Even tied up, her face said, *Bring it on. What you got?* The john would like that, beat her harder, and maybe she would like it too.

Some got into the pain by choice, but there was always more to the story—a heavy-handed uncle with salty thumbs, a stepfather coming into the bedroom too eager, a first boyfriend who couldn't comprehend the meaning of no.

I closed my eyes and turned away, said a silent prayer that they'd leave this grind, go back home. I prayed to whomever or whatever I believed in for them to still be in this world, to have hope. Such was my use for religion.

I could still see their faces in my head, tell by their eyes how hard they'd been used. They were hooked, wanted more. It would be a long way back for them, if they could ever get back to being just girls.

"Donner."

"What?"

Hendricks stood to my side, waving his hand. "You there? That coffee too weak?"

"What?"

"Ibaka just left. She was talking to you, but you didn't say boo."

The studio was quiet, just the two of us and yellow crime-scene tape across the door.

"I'm here."

"Where'd you go?"

I waved at the desk, the pictures, and Hendricks went over. He swore a few times as he flipped through them.

"You know," he said, "perp like this doing everyone a favor. Getting these animals off the street."

Farrow's feet stuck out of the bathroom. I saw his pale, skinny calves and knees. There lay a man who would never take another breath, not another step on this earth.

Hendricks waited for my response.

He didn't believe what he'd said; he was trying to bait me, draw me in. I had crossed the line once with a jerk named Brian Terranella who'd killed his wife, Jeannine. This was when I had first come over to homicide, about six months back.

Terranella got off, walked on the strength of his alibi—that he'd been at a bar with his brother, who was a Mill Valley DA. I had thought about introducing false evidence, wanting to make sure he went away, but Hendricks talked me out of it, convinced me that wasn't how things were done here. I still wasn't sure he did right. In my father's day, you got your guy off the streets one way or another. When you knew, you *knew*. And things got done.

The job might be different now, and maybe that was fine. Or maybe it wasn't.

After the trial, I found Brian Terranella in the hall outside the courtroom and brought him to his knees, broke two of his fingers when we shook hands. I got a reprimand and two weeks' suspension without pay, three months' mandatory therapy, but it was worth it—to me, anyway.

Now I strode a thinner layer of ice, and Hendricks wanted to know if I'd fall through.

I turned to meet his eyes. "Find out who killed these turds, and we'll go lock that bastard up right now."

"Okay. Tell me what you make of this, then." He swept his hand across the apartment with a wave. "What do you see here?"

"I see a lowlife paying for S&M sex with girls too young and drug addled to know better. He's a small part of them ruining their lives. Lately he got off that, onto horse, and now he's dead. You want me to say the girls will be better off? They won't. Someone else will step in to pay for what they're selling.

"Nobody's addictions or habits are getting quenched. Nobody's but his." I pointed to Farrow.

Hendricks lowered his shoulders. "That's what I needed to hear."

"The bigger question is whether we have a pattern. If this ties in with Piper or if Lund and Peters just dumped an extra case on our heads."

"What's your thinking? Just the pictures, or there's more?"

"Those pictures say a lot for the similarity. It's true." Then I shook my head. "The kill is so different though. Body left a mess, a very different mess than at Piper's. What we saw at Piper's was all premeditated, slow. This was fast, an act of rage."

"Maybe this guy pissed him off."

"Maybe."

"Or it's what he wants us to think."

The cheap wood floor creaked under my feet. "Maybe. But if these are the same hand, your butcher theory has to go. This guy didn't even bother to find a knife."

Outside on the street, a light night rain had started. We wrapped up what all we needed to do at the scene and left the rest for the techs. We got into Hendricks's car, and he drove while I watched the corners and the streetlights through the windows as we rode in silence.

I could smell fresh oil on the streets, see visions of the city caught in bubbles of water on the glass.

On the corners I saw predators: buyers, johns, men looking for women or other men they could use to live out their desires. Money could buy anything here, from drugs to souls.

San Francisco offered a marketplace of depravity. Whatever a man wanted, he could get: domination, she-males with postoperative breasts, good sex, bad sex, young boys, girls, women who let them inflict pain. For every taste, a different block with its own set of nightwalkers to satisfy an urge.

I had read that the city's slave trade was bigger than in the South before the Civil War. So far we had come. We should've known better. Someone had to.

My mind's eye flashed to a dried smear of blood over Farrow's bed—not from tonight. What kind of a man would live like that? With blood on his wall?

I still didn't have a clue.

"We talk to the girls, I bet we find something." Hendricks stared straight ahead as he drove.

"We could try that. Might get somewhere."

"They look like a link to me."

It was late enough for us to pass through the city, barely slowing at lights. We cruised all the way east and then south.

When we pulled up outside my place in Potrero, a nice third-floor walk-up with great city views and a deck, Hendricks turned and touched my arm.

"Listen, it was nice working with you tonight, Donner. Full truth, you make leaving a hot date to come out and see a dead guy not the worst thing imaginable."

I tried not to smile, because it was the most backhanded compliment I could get, but I knew what he meant. "Thanks."

I turned to the door to go.

"Hang on a second, okay? About this case, what you think?"

I sat back in my seat, sighed. "I think we got us a potential perv killer. Someone taking scum off the streets in the bloodiest ways. It's a nasty world we're dealing in."

"Maybe it's best you ask off it."

"No," I said. "This guy, he's doing the perps. I want to see why."

It was after three in the morning, and we were on the clock again at nine the next day.

He said, "Get some sleep. I'll see you in a few hours."

I moved for the door, then stopped. "You ever wonder?"

"Wonder what?"

"If this shit really comes out in the wash. If things wind up right in the end, justice served and all that."

"As long as the justice system does, that's what I care. Courts get used, turds tried, cells filled. The cases go up and come down. My checks come. I get paid, even get out on a date once in a while. I see my kid the odd weekend. Have some fun, you know? Something you might try once in a while."

"I hear you." But I was already turning away, opening the door to get out. I stepped up into the night.

"Wait. Donner?"

I turned back.

"What does it for me is I think of their families—Farrow's and Piper's. I think about how I would want this case worked if I was one of them."

I nodded. That was the hook: the humanity in it all. The call to always do what was right for the other good people in this world, assuming they were out there.

I thanked him for the ride and got out. At the curb, I turned back and watched him go, heard his tires roll along the wet asphalt.

Hendricks was going to worry about me. It was his job, what a good partner did. And he was a good partner: picking me up at home, following my hunches, and letting me lead. I was lucky. I'd be fine.

I wasn't sure how I had gotten so tied up in my own head all of a sudden, gone away from having fun and giving Hendricks a hard time. But I did know too: it was the girls. They always got to me, got me down.

I walked up my front stairs to the porch, could still smell the oil, but now something else too.

Ash. Ash and dirt.

In the morning it would all start again.

CHAPTER EIGHT
MICHAEL

The second name Emily gave me was Doug Farrow.

His place in the Tenderloin was only a short walk. I broke in late, and as I came in, he stood at the desk, naked, fondling himself, entirely without shame.

Red anger. I wanted to kill him right then. No waiting. No words.

"Who are you?"

I didn't answer, couldn't speak. I got closer, saw he stood before a table of pictures. There among the others was Emily.

My Emily. My charge.

"No!"

I backhanded him with a closed fist, turned and caught him under his chin with my left hand and drove him back, off the floor and into a wall so hard it cracked. His hand finally left his sex to manage some minor defense but too late. The thrum in my ears blocked out his words, the world.

I held him above the ground, both hands at his neck, him coughing. Threw him airborne into his bathroom sink. He landed, knocked it off the wall. I rushed in and grabbed what I could, found myself holding the faucet fixture in my hand, its odd-shaped metal coming clean off from the white porcelain, jagged grout around its edges.

Then the rest was urge and violence—lack of control, my own abandon, blood. Something else took over. When it was done, there was very little left of Farrow's face to see.

I stepped out of the bathroom into his studio, my chest heaving. I bent, put my hands on my knees, worked to catch my breath. Then stood hands on hips, breathing harder than I could remember. I was gassed.

I counted. Five. Seven. Ten. That was all.

Water poured out of the wall above Farrow's head, gurgling behind me. Running over what remained of his face.

I turned to the table, lifted Emily's picture up out of the rest. A mess in front of me. Too many girls, poses, straps. Filth. Emily was in another shot and another. Her face among a mix of many others, all mired in filth, her thin body contorted to his desires.

I took what I needed—only one picture of her—and left Farrow in his bathroom. Shut the door behind me, tucked the picture inside my jacket, close to my breast. Brushed off my hands, saw the cuts, didn't care. I wiped the blood off on my pants and walked out of the building, onto the street, toward home.

Emily's soul one step closer to clean.

CHAPTER NINE

I lay awake at 3:57 a.m., listening to her breath, longing to touch her in ways I never would. Protector, savior, absolver . . . these were the roles I played for her in the name of our Lord.

But lover? That would never be.

Under the bedsheets, I allowed myself one touch.

I brought my fingers along the length of her thigh, hip to knee—not even. Stopped myself inches from her knee, just touching with the pads of my first fingers. Just two! The softness of her skin. In the dim dawn light, I saw her side move as she inhaled, lowering as she let go. Her soft sounds.

I allowed myself one long touch, put my palm against her side where she felt warm. This, in the night, was where I committed my own sin. I wanted to believe she liked it. My hand burned. I felt the fire of my own urges—more than I could take.

The cold floor shocked my bare feet when I pushed myself out of bed on the opposite side. I wanted to come around and watch her face as she slept, but couldn't risk waking her. Instead, I moved to the sink, where I splashed cold water on my face and under my arms. I knew the

movies where men like me self-punished with whips and straps, flagel-
lating their backs. Silly. Why would I want to do that when the streets
beckoned with a wealth of sinners waiting to be claimed in His name?

Outside on Larkin, I headed north, into the heart of the city at its
worst. At this time of night, I passed addicts nodding on the concrete,
bodies laid flat. Beyond them walked the last peddlers of physical sin—
those too broke, without a home to go back to, barely standing in the
light for the last hopes of a trick that might pay what they needed to
cop. He was in the middle of all this, out here for me to find.

Emily had given me one final name. The one I wanted most.

I knew where to find him. Her instructions were specific: third floor
in the back. The door wouldn't have a lock. This was where he would be.

Taking this route, I saw the city's worst. The smells, the faces, the
questions. They asked for money, even knowing He has a house where
they might go to be helped and fed. But not these; they didn't come for
absolution, only recognized me as a black shape passing at 4:00 a.m.
They had no want of change or saving, death their only end.

I stopped at one I couldn't pass: a black man with foam at his
mouth and an unshaved chin, holding his hand out. His clouded eyes
didn't even recognize me from his meals.

"Quarter? Dollar?" he asked.

"*You,*" I said quietly. I pushed him back against a building with
my hand, close enough to get his smell. He hadn't bathed in weeks.
"Absolution in the face of our Lord. Do you accept it?"

"What, man? Why you coming up on me . . ."

He tried to raise his arms, but I already had both his wrists.

"What do you want?" I asked him. "Do you want to be saved in
the eyes of the Lord? And live in heaven?"

"What you talking about? What is this?" He struggled to break my
grip but couldn't. Not only was he weak, but he was undernourished as
well. He couldn't do a thing.

"I can offer you absolution right now, for a price. Do you take it? Or do you choose to stay in this sinful place?"

"No. Fuck, no. What the shit you saying?" He pulled his head back and angled his face away, trying to see me more clearly through the sides of his eyes. Who knows what he saw? In all likelihood, he hadn't seen clearly in years.

I used my left hand to hold his wrists. With my right, I drew the knife. A sliver of streetlight gleamed against its blade, and he saw this. Suddenly his vision cleared.

"What you—"

"One chance, old man. Don't ask me why I'm giving it to you, but I am. One chance to be absolved of all your sins."

"How is . . . ? How can you?"

"I take them on as my own, my son. Send you to heaven for eternity to live in His presence among angels."

He didn't respond. I slid the knife's tip down his jacket, slicing fabric.

He shook his head, did his best to push me off. This time I let him. He danced away, down the wall, screaming no, over and over.

No one bothered to notice. For all they knew, he was just howling at the night—seeing things, imagining ghosts.

Then he fixed me with the clearest stare he could muster, a clarity of vision I had not seen in some time—from anyone—and he said, "I choose this earth and this life. This is where I'm gonna stay."

"Your decision." I turned away. Perhaps if he had chosen absolution, it would have changed all that came after, kept me away from the pimp, saved us all.

But he had not.

The sinners chose their sins, the path toward faith presenting itself daily and lying untaken. Everyone had free will upon His earth.

Everyone paid.

CHAPTER TEN
DONNER

Hendricks was late Tuesday morning, so I went to evidence myself to check out the pictures from Farrow's studio to compare them with Piper's.

I took both sets to a white-walled interrogation room and laid them out in front of me on the scratched table.

At Piper's, the number of pics was precise, a lineup on his shelf of girls he had hurt. I studied one of the tech's pics, the one that showed how the shelf looked when we arrived. One spot stood empty, as if one of the girls had been removed. The very middle picture. She was gone.

With Farrow, the stack had no order, no way to tell if any pictures had been taken. His collection was just a mess spread across his desk.

The murders were so different: Piper meticulous and calculated, Farrow carried out in anger and with strength. It almost looked like two different killers but with too many coincidences. I was starting to believe in the connection of the girls.

I started putting together matches of pictures, finding the few girls who were the same. There weren't a lot of these. Many more of the pictures didn't have matches, but in all there was a similarity of taste, something that told me there was more here than two dead guys.

Of the few girls who matched, the first was a blonde with shoulder-length hair and streaked mascara. I put the two shots side by side and stared at her. She had aged maybe six months between the two pictures, but that could've happened in three weeks on the street. Her eyes were tough in the first, hardened in the second. Perhaps at that point she was already beyond help.

The next girl to match stared back at the camera, trying to look sexy-mean, wanting to project a sense of anger that might hide her fear, maybe even protect her. In the first picture, her fear was still there, then less in the other. Fear was now apathy. She could've been eighteen or as young as fifteen. Her shoulders were narrow enough to fit through the neck of a dress.

I wondered if I had ever been that frail. Not since junior high, if then.

Farrow's set was harder to put into a chronology. I spread them out to get a better look. He'd had more girls, been at it longer; he was less selective. Some of the pictures were yellowing around the edges, starting to curl. They weren't Polaroids, which meant he went to the trouble of having them printed. Or maybe he had a color printer somewhere in that craphole. I almost admired them both for going to the trouble of making tactile products of their efforts—physical pictures, instead of just looking at everything on a screen. It showed some kind of dedication to a connection with the physical world. Or maybe I was kidding myself; the real pictures were probably just better for beating off.

I tossed the ones I was holding down onto the table, glad I was wearing gloves. My disgust for these scumbags rushed back.

Studying these could wait. I needed to sit it out for a while and settle my stomach, figure out what I was trying to do.

Working in homicide had always been my goal, ever since my father told me it was no place for a woman. But that was in high school. Now, here of my own accord, I still carried my hurt and prejudices from vice.

I stood up and stretched my shoulders and arms.

My dad had been a homicide investigator himself in lower Manhattan in the eighties, should've been forward-thinking enough to imagine a woman doing the job. He would've pushed me toward this it if I'd been a son. But a daughter? Not ever.

Here I was then, essentially in the career I had because of him—a man who never thought a woman officer should be anything more than a meter maid.

A parking ticket maven.

That wasn't me. Never was.

I stacked the pictures, clapped them down a few times on the table to organize the piles, and put them in their bags. They could go back to their shelf in the evidence cage and wait.

CHAPTER ELEVEN

Hendricks came in around ten thirty. He could tell by my face I'd had more than enough coffee and wasn't working on either the Piper or the Farrow murder.

He came around to look at my computer.

"That went off the board last week."

"Paperwork," I said. "Got to be done. You might try it sometime."

He sighed and dropped himself into my extra chair. "How long you been in already?"

I lied, told him fifteen minutes so he might think I'd slept well and stayed in bed like a normal person.

"I got a few ideas about our killer. Mind I run them by?"

I saved my work. "Go ahead."

"For some reason I thought you'd resist this. I don't know why. I think it's the girls. We trace it back through them, we find who's pulling strings."

"How do you mean?"

"What if one of them came into some money? I know the work on both vics needed muscle. What if it was a hired job? One of these girls starts hiring killers."

"It's possible. Why a girl though? What if a pimp starts hitting his johns?"

"Why would he be taking out his customers?"

"For damaging the merchandise."

Hendricks shook his head. "I don't see it. No. But if a girl came into money, say . . . maybe she found a guy she liked, someone who put her up with some dough? Say she wanted to get back at her johns. What you think?"

"Sounds too much like *Pretty Woman*. There's no Julia Roberts here. We're talking about some teenage runaway on drugs. She's going to care about revenge? Don't think so. She just wants another fix."

Hendricks sat back in the chair, crossed one leg over the other, his boot almost touching my desk. "It's an idea," he said. "I don't know about the money. Maybe she robbed it. Maybe not a benefactor."

"Maybe I should finish this paperwork."

"These girls could turn themselves around, you know."

"I'd be the first one to say that, if I believed it." I stared at my screen, grinding my molars. Anything to keep from getting further into this. For these girls, it was all one direction: down. "Or maybe they do clean up. You think they'll care about these turds? No. They're long gone."

Hendricks stood up. "I'll look over the pics from the scenes then. Maybe find some matches."

I sat listening to the buzz of the station around me. Hendricks could piss me off, but his heart was in the right place. He cared about the girls, the vics of both sexes. The job meant more to him than the pay. He cared about the families of the victims, the ones left behind.

No one could last at what we did if it was only about the pay.

I finished with my paperwork and then went down to evidence to see if I could help.

I found Hendricks in the file room, staring at the same pictures I started on earlier.

"Who you care more about?" I asked him. "The girls or the freaks?"

"You mean the vics." He flopped a handful of pictures down on the table. "Farrow and Piper are the vics here. They're both dead."

"Yeah." I leaned against the wall. "Vics, freaks, whatever. Look at those pictures and tell me they're not both."

"That's fine," he said, "both. What difference does it make?"

I didn't have anything to say to that. We were quiet under the hum of the fluorescents.

He pushed back from the table. "I hear you, Donner. I do. Just promise me we keep things right on this one, don't let anything get out of hand. Like on Terranella."

I nodded. He could've just said "that time" or "the other," and I would've known what he meant.

Now I wanted a drink.

"I hear you, Daniel."

Using his full first name was a good tactic for stopping Hendricks cold; he'd once told me it made me sound like his mother.

Terranella was a mistake, one I wouldn't make again. I'd just given a bad man a little of what he needed. My father would've done the same. In his eyes, it was part of the job.

But those were different times. Doctors, police, firemen, all of us now operated in a new world of liability and litigation. Not that it helped.

"I get it," I said. "By the book here. Strictly."

"What happened to these guys is wrong. Even if what happened to *them* is wrong too." He waved at the pictures. "We're here to stop murders and put murderers behind bars. Someone did Piper and Farrow. We need to stop him before he kills again."

"Any new theories then?"

He shook his head. "There's nothing here. But something tells me there's a link."

I sat down, shuffled pictures into order, showed him the matches I'd found earlier, the chronology I made at Farrow's place. You could see the progressive buildup of grime on his walls.

Best I could, I put them in order of what I thought was time, judging by the condition of the prints and the color of the wall. A few had dates printed on the back by a developing machine, but not all.

When I finished, I had twenty-four pictures laid out in front of us. A catalog of what a disgusting man had done with his life.

"So what do you make of that?"

Hendricks swore. "Not much. I think we track down these girls. Maybe one tells us something."

I held up my hands. "Let's do it."

CHAPTER TWELVE

We took to the streets to canvass the girls, found them using connections I'd made working vice and from volunteer work I did at a battered women's shelter in the Tenderloin.

We started on the corners they usually worked, but it was too early in the day for them to be out on the job. I knew a couple of coffee shops they frequented, found a handful of them talking over breakfasts, coffee, having just woken up from a night's work. It was just past noon.

Three girls I recognized sat in a back booth at It's Tops, hair unkempt and makeup-free, not yet ready to work or even dress for the job.

"Hey, Shane," I said, walking over to them. I nodded at Hendricks for him to hang back, grab a stool at the bar, and enjoy a cup of the diner's weak black joe.

"Here's Clara Donner," Shania said, "our avenging angel." She seemed underwhelmed.

The girl sitting across from Shania, who had a side of the booth to herself, didn't make room for me to join, so I slid into the booth adjacent.

"What's the matter?" I asked.

"Same old same old. Just the work, the life. Makes me tired."

"Mmm-hmmm." Her friends nodded.

"I could say the same," I said.

She went on. "Even now, waking up at noon getting harder. Shit, we out till five last night. Girl needs her full eight hours."

"We caught a bad one last night, kept me out until three thirty. Then I'm back at my desk at nine."

The girl closest to me turned to regard my makeup and to see how I held up. I passed some kind of test. She went back to eating her eggs.

"So what's up?" Shania asked.

I reached into my blazer for the pictures of Piper and Farrow, flopped them onto their table. Farrow's was a shot of him blown up from his driver's license—I wouldn't ruin their meal with a pic of him from last night. "Know these guys? Any of you ever trick for them?"

They spun the pics around to all get a look, checked them out, shook their heads.

"No, ma'am. Honestly, I don't think we his type."

Shania was Latina, but her two friends were African American. "You can tell just like that?"

They nodded. "Just like that. They looking for something else."

"What?"

The girl next to Shania smiled. "I could tell you that, I'd be working some other line, girl."

"What about girls? You hear of anyone disappearing? Leaving the life?"

"Happens all the time here. What can you do?"

"People move on."

Shania leveled a hard look at me. "Now what you gone do about helping us with this dickhead coming around from vice?"

I sighed. "Give me a name."

"Owens. Steve Owens. He the one. Get him off our ass, girl."

I reached to their table for the pictures. "You sure? Nothing?"
Same response.

I reached inside my jacket for my pad to make a note. "Owens," I said. "Will do my best."

"Better, girl." Shania raised her coffee in a form of toast. "Or next time we won't be so forthcoming with you." She winked.

Getting up, I slid two twenties onto their table, enough to cover the breakfasts and a nice tip, told them the meal was on me. I'd get nowhere with Owens in vice, if I could even get time with him, so this was some consolation to that, a fact we all knew too well.

I walked back to Hendricks just as a BLT with a side of fries arrived in front of him. "Any luck there?" he said.

"No knowledge of our johns whatsoever." I stole a fry and ate it. This wasn't the place to worry about it being too hot. Here the oil and salt had already soaked in. For better or worse.

He poured ketchup onto the side of the plate farthest from me, so I moved around to his other side once I'd stolen another fry. I dipped it in ketchup.

"You know anyone in vice who owes you a favor? They got an issue with Owens."

Hendricks laughed. "Old Squeaky-Clean Steve? Not much *anyone* can do about that jackass."

I knew exactly what he meant; through most of my time on vice, the man Owens and I weren't even on speaking terms. Call it a difference of opinion on how to enforce the law. Call it whatever you wanted. It was another good reason for me to find pleasure in the fact I'd moved on to homicide and had a new home.

CHAPTER THIRTEEN

A few other girls we spoke to either knew nothing or didn't want to talk. Only one told me she knew the guys in the pictures. "They're around, yeah," was the depth of her response.

No, they hadn't seen any strange john who might be hunting the others. Yes, some of these girls had disappeared of late; of course that was likely to happen; and no, they weren't sure which ones. I tried to parlay some of the credit I'd earned on the corners, but mostly these girls weren't having it. They knew I was a cop, and they didn't want cops around. Even without Hendricks, I didn't have any luck.

We found one girl down enough on her luck, needing a meal so badly that when we offered, she accepted it. She gave her real name as Jennifer Hathorn, but everyone knew her as Destiny.

She didn't fit the mold of the pictures we had from Piper's and Farrow's: her hair was brown and not blonde, and she came in maybe a touch on the older side, but she was white and looked like she'd come from a good family somewhere, once.

She clearly used too. But not for so long that she was completely gone.

I bought her a burger and fries at one of the Chinese coffee shops that had a lunch buffet but sold mainly donuts and burgers. J. Georgie's. There were a string of them, offering this strange mix: burgers, donuts, teriyaki. It never made sense or seemed right to me, but then I wasn't the one eating the food.

The man and woman behind the counter fought in their native tongue. Hendricks sat next to me, drinking a greasy coffee. Mine was untouched, and Destiny had already finished hers—she'd put enough sugar and cream in it to satisfy a six-year-old's sweet tooth.

I started out setting pictures of girls on our table—ones from Piper's and Farrow's.

"Yeah, I know them," she said. "They all right?"

I told her they were, so far as I knew. "Any of them drop out of sight lately? Would you have reason to worry?"

She stared straight ahead, deadpan. "Can I have more coffee?"

I laid out the dead men's pictures.

"How about them?"

"This one. Him." She pointed at Farrow. "He comes around. You know. He dead now?"

I turned to Hendricks for a moment, then back to Destiny and asked, "You just guessing here? Or do you know?"

"Word gets around."

"Anything you can tell us?"

"He went with the girls in those pictures, yeah. Much as I know, these the kind of girls he liked. I ain't never been with him." She gestured to her hair. "Guess I'm not their type."

The chef rang a bell on the counter, and Hendricks got up to get Destiny's food. I watched her eyes as he brought it back, aware she hadn't looked directly at either of us yet. Whether we could trust her or not was still very much up for debate. That, and if she had anything interesting to tell us.

When Hendricks slid the plate onto our table, she smiled. Her teeth had yellowed, the gums pulled back in a sure sign of meth.

Her fries steamed in their grease, and I wasn't tempted at all. Her burger looked just tastier than a hockey puck.

"Sure I can't get you something else? Maybe a salad?"

She was already shoving hot fries into her mouth, her head down and hair hanging in front of her face. "Thanks. This good."

"Anything else you can tell me? Maybe something that sticks out as strange in the last couple, three weeks?"

When she came up for air, or to let her mouth cool, she turned her head as if thinking it over. Then she said, "There was one thing this weekend. Girl got beat up, lost a piece off her tongue. Pissed a couple of us off." She frowned, put down her burger, and locked her eyes on mine.

My trust and interest level shot up. "Her tongue?"

"Don't matter what you pay, you don't get to do that. Nothing that lasts. No way."

She moved a mouthful of burger out of her cheek and resumed chewing. I hadn't even known it was there. Maybe Squirrel would be a better name for her than Destiny.

I thought back to the piece of Piper's tongue on his floor, the Achilles in his mouth.

"You saying a john did this? Remember his name?"

She shook her head. "Nah. Just heard this from her man. You know." Her focus had gone back to the food, almost as if any sense of ire had never arrived.

"Her man?"

"Dub. Her pimp."

Everybody who'd ever worked in the Tenderloin or vice knew Dub, a.k.a. Richard Webster, a.k.a. Richard Dubya, Dick Dub, Just Dub, or Dick D. He was as much a feature of vice and the 'Loin as the officers who worked there. Tall and white with long dreads, a scar slashed across his face that you never forgot once you'd seen it. The biggest surprise about Dub was his longevity, the simple fact that he hadn't been killed in the game for as long as he'd been around. He worked alone, didn't use muscle, and got to his women with the drugs he sold out of his apartment. Somehow he never got rolled or bumped off for his stash. He seemed immortal. The collective speculation had him as some kind of made man from an East Coast mafia family with enough juice to keep him safe by the implication of their might.

Hendricks tapped his fingernails on the table; I could feel his knee bouncing with more than the caffeine.

"Who was the girl?"

She shrugged, already lost to us but for the burger.

"She dropped out. Ain't seen her."

"But I asked—" I stopped myself; it wasn't any use. Maybe the food had woken her brain.

"She gone now. Dub put word out. Ain't nobody seen her."

"You don't have her name?"

She chewed and thought about it for a moment, then said, "Silver. That's her name. Silver."

Hendricks asked her a few questions while I thought it over. When it was clear she'd given us all she knew, I slipped a twenty and my card across the table. "This is in case you think of anything else, okay? Anything at all."

She nodded. The burger was half gone, but her eyes had dulled like a light switched off. The money and my card just sat there.

"Anything else," I said.

She waved like we were already moving on. So we did.

Outside, I asked Hendricks if Dub's name rang a bell.

"You know it does."

"Then I guess we go see the man."

He jangled his car keys, spun them around his finger. "I guess we do."

CHAPTER FOURTEEN

The ride to Dub's apartment wasn't a long one. We were just off Market, down the hill and a few streets over from his apartment when we left Destiny and her burger.

In the car I asked Hendricks what he knew about the man.

"Not much. I mean, I heard of Dub, but he's no killer, so homicide don't rightly give a damn. And that's my stance too."

I filled him in on what I'd picked up in vice, the background that had him as a satellite scumbag for the mob.

When we cornered Larkin onto Ellis, we came up behind two patrol cars, and my stomach dropped. I had a bad feeling right away, even before I knew they were in front of Dub's. Two black-and-whites and an ambulance in front of them, all with their lights flashing.

"What the—?" Hendricks pulled up behind the black-and-whites. I was already half out of the car by the time it stopped.

I slid between the parked cars to the curb and saw something else I didn't like: Lund and Peters's unmarked sedan parked in front of the ambulance.

I swore. Hendricks came up behind me and saw it too. "The hell are they doing here?"

I asked if he wanted to guess. "Because I don't."

"Damn."

We badged our way past the officers on scene and made our way up the stairs, then to the dirty apartment in back on the third floor. I'd been here once before, when I was with vice, but that was just my partner and me. This was a full-on gathering. When we came in the door, stepped into Dub's dirty living room, Lund, Peters, and Ibaka were all there, standing around what appeared to be a battered mess of the man that had once been Dub.

"Looks like his luck finally ran out," I said. When Lund smiled, I added, "And ours keeps getting worse."

Hendricks swore. Lund and Peters swore, but then they smiled. Any chance of them giving up a case as messy as this one would brighten anybody's day.

"What are *you two* doing here?" Peters asked.

Lund said, "For real. You get doubled up on this call?"

"No. I—" I looked to Hendricks, but we both knew it was no use. Even if we wanted to walk back out and forget the whole thing, we couldn't now. We'd be taking this case and adding it to the others we'd already caught, making us three for three and our secondaries, Lund and Peters, still working a solid donut, a zero-for-three performance that was one for the record books.

"Would you two catch a case already?"

Lund furrowed his brow. He still couldn't believe it. "Are you taking this one too?"

"We're following a lead. Dub was a possible connection between the other two cases."

Lund laughed. "Bowen is gonna *love* this."

"Like I said, catch a case already."

Peters started ripping pages out of his pad. "We'll be glad to help you out though. With our notes. And anything else you might need. You know, if there's *anything*. Just call."

Lund patted me on the shoulder as he headed toward the door. Ibaka stood and watched, shot me a knowing smile. We were getting the royal screw on this deal, Hendricks and myself, and there was very little we could do.

"You're gonna owe us for this, hear me?"

They waved over their shoulders.

Hendricks turned my way. "They'll get us back. That's how it works, Donner. Calls come in, murders go up and come down. It all washes out in the end."

"Are you serious right now?"

He sucked his lips in tight against his teeth. "No. No, not really."

Ibaka smiled. "Well, it's nice to see you two, also. Anyone want to see the body?"

CHAPTER FIFTEEN
MICHAEL

I knocked at the door, and he opened it, simple as could be—no fear or hesitation. Shirt open, actually a bathrobe on his shoulders, with baggy pajama pants and a gun parked at the waist. When he smiled, gold caps shined among his teeth, stains of neglect on what was left of his originals.

"What you need, my man? My playa?" He strung out the last syllable, eyeing me up and down. Long dreadlocks fell over his shoulders. He wore shaded glasses, but even with these, I could see one eye had gone bad.

He lowered the glasses to stare me in the eyes, squinting his good eye, sizing me up. Some sign of recognition passed over his features.

Then he laughed. He mocked the act of straightening up. "Welcome, papa." He winked at me and placed his glasses back over his eyes. "What can I get you? We ain't got no little boys here."

Mystified, I wanted to know how he knew me. He had never entered the church.

He stepped inside, baiting me. "Well? Help you, padre?"

"I'm here about a girl."

He laughed. "That we got!" He turned, left me at the door, let it stand open. "Girls what I got. You let me know."

I followed him, watching as he packed a large bowl of dark hash for his pipe. He was far enough gone already that the hash wouldn't make a difference.

A blonde girl sat on the couch, wrapped in a robe that hung open to her navel. Below that, a sash tied loosely. The robe barely covered her sex. I saw opaque pink underwear, the soft inside of her thigh. She smiled up at me, revealing teeth treated as badly as his.

"Hi, sugar," she said. "You want some love?" Whatever she saw in my face, she didn't like. "Okay then."

"Get up," I said, then to him, "Let her go. She should leave. The two of us have to talk."

"Oh, *do* we?" His face turned sour, ashen, and his hand went to his belt. I saw the gun, its handle.

She asked, "What you say to me?"

I told her, "You're free. Go. Leave and find salvation in God. He loves you. I give you love."

The pimp stepped to me, hand at his belt. "What you—"

"No," I said, "no." Before he could do anything, I took him by the throat with one hand, held his wrist with the other to keep the gun in his pants. I pushed him back against the wall hard enough to knock down a framed picture of a girl.

He called me a name through gritted teeth, a racial epithet I'd never been called before.

I hit him in the gut with a left, then she was coming at me, arms windmilling, punching, her robe wide open. I covered my face, let her hit my arm, leaning into the pimp so he couldn't lift his gun. I brought my knee up hard into his stomach and then again to his groin. He doubled. I grabbed the back of his head, his Medusa's mane of dreads, and thrust his face against my knee. He crumpled, down, out, and I turned my attention to her.

I caught her wrists and held them. "Be still. I am here to save you."

"I don't want saving, you perverted—"

"I give you love, child. Take it."

She spit in my face.

Like the man on the street, she chose her own way. We are nothing if not our habits. She writhed in my hands, tried to kick. I turned away, wanting to ask how much he meant to her, why she would protect him. She tried to bite my neck, berserking, gnashing teeth.

I shoved her back onto the couch, harder than I meant to, and she went limp.

"Are you all right?"

This was for Emily—Emily and what he did to her—and it had little to do with this girl. She had chosen her own path away from God. And this was what it wrought, this result in a place she shouldn't be.

I stood over them, watching them breathe. Under her head, I saw a metal box, realized this was what she'd hit her head on. I pried it out from under her and opened the lid. It was filled, of course, with drugs and money. The money wasn't a lot: twenties and crumpled, dirty tens, even change. Bags of white powder, rolled into tubes pushed against a bag of weed, cubes of hash, clear plastic boxes of pills. I closed the box, put it aside.

Something moved inside me at the sight of her bare thighs, something I didn't like. I reached down to wrap her robe back around her, but it was caught underneath. I had to crouch down, so close, to lift her and pull both sides closed. I smelled her scent: unavoidable, earthy like sweat, sweet like cheap candy. For a moment I wanted to touch her.

"No." I shoved the word out. Her teeth, dark, stained, unkempt, pushed me away. I could barely see her gums. I tied the robe tight with its sash and pulled her up off the couch by the arms, got her on her feet and then over my shoulder. I carried her back through the apartment to a bedroom, flopped her down on the bed. It sloshed and moved under her.

A water bed. Funny. I almost laughed as she swished around on its waves, thinking how good it was for Emily and so many others that soon he would be gone.

CHAPTER SIXTEEN

In the pimp's living room, I slipped my knife out of my pocket, opened it with care, and slid it up the back of my hand, watching as it trimmed black hairs from my skin. It was ready, and so was he.

I took a pillow off the couch and wiped blood from his mouth. He still didn't respond. Not until I pulled him up by his hair, held him in front of me, slapped him. Then, when he started blinking, I lifted him higher and smashed him facedown into and through his glass-top coffee table, making one big mess on the floor.

He scrambled onto his hands and knees, the fight rising in him, and I let him stand, seeing I'd made an even worse mess of his mouth. He flipped hair out of his face, an action that took a full movement, a swing of his body. His hair so thick and heavy.

He saw the gun on the floor. I didn't know how stupid he thought I was, but I wasn't that green. I dipped into a right uppercut and pivoted from the hips, brought my fist up hard under his chin, sent blood flying. I dropped a left hook into his ribs, an easy move since he was fully unguarded, didn't even attempt a fighting stance. When he reacted to the hook, left his face open again, I knocked him down with a right cross.

I had questions, wanted a list of names, but I could barely control myself. I dropped on top of him, straddled his chest, and reached for the metal box. I lifted it over my head and brought it down. It gave a little, the box, and I lifted it to smash down again.

Later, I held the box aloft. He blinked slowly, focusing on my hands, then smiled through the blood. I still had him; he had enough left to give me what I wanted.

When the pimp came to, I'd calmed enough to do my work, to get what I needed. I'd cleaned and scrubbed his coffeemaker and used it to make a dark pot, finding old coffee that I forced myself to consume. When I'd had enough, I tied up the girl and gagged her so she couldn't scream. I woke him with cold water on his face and chest, forced some down his throat.

He spit it up on the floor, coughed himself awake.

"Ready to talk to me?"

His eyes flitted around the room, then focused on his wrists, which I'd tied.

"You can't do this."

"I want names." I brought the knife to his forearm, played it against his skin. "We're going to play a game you won't like."

He swore, and I admired that attitude. It made what I had to do even easier.

I sawed the knife harder, broke skin, then worked its tip into the cut.

He ground his teeth, and something came loose. When he spit it on the ground, I could see it was a piece of thin, cheap gold.

"What you want?"

"Names. Everything about a girl named Emily. You called her Silver."

He shook his head, grimacing at the pain. "Don't know her. Too many tricks, man."

I slapped him with my open hand. "How do you know me?"

He squinted. Thinking. "The church, man. I been to your church. Seen you there. You can't do this. What would God do?"

I punched his mouth, bouncing his head back.

"Who did that to her?"

"What?" He focused. *"Who?"*

"Emily. Her tongue."

It came to him then, slowly but definitively. He got it, remembered exactly who I meant.

"Did you do that?"

"Me? No. Huh-uh. That made her worthless to me."

"Who did it?"

"Who? Right." He was scared. "A trick. A john."

I pushed the knife in.

"Johns. You got to believe."

The knife formed a distinct outline under his skin, almost an inch of it now.

"That was a ways back. Silver, she—"

I slapped the word from his mouth. "Emily."

"Emily. She wasn't here that long. She young, man."

"Too young."

"Damn." His eyes came into focus. Blood dripped from his lower lip. I pulled my arm back to hit him again when he said, "How you know her? Who she to you?"

Time passed without my answer. His breath wheezed in and out through his nose. In the bedroom, the woman strained against her bonds, screamed into her gag. I removed a small black notebook from my inside pocket and flipped it open, readied my pen.

"Tell me who did it to her. Tell me their names and how I can find them."

CHAPTER SEVENTEEN
DONNER

Ibaka led us back into Dub's apartment, past a shattered coffee table and a turned-over recliner. There, on the floor, his dreadlocks matted with blood and flecks of bone, was our man Richard Webster—Dub. In truth, he'd been lucky to live as long as he had.

I wondered if we had gotten here sooner, if maybe something would have changed. Maybe we could have helped him, even caught our guy. I didn't waste long on that line of thought. It wouldn't get us anywhere.

And this wasn't a loss I would mourn.

"Here lies one dead pimp," I said. "Adios, pimp."

Hendricks said, "Dub got dead. Things shake out. Scum claiming scum. And still we work it."

Ibaka wore her gloves already. By way of confirming his identity, she lifted a wallet off the top of the TV and worked her way through it. She found and held out a New York driver's license toward me. "Richard W. Webster," she said. "Address in Harlem. Can you believe it?"

"He tarnishes the neighborhood's fine name."

"This stain's been here long enough to have a sheet like he does, still never bothered to get a California license."

It was ironic. I gave her that. Illegal too.

I looked at the address, somehow relieved to be looking at an old New York license, even after all this time. Dub was from a bad block in Spanish Harlem, way over on the West Side—home to some of the city's worst crack hustle. Even dead in his pajamas on the floor of a dirty apartment in the Tenderloin, Dub had done well to get away from there.

I saw the scars on his face: old scars, long-ago cuts that had healed and only added to his persona. He was like that old tortoise, its shell scraped and gnarled, who still plodded along—until that one fateful day.

Hendricks toed Dub's leg with his boot. "Real looker, this guy."

One cut went across his forehead, clear down over one eye and onto the cheek below. The eye was milky white, pupil and iris washed out from the wound.

"Oh yeah. No way anyone would know him but as a pretty boy."

"Pretty boy with a lot of women." Ibaka read off her sheets. "This Cyrano held down half the women in the 'Loin."

I said, "Don't I know it."

She glanced around the apartment at the filth and the wreckage. "Though calling the hookers in the 'Loin *women* might be stretching the truth."

"Still, he had some run regardless."

Hendricks said, "Chicks with dicks. Guys with fake boobs. Love this city."

I thanked him for the clarification.

Scanning the wreckage, if Dub was actually a major player, controlling a lot of women and money, he didn't live like it. Some people like a low profile, but this was gutter profile. Too much of the proceeds into his veins or up his nose.

He had a fake polar-bear-skin rug on the floor, now soaked in blood, and a TV that wasn't even sixty inches.

"Makes you wonder what went down here." Hendricks stooped to get a closer look at the body.

Ibaka clued us in: "This took some time. Look at the hand. Every finger broken, sometimes twice. You know how hard that is to do?"

It looked like a handful of sausages. Hendricks tested the fingers, wiggled each one to tell what was intact under the skin.

He said, "Never seen anything like this."

"Call it a new form of waterboarding. Next thing they'll be using it up at Homeland." She pointed to Dub's arm, pulled up his sleeve to show the skin above the wrist. I counted four cuts, going up toward the elbow, each deeper than the last. The topmost one, closest to his elbow, was more than an inch wide. It made a rectangle about three or four inches long where the skin had been peeled back to reveal muscle. Then the muscle had been cut again, and a cube pulled out of it.

This level of pain had never occurred to me.

Ibaka straightened. "This was just the start, I'm guessing. We roll this boy over to see where he bled out, I think we'll find a whole new interpretation of dark ages."

CHAPTER EIGHTEEN

Hendricks and I sat in our car on O'Farrell, trying to let the violence of what we'd seen wash away. We each had a coffee and donut from a trashy place on the corner, basically the best of what you could expect from this part of town.

I checked the clock on the dash, trying to imagine myself going home and having a normal night, even getting to the gym to shoot around. Didn't seem likely after what all we'd just seen. Ibaka was right about the damage done to Dub; it was worse than we'd seen, Farrow included.

This was turning into some kind of a single-nutjob case, to use a technical term, a possible killing spree by someone bent on taking out parts of the filth in the city's sex-and-pain-for-hire racket. This went way beyond any normal on-call week in homicide. A killing spree meant talking it over with our lieutenant, Mike "the Knife" Bowen. If that went well, he'd start a separate detail to handle the case, take us off call to let us focus. He'd even give us some support, if he felt generous.

Any chance of me getting time to myself was fast disappearing. I'd be lucky to see Alan in two weeks.

But who was he? Just some guy I'd barely met. There was no reason for me to even be thinking about him when I had active profiles on Match and OkCupid. Was there? Tons of guys in this city, and I could go out with one any night of the week I could get free time.

Still, thoughts of a guy I'd barely played one game with kept tumbling back.

I tried to shake it off, physically shaking my head to clear it.

The coffee helped. I told Hendricks it wasn't half bad, offered a toast.

"You and your high-priced lattes, Donner. You miss out on the quality of an old brewed pot of crappy French vanilla." Hendricks tipped his cup. "Or hazelnut."

"Awww. You're such a sweet tooth at heart."

"Exactly. Nothing wrong with a cruller now and then." Hendricks held up his old-fashioned. "So long as the civilians don't see. Can't live down to our stereotype."

"So what about this case? We need to go to Bowen."

He took another bite, said through his mouthful, "I was just thinking: it's the little things in life that make it all worthwhile. A little perk given all the caloric requirements of our work."

"The little things." Something I'd said a hundred times in the months we'd partnered. I tried to convince myself to have perspective each time, saying it for myself as much as for him. Now he turned it around. This reminder to keep up a healthy awareness of the present, life's small offerings.

If I believed in anything, this was it. This was my faith.

At least, that's what I tried to convince myself.

Maybe I could make it to the gym.

He drank more coffee. "Here's to having stomachs like iron."

We toasted. I had added two spoons of sugar, but the coffee still tasted bitter.

"So what do we do?"

"I say we step away for a minute. This freak's out there doing his damnedest to make it a bad week in homicide, in the city, but maybe we miss something if we go rushing in half-cocked. Let's let it all wash over us with a night's rest, see what shakes out."

To say this was an unconventional approach would be an understatement. But then, Hendricks had been accused of doing things his own way for years, since long before we became partners.

"So we don't tell Bowen yet?"

"Let's let Lund and Peters catch a few cases now. We focus on this ourselves without getting the big man involved."

"What's the benefit?"

He drank again, sucked anything extra off his upper lip. "I need to think a bit."

"So now you're getting all Zen-style on me?"

He lifted and dropped his shoulders. "Maybe I am."

I stretched in my seat; I was on the passenger side, with the laptop bolted in front of me. Maybe Hendricks wanted me to read between the lines. If he was letting our guy have the night, wipe out another sleazebag maybe with some additional time, then why would I go against it.

But really I had no idea what to think.

I touched my lips, thought about smoking a cigarette. I'd given it up over a year ago, both at my own urging and Tim's insistence that it left an awful smell on my hair and clothes, but all of a sudden, I missed it.

Even without Tim, I was glad I'd quit. I felt better and liked my new nonsmoking life—being a smoker had turned from a night-out anomaly into something I needed. That had real effects. Now I had better wind and felt physically stronger.

"Go outside and smoke," he said. "If I thought it'd help me get past that scene, I'd do the same."

"I'm good."

He laughed. "I was just thinking, won't this make a good story on my next date?" He reached down for the starter and revved the engine.

"Especially if you never want to see her again."

"Oh, Donner. You're the only date I could share this fine moment with." He batted his eyelashes.

"Harassment. Seriously. *And* you're making me ill." I put my coffee in a holder. "I'm going to start carrying a recorder in my purse."

"Please do."

He popped the last bite of cruller into his mouth. With his coffee in one hand, he shifted into drive and pulled out onto the street. It was just about rush hour in San Francisco, and we were headed toward the worst of it.

"So what's next?"

"We go home for the night, come back at this again tomorrow."

"You're sure?"

Hendricks nodded. "What you have planned for later? Anything good?"

"Tonight? Nada. I'll probably check email and see if I can drink myself to sleep."

"No. No. Do something good for yourself. Clear your head after that scene at Dub's. It'll do us both some good." He smiled. "Partner's orders."

CHAPTER NINETEEN

So I followed what Hendricks said. I went home from the Hall and ate a salmon filet with a side of steamed kale and quinoa. I checked in with my online dating, saw nothing I felt any need to respond to, and left it at that.

At seven thirty, when the youth league practices ended, I was the first adult out on the basketball courts at the rec center. Dribbling my own ball, making layups from both sides, it took me only a few minutes of activity to break a sweat and start feeling better. I felt the rush of breathing hard, transitioned to knocking down jumpers from the wings and picked up the pace a notch.

Two guys came on at the other end of the court, started a game of one-on-one. I was only peripherally aware of them; my focus was on the case in the back of my head and the ball in the front. At times, the best and biggest breaks on cases or realizations of life happened while I was doing something athletic, getting my mind free and clear.

Maybe this was what Hendricks meant by doing something good for myself, clearing my head, why he'd insisted we take the night off. At the same time, if a lax attitude led to another dead scumbag, I wouldn't be the first one to sound an alarm.

But there *was* something that nagged at me about it. I spiked the ball with my fist; it bounced up hard, just missing my face.

"Hey, watch out there."

I turned and saw Alan standing before me. He and a few of his friends had just arrived. No Mustache, but I recognized one of the others from our game.

"Hi. Yeah, don't want to hurt the ball, do I?"

He smiled. "To say nothing of your face."

I could feel myself blush, which made me say something fast: "Not that."

"Listen, I—" He paused, and in that moment, my phone rang. I had set it on a bleacher under the basket. That was part of the job: to stay by the phone. We were, after all, still on call.

The ringer chimed again.

"That's your phone?"

If Lund and Peters were dodging another body, I would kill them.

I said, "I should get that," and jogged over to it. Picking it up, I saw Lieutenant Bowen's number on the screen and knew my night of relaxation had come to an end.

"Sorry." I pushed to talk and held the phone to my ear. "Donner."

Alan shifted his weight from one foot to the other. I hated being *this girl*, the one who could never give herself in to what was happening, who always had to answer her job's call.

"We got a potential wit for your body on Ellis. Says she was on scene as it transpired and saw your suspect. You'll want to get down here and get whatever you can from her."

"Roger that, Lieutenant."

He had already hung up.

I would have to rush home, take a shower, and get down to the Hall fast. Hendricks would be on his way too, and maybe he'd offer me a ride. If not, I'd call a cab.

Alan said, "You have to go."

"It's that obvious?" I reminded myself to enjoy the little things, that this guy had actually come over to talk to me. I checked out his black-with-white-trim Kobe high-tops and baggy shorts. Tight shirt. He was all right.

But my internal Bowen clock ticked.

"Yeah," I said. I pushed my hair back behind my ear. "I do have to run. Wish I could stay."

"Light up that jumper again."

I laughed. Complimenting a girl on her game—he could do a lot worse.

"What are you?" He gestured at my phone. "Do you work for a startup? My friends with startups work *all* the time."

I started shoving my basketball into my duffle, pushed an arm through a jacket sleeve.

I wanted to ask his number, get it, and run, but being so forward scared off more guys than it didn't, in my experience.

What was even worse at scaring guys off was the truth of my job.

I drew in my breath and gave it to him straight. "I'm a cop. Homicide."

"Oh." His face showed surprise, then tension, then pleasure. I could live with that. Better than the usual scared reaction. "Must be something important then."

With my jacket on both arms now, I sat to yank my sweatpants up over my Jordans. "It's a case. So yeah, kind of."

He turned to check his friends, who appeared to be more interested in shooting buckets than their friend talking to a woman. Maybe I really was becoming one of the guys. That or these were real ballers. I knew there was a reason Alan kept popping into my head. He wasn't fake; he really had game.

"So, think I can get your number?"

I stopped what I was doing, sweats at midthigh, and looked up. Not my most attractive moment, I'm sure, but I'm not sure he didn't feel as awkward as I.

I might have giggled, just a little.

I know: Clara Donner, homicide cop, is not supposed to do that, but it happened. It did.

He shrugged. "Maybe we could play ball or something else. Get together for a movie."

"Even dinner," I said.

"Yeah. That's cool too."

I stood up and showed him my phone, went through the routine where I called him so he had my number. Then I had his too. I'd add his name to it later.

Then he said, "I'm Alan."

"Clara. Yeah. I remember." We shook hands. Awkward. I wanted to give him a pound or a knuckle bump, but that'd have been even worse. What I really wanted to do was kiss him. But not yet.

I'd see what happened when he called.

CHAPTER TWENTY

When I got to the Hall, I found Hendricks already waiting for me at his desk, pushing paper around with a pencil. Bowen's office was dark, blinds drawn.

"Witness in four. So much for us thinking about it, huh?"

"I was surprised it was Bowen who called us."

Hendricks frowned. "Yeah, well. Bad news travels. You ready for her?"

He handed me the file, and I buzzed through it. Her name was Deborah Szajngarten, and I'd be damned if I'd try to say that out loud. She had walked in off the street about two hours before, talking about Dub, details of the murder scene she couldn't have faked.

It was strange to actually get a witness, especially one who came in. Maybe that's what interested Bowen.

"Come on." Hendricks got up and led me around to the viewing room. We checked out Szajngarten through the two-way glass while she waited. She looked worse for wear, like a seven-month street zombie who'd gotten there in four—and was pissed off we'd kept her waiting.

I felt my adrenaline rise. No need for caffeine now.

"Let's do this," I said, and Hendricks led us in.

"Why you got me in here like this?" she asked as soon as we'd opened the door. "I'm not a suspect." She pointed at the mirror. "Who's behind there?"

"I apologize, Ms. Szaj—" Hendricks stopped. "How do you say that?"

"Just call me Shine," she said, "Debbie Shine what everyone calls me. Or Sunshine."

He smiled. "Nice. I can do that, Ms. Sunshine."

I leaned on a wall, watching her body language as he asked for her particulars, went over what was already in the file. When I saw he was making her uncomfortable, I sat down.

"What my partner's trying to say"—I reached across the table to show her my empty hand, a peace gesture—"and you'll have to excuse him for being so male tonight. He's not always like this." I winked. "We dragged him away from some private business."

I shot Hendricks a wink of apology but knew he was happy to be the sacrificial lamb if it made her more comfortable.

"We can take you back out to talk at our desks, but this room is more quiet. Outside can get pretty loud."

Hendricks said, "There's no one behind that mirror. I promise."

She pushed her lips out, nodded like it was settled. "I'm all right."

She started rummaging through her purse, brought out a crumpled soft pack of Camels. "Mind if I smoke?"

I pushed an empty paper cup toward her to use as an ashtray, the ring of old coffee long dried on its bottom.

"How about if you tell us what brought you in tonight?"

"My friend got killed. I saw who did it." She massaged her face, rubbing around her eyes. I wanted to know if she'd slept, what all she'd done, and where she'd been since Dub's death the night before.

"Your friend?" Hendricks said. "Dub."

She turned away, lit her cigarette, and inhaled hard enough that I could hear the tobacco crackle. Squinting through the smoke, she said, "I seen the guy clear as I see you two right now. I cared about Dub. No matter what you heard."

"Would you be willing to identify him? Maybe look through some mug shots or sit with a sketch artist?"

"Yeah. I could do that." She nodded. "I would."

Hendricks asked if she knew the man she'd seen, and she pulled her lips away from yellowed teeth like they hurt her—or the memory did. Her gums weren't as far gone as some of the others'. The cigarette burned in her hand. In truth, I liked the secondhand smoke. "Had you ever seen him before last night?"

"I thought Dub maybe recognized the dude. He said something to him." She coughed. "I don't know who the hell this guy was."

"How did he get inside?"

"Dub lets in guys. Dudes that needed a quick fix." She shrugged. "Maybe." She stopped, unsure what was all right to tell us.

I touched her hand. "Go on. It's all right. Whatever you tell us is okay."

"Time to time. Usually someone he knew real well, but last night we was partying hard. What was Dub thinking? I don't know. Never seen this dude before last night."

Her leg started bouncing double time under the table. "Why he let him in, then? Dub. Why he do that?" She smoked. "I really can't get in trouble for what I say here, right? No Carmen Miranda?"

It was all she could do to stay seated at the table.

"You're safe, Debbie. Nothing you say can get you in trouble here. We're just after the man who killed your friend."

"That's good. Good then." She inhaled, nodded as if settling something inside her. She tested the surface tension of the tabletop with her fingers, as if trying to draw reassurance.

Then more words came out in a rush. "I asked if he wanted something from me. You know? Like, he was staring. So I asked. Right? Said he wanted to get me out of there. *Save me* from Dub. I laughed. Who's he gonna take out of there?"

Hendricks asked, "You said Dub called him something? Can you remember what it was?"

I touched his wrist, trying to ease him off, get him to let her tell it. The story was coming out; we just had to give it space to flow.

"We both saw his face then, saw he wasn't right. No." She closed her eyes for a moment. When she opened them again, she said, "Something was in his eyes, like, you know when you see something in a person real bad?"

I told her I did, though from the looks of her, she had already seen plenty of hard, bad things in her world. More than I. This guy must've been a real prize. "His eyes?"

"Yeah, creepy. Maybe Dub did know him. I don't know. He called the dude 'Father,' I think. 'Padre.' This guy didn't like that one bit. But then Dub just did it again. You don't kill a guy for that though. Uh-uh.

"Maybe he knew the guy from somewheres, I'm figuring. Then the dude looked angry. His clothes was all black. This white dude. He was white. Did I say that already? Clean cut, you know?" She bit her lips, nodding to herself.

"Then he got this look. He stared me right in the face and told me he loved me. *Loved* me, he said. The fuck is that? What kind of love?"

She had smoked her cigarette down to its filter, then lit another off the butt.

"Then he grabbed D and threw him against the wall. Broke things. I tried to fight him off, to help out D, you know? But the guy tossed me. I hit my head."

She fingered the back of her skull.

"We can get that checked out for you," Hendricks said.

"No. No hospitals. I'm fine." She paused, studying the table again. "When I come to, I was tied up in the bed. Then I just heard what he did. To Dub. I couldn't move."

She stopped for a time, gathering herself, smoking, her hands shaking.

"I couldn't hear what the guy was asking, you know? But I heard Dub saying names between when he was crying out. Just some names.

"Why he did that to D?"

We looked at her without answers. She paused as if she might cry, but didn't. I wished I'd brought a box of tissues in with us. In my jacket I kept a handkerchief, but didn't offer.

"Then the guy come in and untie me. It was done. Dub been quiet for a while. He told me to wait fifteen minutes before I moved. Said he didn't want to hurt me, but he would though. He told me again that he loved me. Said I could be all right if I left the city.

"So I waited. He left. I heard the door close. I still waited. Like, you know, it could be a trick or something."

I nodded, but she was already into it on her own.

"Then after what I thought was fifteen minutes, enough time, I come out and seen what he did. How he done Dub. *Man.*" She squeezed her eyes shut and tears spilled over.

When she was calm, Hendricks said, "You said he wanted to save you? Why would he say that?"

"Man, I don't know. Some strange shit, right? But not like save me take me to the country or something, more like save me in like a Biblical sense. He said, offer salvation. Like he was a preacher man or something. A freak what he was."

"Anything else you can remember? Anything at all?"

"He took a picture. I saw it when he was leaving. Had one of Dub's pictures, framed, under his arm. I don't have no idea why he would."

Hendricks leaned in. "What was it a picture of?"

"Who," she said. "Just one of Dub and some of us girls from a Christmas party."

"A picture?" I said. "Anything else?"

She shook her head no. Then when we asked her again about working with a sketch artist, she nodded.

She ground out her cigarette in the paper cup. "I don't care. Tell me who I talk to. I can describe him. I want you to catch him."

CHAPTER TWENTY-ONE
MICHAEL

In the end, Dub didn't give me everything I wanted, but he gave me enough. He said there were four men, some kind of a party. These were the ones I wanted. I got descriptions, locations, who they were, but not their full names. With Dub it was as much as I could expect, as much as he would give.

Four.

And whatever disparate connections there were between them I'd have to uncover. I had to find them, then make them pay.

When it was done, I delivered Dub, sent him on. At that point, would have been crueler if I hadn't. I said a silent prayer over his body. This sinner would need more than my absolution to walk through heaven's gates.

I untied the girl, left her waiting on the bed. She'd have to pass his body, and perhaps that might be a message to her, one she'd hear. But I didn't hold a lot of hope. From the way she fought her ties and the look of her teeth, eyes, and skin, I knew she was already gone. Not that the devil had claimed her yet; she had chosen her path.

She was far down that road.

What I saw as I walked back to the rectory was more of the same: sinners. I saw so many of them in this city, on these streets. Only a small few came to God. Those who came to ask for absolution, such a small piece of the whole, a tiny fraction; it was hard to understand why more didn't take matters into their own hands. What drew me forward was my love for her and the need to cleanse her for heaven. But I also wanted the men who hurt her to pay.

I did it for Him. In His name. As Sodom and Gomorrah fell, and the flood cleansed the world in Noah's time, I would do my part to the city's filth. Whatever I was able.

It was dawn, and the streets had emptied as I headed back, pale light showing only the few homeless who slept in plain sight. Most retreated to alleys, doorways, or underneath whatever they could find.

We offered a place for them in the church for parts of the day, to sleep in the pews. The Gubbio Project. But now they had the shelters and their own haunts. The shelters could only take so many, and they had to be in by a certain hour. The laws helped the city to go on eating itself. Nothing new.

I didn't have time to stop in and see her, though I wanted to very much. I wanted to see she was all right, that she had slept. Instead, I had my duties: lighting candles and the preparations for morning mass to tend to.

Father Kevin was there, filling the prayer altar with fresh candles. He whistled. He had already set out the sacrament for our service: His body and blood.

Inside the church, protected from the world outside, Kevin was cheerful. Always cheerful.

I wanted to ask him what he made of the sinners on the streets, how he could forgive in the name of the Lord, or how he could even walk past them without getting sick. I wanted to know how he could omit them from his heart, avoid carrying them in it.

Somehow, he did.

"Good morning," he said.

"Good morning."

We smiled at one another and nodded. Then his face changed. He saw something in me, noticed a scent or a mark or blood. Or perhaps he felt my energy, knew it had changed. Maybe he suspected me of keeping Emily in my room, or heard me slipping out late at night.

"Everything is right with you, Michael?" he asked. Grave concern.

"Yes. Yes. Everything is fine." I hadn't slept more than a few hours in the last two days, didn't know what he might see, or think he saw.

"Sometimes I worry for you," he said. He stepped to his left, stood in front of me, meeting my eyes. "Since you come here, you do excellent work. Still, I worry. You come in trouble, on drugs. I concerned. Now you with us long time. Still, I ask when I see you not okay."

"Yes. I understand." He waited for me to say more. "I can assure you, all is well. Thank you, Father. There is nothing to cause you worry."

He nodded, though still grim.

Our eyes met, and I smiled. "I am all right." I reached out to his hands, squeezed them, and he seemed relieved. He smiled too.

"Very well." He turned then and was gone.

I wondered at his comment, his concerns and what I was showing, but there was no time for that. A long time ago he had saved me. Now was my time to save another.

I doubted if Father Kevin directly heard His word, if anyone did. I was chosen for a reason, for a specific path. Myself alone.

I often wondered at the other fathers: how they could live in this desolation and not become ill with it, how they could tolerate the filth on the streets outside our walls. Somehow, they did not feel forced to do more for Him. He was sick with it, I knew, for He had told me. I needed to do more to make things right.

He didn't speak to them.

I watched Father Kevin's back as he walked into the sacristy, whispered after him, "Forgive me, Father, for I have sinned."

CHAPTER TWENTY-TWO
DONNER

When we were done, we let Debbie Shine go. She was stubborn, refusing treatment for her head injury, as if a visit to the Hall of Justice was more than enough, let alone men in white coats and nurses touching her. I couldn't entirely blame her. By the time we'd had her sit down with a sketch artist to get a representation of our man's face, she'd been with us nearly five hours. Open gym at the rec center was long over.

I sat at my desk, drinking coffee, looking at the drawing, feeling the usual brain scramble at the back end of a seventeen-hour shift. A night of hell, to be precise. From the scene at Richard Webster's apartment to hearing Debbie Shine tell her story not once but twice and then a third time for consistency, drinking coffee all the way through, I felt like someone had run hot lead through my veins and scraped them out. I could barely get my legs to stop twitching.

"You should get home." Hendricks stood above my desk, jacket on, tie straightened, ready to leave. "We come back and go at this tomorrow early, we'll have fresh eyes. Be more logical, sensible. I can barely even think straight."

"Yeah, partner. Maybe you're right." I wanted to say more, ask him what he thought of the guy saying he loved her, what he thought it meant about saving her, or the line about "salvation," but I didn't.

"Listen, we come back later, put this into the Clip, see what comes back."

"I hear you." But I didn't look away from the drawing. I was trying to get a sense of the guy, burn his face into my memory.

Our perp had dark coloring with hair cut short, a heavy brow, and eyes set apart in an appealing way. He wasn't bad looking. He had the scruff of a three-day growth, what some considered a beard these days, a Roman nose that most would consider strong. Nine times out of ten, an artist's rendition from witness testimony carried a look of anger or something resembling fear, but his face appeared calm, at peace. Maybe Debbie Shine's description had captured something there.

The artist had drawn in the top of his black shirt, just the outline of his collarbones, not even shoulders.

"A preacher," I said. "A priest."

Hendricks was gone. I didn't know for how long. The night squad was coming in and putting their notes together for their shift. They were on the opposite end of a world.

A preacher was what she'd called him. "Father," Dub had said.

So what if he really was?

I put the drawing down on my desk and exhaled hard from the top of my lungs. Bright fluorescents shone on me from above, and I realized I was barely awake. I needed to get home. I didn't go anywhere. I was stuck in one of those moments where your mind knows what you're supposed to do next physically, but your body isn't ready. I didn't move.

What happened to time in these moments? I wondered. Does it get counted against you, or are you just on a time-out? What did these moments really mean in our lives?

I suppose I was merely feeling the effects of the night, letting exhaustion work its power. I knew that a part of this thing was him, not only what he'd done, but who he was. I felt like I was starting to put pieces together and make progress.

I was waiting. I waited. Sometimes it can be important to just sit and wait.

But for what?

From whom?

Divine intervention? I don't believe in anything like that. Instead, I try to figure it all out on my own.

Wish me luck.

In the waiting, important things can come, even if you don't feel them coming, I believe. These are often the moments that I remember much later as relevant.

That moment, late at night after having a man's face rendered for the first time, sitting still at my desk, watching the sunlight just start to shine over the East Bay—those moments I still remember. That was when it struck me like a bolt from the sky. You could call it Occam's razor, or the shortest line between two points, or the inspiration I'd been waiting for.

Basically, I decided to look at things for what they really could be, try the simplest explanation for what Debbie Shine had just told us: that our perp actually could be a priest—a real one. Not just a lunatic, but an actual man of the cloth.

PART TWO
WEDNESDAY

CHAPTER TWENTY-THREE

I blamed Hendricks for leaving, acting like our shift was over and just going home. Sure, I needed to sleep, but whatever it was that made me stay in the chair and wait it out, waiting for *something*, that was the part of me that knew where this was headed, that there was still work to do.

"Hey, hey!" I said, getting the attention of two fresh-faced investigators from the night shift. It was Dale Bennett and Mark Coggins. "Either of you two religious?"

If I'd processed that it was Bennett and Coggins before asking, I wouldn't have bothered. Bennett was the guy to send out dirty jokes through the departmental email, and Coggins routinely bragged about going home with women he met at investigations, not infrequently describing them as barn animals. "Man, this one hog," he'd tell us, "we rolled in the mud."

I could barely stand the sight of him.

They laughed, shaking their heads. Coggins winked. "Ask Meyers," he said.

I caught Josh Meyers brushing cruller crumbs out of his beard by the coffee machine.

"Yo," I said. He blanched, maybe more from how I looked than because he'd been caught eating crullers. This was his usual. "Does a preacher wear a robe and a collar?"

"*A preacher* generally refers to one who preaches," he said. "Someone like a minister or a pastor. No, they don't wear the robe."

"How about that nice little white collar that goes at the neck?"

He shook his head. "Not that either. Not usually. *Preacher* usually refers to congregation leaders in the Protestant, Baptist, or Evangelical faiths. So sometimes collar, sometimes not."

"But a priest, he's got the collar, right?"

"No. Not so much. The collar isn't big these days—not since Vatican II."

"Right," I said. "Vatican II. I didn't know there was a sequel."

He laughed, then started into a lengthy explanation, but I was quick to thank him and leave him be.

I started my second day of work in a row that morning without going home, just washed my face and brushed my teeth and kept drinking coffee as I put my nose to the grindstone, started making copies of the sketch artist's drawing and putting them up around the station, faxing them to other districts, and uploading them to the database to go into the Clip.

After that, I started looking through church information online, trying to find a priest who looked like our goon, coming up with lots of nothing. One thing I found out: we've got almost five times as many churches out there as police stations. You might think district stations cover a city, especially a big one like San Francisco, but churches cover it that much more. In any case, there were a lot of priests to be checked.

I sat at my desk, making calls, faxing the picture, working with little help from the other investigators, who were all working their own cases, trying to get clearances to up their own solved rates and protect themselves from fresh budget cuts.

I thought about calling in Hendricks, getting him out of bed or back from wherever he was, but didn't do it. Call it love of a partner or negligence or respect, or just that I was too bleary-eyed from the coffee and lack of sleep to stop long enough to think it through. I guess I needed him more than I knew.

I did what I could, and around six or seven, I retreated to the bunk room—really just an old files closet without windows that had a few cots—and passed out for a couple of hours.

When I woke up, my mouth tasted like boot leather and my clothes felt days old, but physically I felt about eighty-seven percent better.

I was headed down to the lockers and a shower when I passed my desk and saw the red message light blinking. I wanted to ignore it, take care of my physical needs, and come back to the desk later, but before I knew it, I was in the chair with the phone at my ear, punching buttons.

I had four messages from cops at different districts, guys who said they could recognize the man in the picture from a church they knew. The first one said he had seen the guy at a church in the Mission, on Van Ness and Twentieth Street. I knew the place, pictured it across the street from a dive hamburger place called the Whiz that I used to walk past when I'd lived in the Mission. Most of the observers I'd seen walking into or out of that church were Mexican cowboy types who wore ten-gallon hats and pointed boots as part of their Sunday best. These weren't sex workers. These were family folks: the men went to church with their wives and children, holding hands as they walked across the street. This one didn't have the right fit. Even if they had a priest who fit the description, which I doubted, he wasn't going to be my guy.

The second was from a cop in the Richmond calling about a Roman Catholic place. He said they had a priest who matched the drawing almost perfectly, but that he had a mustache and different hair. I wasn't sure how that made him fit the description, especially from an eyewitness account less than forty-eight hours old. And again, not the right fit. Roman Catholic in the Richmond? Maybe Point Richmond in the East Bay, but not north of Golden Gate Park. No, for this guy to care so much and get so involved with hookers, young S&M types, he had to have a close connection.

My third call was from a cop who walked a beat in the Tenderloin. This felt on target right away. He said he knew the priest in our drawing, saw him most days at St. Boniface Church on Golden Gate at Leavenworth. This was a guy he knew from bringing in homeless to the shelter across the street from the church all the time, or bringing them by to get fed. Said the man was reasonable enough, nice as a priest was bound to be, but with maybe an edge on him, like he'd done a few wrong things or been around the block a bit himself before turning to the cloth. I found myself nodding as I listened, but then I got worried when he said he'd take a walk over right away. I skipped to the start of the message and got the patrolman's name as Officer Cope.

I hung up and dialed the Tenderloin district station, got the duty officer, and told him I was calling from homicide down at the Hall, needed Officer Cope.

While I waited, I tried to get a sense in my head of whether I'd seen this guy. His voice didn't sound familiar. We went all across the city on cases, but it wasn't often I remembered the rank and file. Blame my too-intense focus on the details of an investigation and the fact that I tried to avoid anyone who might know Tim.

When he came on the line, I could tell right away he was talking into a shoulder mic, wasn't in the station. "Donner at the Hall. You're not at St. Boniface, are you?"

"Not yet. I'm heading over."

"Don't. This perp isn't a guy you want to confront on your own."

"I talk to him all the time," he said. "Seems about as vanilla as any other priest in this precinct. Not without his demons, but we're on a first-name basis, you know?"

"Doesn't matter. I'm putting together an apprehension team and coming at him myself."

"I'm less than a block away. They close up for the day in less than twenty minutes. One o'clock. Want me to at least poke my head in and see if he's around?"

I thought about it for a moment. If this cop stops by all the time, maybe our man wouldn't think it odd if he came in for a look around, not asking any questions. But I didn't want to chance it.

"Negative," I said. "Just get out of there. Stay away from the church until I get there. We'll find a way in."

CHAPTER TWENTY-FOUR

I'd told Cope to wait for me at the Tenderloin station with as many other beat cops as he could find. Told him they'd better be wearing vests.

Before moving out, I went to Lieutenant Bowen, waited outside his office while he barked into his phone. In a minute or two, it became clear he wasn't getting off any time soon, so I knocked, and he looked at me, raised his eyebrows. This was his way of inviting me in, such as that was. He held the phone away from his ear while someone talked on. His nod was the last invitation I would get.

"Got a lead on the cases I've been working. Heading out to the Tenderloin for a possible apprehend. Bringing—"

"Hang on," he said into the phone. He checked his duty roster to see who else was on, ran his finger down the list. "Take Bennett and Coggins with you. And be sure to wear your vests."

"Yes, sir. Thanks."

"Donner." He called me back. "Take these." He tossed me the keys to the special gun lockup where we kept the real firepower. "Use the Benellis if you need them."

I one-handed the keys out of the air and walked out before he could change his mind.

Bennett and Coggins were in the bullpen, pretending to do work, when I came back.

"You're up," I said, jangling the keys. "Put your vests on and protect your peckers, boys. We're going to the 'Loin. Heading out for a possible apprehension of a killer with at least three bodies behind him."

"Amen," Bennett said, slapping his monitor on the side. "See *you* later."

Despite his affinity for email forwards, he was not one who had a way with machines.

Hendricks walked in then, rubbing his hands. "Looks like I'm just in time."

"Long as you got some beauty sleep, partner."

"Donner, Jesus. You look like hell."

I touched my hair, gauging its shape and size. I hadn't paid attention to either in twelve hours. "Yeah, baby. Just like you like it."

I brushed past him to the gun room, offering an air kiss as consolation. Inside, I could smell the oil and cold steel. These made me more than a little bit happy. Along the left wall were the SWAT team carbines and the guns we had confiscated in raids or arrests. These were on hand to try out at the range, so we knew what was out there, how it felt to fire what the other guys might be packing. Someone had even picked up a military-grade Barrett Browning, a .50 caliber cannon that would cut through a wall. I hadn't gotten a chance to test it out yet, but Hendricks said it almost took his shoulder off with the recoil.

"That's why it's supposed to be mounted," I had told him.

The carbines, AR-15s, were all reserved for SWAT. We never got our hands on these unless we put in for the extra detail.

The weapons on the right wall were what caught my attention: our Benelli M2 semiautomatic shotguns. If Bowen knew we were headed to a church, he never would have given me the keys. If any of us fired a shotgun in or near a church, our careers would be short.

I imagined the headlines and media attention that could draw.

Hendricks waited. Bennett and Coggins were right behind.

I turned around. "Ah, our suspect. He's a priest. We're heading to a church for the possible apprehend."

"Oh." Hendricks lowered his hands. "Guess we'll have to do without the artillery," he said.

We wore our bulletproof vests but only packed standard sidearms, Sig Sauer P226R, which I had gone to after deciding the 229R was too small for my hand. Given our destination and that none of the crime scenes had involved shootings, I figured we'd be all right.

The drive to the Tenderloin station was a quick eight blocks north on Seventh, but we crossed into a whole new world by just going that far. Not that 850 Bryant was any paradise, but crossing Market on Seventh put us right at UN Plaza and Civic Center, the heart of the city's worst homeless encampment and junkie zone.

"Jesus," I said, staring out the window as Hendricks drove. "Land of the living dead."

"Never ceases to amaze me how far they let this stretch go."

"Are you surprised our killer would come out of this?"

"A church? Yes. The 'Loin? No. But we'll see what we find."

I shuddered at the thought of what a beat cop on these streets must see on a daily basis. Then again, I probably spent more time with corpses.

We drove up Leavenworth past Golden Gate and turned right onto Eddy toward the district station. Out front, patrol cars lined up along the right side of the street, creating their own parking lot. When I radioed inside to Cope, he came out with three other officers, two cars' worth. They fell into line behind us as we looped back down to Market at McAllister, then to Leavenworth again to reach the block of Golden Gate where St. Boniface was.

We set up a perimeter outside the church with our two homicide units and two black-and-whites from the precinct. I looked up at the big tan church, its bell tower and rose window. The entrance was set back from the street by a courtyard with a big palm tree in it.

As I got out, Bennett and Coggins were already closing in on the big wrought-iron gate. It looked closed, locked tight. They'd already drawn their weapons.

"Guys," I said, "guys." I waved them down, trying to calm them.

A patrolwoman came up to me from the last black-and-white unit. She said, "They're open until one o'clock, letting the homeless inside to sleep. Then they close up shop." She had her hair pulled back tight into a bun and looked killer serious, a necessity of the job. Her nameplate read "S. Bruce."

I checked my watch: just after two o'clock. That explained the gate being locked.

"So how do we get in there?" I asked. "Where's the doorbell?"

"Shelter and food kitchen across the street." She turned to show me a big, modern building with "**St. Anthony Foundation**" across its facade. A short, rough-hewn guard was already crossing the street.

"What happening here, Officers?" His mustache might've been trimmed with a Weedwacker. He wore a dark-blue nylon jacket that said "Security" on it and looked like he was used to handling a lot.

"We need to get inside the church. Any chance you can help?"

"Nobody in there but the priests, Officer."

Officer Bruce told him to call inside, get someone to open up, and he went off like he'd been given a mission.

"This place have any back exits?" I asked.

She shook her head. "Old as this building is, I wouldn't even know who to ask. But I don't *think* there's any way to get out to McAllister. That's the next street over."

Hendricks came around the car, and I pointed up at the towers, two columns of evenly spaced narrow windows climbing five stories high between a larger central bell tower that probably went up eight stories.

"Hate to chase someone up those if they're running. Let's hope it doesn't happen."

Hendricks looked up. "Amen, sister."

I checked his face, trying to tell how aware he was of his religious terminology, but he didn't crack a smile.

I fingered the safety strap over my holster, unsnapped it, and felt along the handle of my weapon. I hadn't used it in a long time and didn't want to.

A forties-ish Asian priest opened a side door off the church's central facade and began his walk across the courtyard. He wore dark jeans and a gray sweatshirt, brilliant white sneakers. Definitely not our man.

I breathed a sigh of relief and inhaled deep. I had no idea what we might find inside.

CHAPTER TWENTY-FIVE

The priest who came to open the gate was gray around the temples, with thick black hair above them, an older man, weathered but tight skinned, like he could deflect so much of what life threw at him with just his face. This was a man to stare down the world and let its problems wash off his back.

I assumed he was the head guy. Or the head guy under *the* head guy, to be more precise.

"There is no one inside now but us," he said, coming up to the gate. "All parishioners across street eating lunch."

I leaned down closer to him so I could speak quietly. "No, Father," I told him. "We're here looking for one of your own."

His eyes cast down immediately, past the locks to wherever it is that you look when you know something you don't want to tell the police. I'd seen this look before on a thousand witnesses and criminals, but never from a priest. Guilt rushed over his face in a hot flush. He had something to tell us but wouldn't give it up until he was ready. I could wait. If all went well, we'd find our man first and talk later.

"Father Kevin," he introduced himself as he opened the gate, and we shook hands.

I told him my name and rank, and he let something else pass behind his eyes, something like fear.

"What's happening here, Father?"

He stepped back and away, laughed. "Isn't that what I should ask you? Why you are here?"

I smiled despite it all, pulled out the artist's sketch, and showed him. He nodded, too quickly, and held his arm toward the chapel. He wasn't sure what was happening or what his man had done, but he had known whom, that this would be the one.

"Do you know this man?"

He nodded. "That is Father Michael."

I waved to Hendricks to get in close, to be sure he was hearing this.

"He should be done with chores now. I show you to his room."

I waved our guys in and had Officer Bruce and her partner hold the perimeter in case he managed to slip out. Bennett, Coggins, and Hendricks came with me. We followed Father Kevin across the court-yard. He moved none too quickly, but what could we do? I'd be damned if I was going to rush a priest.

Church was something I hadn't been to since before high school. I dated a guy who was Jewish for a little while, and he liked to go to temple a few times a year at the high holidays, but church? Not in my world. Not even Christmas or Easter. Being in the quiet and austere space was more foreign to me than dealing with the anarchy and desolation on the Tenderloin.

Hendricks came up alongside. "Think he'll come easy?"

"Shit, I hope so." Immediately I regretted swearing inside the church grounds, thought about crossing myself as a request for forgiveness, but that would feel more strange. Instead, I waved for Bennett and Coggins to keep their guns down.

"Oh my," said Father Kevin. He stopped. He had led us to a small alcove off to the side. The sounds of kids playing echoed from a nearby courtyard. "Please do not use those here. Can you leave?" He gestured with his hand back out to our cars.

"No. I'm sorry. I'm sure they won't be necessary, but we can't leave them outside."

"I wish . . . ," he started. "You would not have them here." He pointed up toward the chapel.

We waited a beat.

"I'm sorry. We can't leave our weapons outside. They're part of the job." I didn't want to tell him Father Michael was suspected of taking people apart with knives, anything to indicate the violence of the crimes.

"Yes." He waited again, I suppose hoping that something would change. Nothing did; these were the paths we each walked, the worlds we lived in.

"Very well," he said, turning toward the interior.

"Believe me, Father, I recognize that discharging a firearm inside a house of religion is about the worst thing an officer could do. We'll take every precaution not to."

"Yes," he said, "well."

He opened the door and let us inside a dark hallway with white walls. I could see off to our right where a door led to the main chapel, possibly its towers, and the long winding stairs up. We were in some offshoot that the public didn't use. Father Kevin led us to the left, down a hall toward what looked from the outside like residences—maybe what they'd call the rectory.

Bennett and Coggins still had their superagent routine going, and Hendricks looked as uncomfortable as I'd ever seen him. He crossed himself as soon as he passed through the doors, and I had an image of him growing up going to Catholic school and attending catechism one afternoon a week. I didn't see any sign of his weapon. It occurred to me that something in his background might be why he hadn't suspected Debbie Shine might be talking about a priest.

Father Kevin said, "I take you to rectory. Perhaps he in his room."

We entered a stairwell, and the priest led us down one flight to a dim basement level. The thick stone walls held the cold; it was probably ten degrees cooler in here than outside.

He pushed open a door and stood to the side. We exchanged a glance. Beyond him, I saw a narrow hallway where brown wooden doors lined each side, breaking spans of white-painted walls. Small lanterns, electric fixtures made to look like old lamps at just about head height, offered the only light.

"Father Michael room is second door on right."

I ran the scenarios through my head, considered asking Father Kevin to knock and ask Father Michael to step outside.

As if he knew, he said, "I go no farther."

"You could help us by asking him to step out. It might save someone getting hurt."

I waited a beat for him to change his mind, just like he had waited for us to leave our guns. When nothing happened I proceeded into the hall, with Hendricks right behind me. As I walked, my flats clicked on the floor. I figured it had been quite some time since anyone had worn women's shoes down here.

I tensed up, thinking about the scenes Father Michael had left behind: Doug Farrow, Dub, Jay Piper. I didn't want to take any chances on scaring him off. Butcher or not—priest even—this guy liked his violence.

I slipped my shoes off and stepped down onto the cold concrete in my thin socks. I felt my bones chill. Down here, in this building made of stone, it likely never got warm.

Now I stepped quietly, sliding my feet and using my toes, conscious of the perspiration I was leaving behind. I raised my weapon. Hendricks still hadn't drawn his. At the second door, I waved him across to the other side. He still had his shoes on but did his best to walk softly.

As I lifted my left hand to knock, Father Kevin started down the hall in a hurry. He waved me back, met my eyes, and nodded. I mouthed a thanks.

Now he knocked at the door, and I stood to his side. He was between Hendricks and me. I stood back across the narrow hall's other side, my gun low but ready.

No sound from behind the door.

"Father Michael? Are you inside?" More knocking. "I'd like to speak to you."

We all waited. Nothing.

I was aware of Bennett and Coggins waiting eagerly behind the priest. Bennett pointed commando-style at his eyes and then mine. I snorted.

Silence.

Father Kevin knocked again. "Father Michael?"

I tilted my head at Hendricks, angling him at the door, and he pushed the priest aside gently, started to lift his leg to kick it in.

"No," Father Kevin said. "Please." He reached for the knob and turned it. "We do not use locks here." The door opened only slightly.

"Father Michael?"

I nudged past Father Kevin into the doorway, then pushed the door open with my toes. What I saw at first was just a small room with a table in the middle of it, like something that hadn't changed since World War II. Pale morning light shone in through a window above a bed that lined the far wall.

Then I saw her: a woman sitting in the bed, kneeling in a prayer position.

She had bleached blonde hair. Just like the girls in the pictures. But hers was short, thin, stuck out at odd angles. Something was off about her.

At first, she had her back to us, faced the window like she hadn't heard us enter, or wanted to pretend we weren't there.

"Hello?" I said.

She shifted slightly and turned to see us out of the corner of her eye. I could only see her cheek from across the room, the skin creased and pockmarked. When she came all the way around to face us, her head held dark eyes set deep into their sockets, peering out at us. Her face was scratched. Maybe they were bites. Her neck had the remains of a wide bruise, now just brown and yellow.

I didn't recognize her from any of the pictures I'd seen in the victims' apartments, but she would've fit right in with the others—once. Now she looked like those had been the good times, before the lean. She'd lost too much weight, likely snorted too much meth to ever get back an appearance of "health."

But something else had happened, something worse: this girl had been beaten, perhaps to within an inch of her life. Now she was halfway healed.

She offered us her arms, wrists up, scarred and scabbed, as if we should cuff her, even though she hadn't done anything wrong, yet. So far she was the only thing right about any of this.

Maybe.

I knew I should go to her, protect her, and greet her like a hostage, but I was paralyzed. I didn't know if the room was clear, and I also felt like an intruder in a place where I didn't belong.

A quick scan showed a kettle, a hot plate, a large dresser, two straight-backed wooden chairs by the table.

Behind me, Hendricks said, "We're here to help you. Do you know where Father Michael is?" He nudged me forward to enter the room.

Then she stepped down from the bed, one thin leg at a time. I could tell by her gauntness and the way she moved that she wasn't all there; something was wrong. She had an air of discomfort about her, like one leg was longer than the other. Maybe something was broken. I wondered at what all she had been through.

Her arms clenched around her ribs like something inside her hurt.

"Get an ambulance down here," I said to the officers in the hall.

Her cheeks were pinched in, hollow. She didn't smile. Her gaze stayed on the floor.

Then a low whine started in the back of her mouth, almost her neck.

"Stay where you are," Hendricks said.

She didn't act like she could hear, just kept coming. By the time she reached me, she was crying. Then she fell into my arms, and I caught her. She surprised me by how little she weighed. I held her there at the entrance to this small, strange room with my feet on the cold floor.

Noises came out of her throat, sounds like she was trying to say no over and over but couldn't make the word. She kept her mouth closed the whole time. It sounded like she didn't have a tongue.

CHAPTER TWENTY-SIX
MICHAEL

In the courtyard of St. Boniface, just beyond the palm tree, was a large azalea bush that needed trimming often. Someone had to keep it looking neat and tended to, and I took pride in that being one of my contributions. Over the years, I changed its shape, pruned it back, even rooted it more solidly. I took my duties regarding the general facade of the church most seriously.

As I snipped at the azalea with my shears, I watched the lunch line across the street. All sorts of sinners waited on the sidewalk outside St. Anthony's with blank, guilty faces. They were cast aside by life time and time again. Not of their own choosing. Still there was responsibility in them all—their choice of certain ways.

Some of them were worth pity and love. Sadness and shame. But He didn't feel shame for them; He imposed His direction and will toward all equally. It was our lot to make the most of both sunshine and rain, treat them equally as gifts.

Some of the needy held wet cardboard over their heads, hoping to deflect the rain. Still their jackets were wet.

Suddenly He blessed me with a new vision, a message. I saw the world clear-eyed as I hadn't in some time, almost as if I'd received a new day's vision on His earth.

He told me to focus on a certain police officer as he walked the street toward our church. I watched the servant of the law when he stopped, talking into his shoulder mic, less than a block away. His name was Cope. We had met before, spoken to one another about this very bush. I cut back a few protruding sprigs. His look showed concern.

He watched the church. I bowed slightly, stayed beneath the line of our courtyard wall.

The officer scrutinized the chapel so closely, as if examining who we were and what we offered. Then he checked his watch, spoke into his mic again, and turned away. He walked back up the street the way he had come, heading toward the station.

Something was wrong. I knew God had shown me this for a reason. I knew I had to run.

Emily? I asked Him. *What about Emily?*

He didn't answer.

Sometimes His instructions had to be enough, even if partial. Anything He offered was truly a blessing—His gift.

I tucked the shears into my vest and retreated inside the chapel, down the stairs to the rectory. No one saw me slip into my room. She was here, sat up from the bed as soon as I entered, concerned, almost as if I'd woken her, though it was well after noon.

Her eyebrows came together. She saw it in my face, wanted to know if I was okay.

"Yes, my dear. I'm fine." Something in my face betrayed me, but she didn't inquire further. For this once, she didn't press me. Perhaps this too was His gift, Him watching over me, over us.

"I love you," I said, crossing the room to give her a kiss on her temple. Pulling the covers up to her chin, even just a little above, I said, "Stay warm. Your fever is high." I touched her forehead, felt the heat. She was not well. I worried, but He didn't direct me to stay and watch her care. I would help when I returned.

I took my jacket out of the wardrobe and slipped it on, my wallet still heavy in the pocket. On the shelf at the top of the wardrobe were my things: my Good News Bible, a small pocketknife, my various keys. The pictures of Emily that I had taken from Piper's and Farrow's apartments. From Dub's. I wanted to travel light but didn't know when I would be back, the whole of His plan. I left the knife and the Good Book, took the keys. He told me to hurry. I tucked the pictures inside the front cover of the Bible.

At the door, I looked back at her again. She had fallen asleep or pretended to do so.

"Be still, my love," I whispered. "I'll be back soon."

Out in the hall, all was quiet. I was alone. I slipped up the side stairs and outside without anyone seeing. Perhaps many of the priests were in confessional or tending to their chores. Some surely were out helping the city's poor.

I slipped through the gate and looked across the street to St. Anthony's, where He told me to go. I saw Gus outside and knew Jermaine would be manning the front desk until three o'clock. I shouldn't involve them, I knew. He wanted me to go around and enter through the back, as if making a delivery. This was why He had told me to take my keys. I did my best to follow, walked to my right, taking the long way around the block so as not to be seen. No one should notice that I'd left; they knew I was at my work, completing my duties and chores. They would never understand my obligations coming directly from Him, that it superseded whatever plans they had for one another.

Even those who carefully read their Bibles, sometimes even they didn't believe or understand the machinations of God. Truly, I didn't either. But I knew when to follow Him and be led.

CHAPTER TWENTY-SEVEN
DONNER

The girl made a mewling noise in the back of her throat, like a lost cat.

"My child." Father Kevin tried moving into the room past Hendricks.

"Someone get him out of here," I said.

"Right behind you," Hendricks said. He left, taking the priest. I could hear them talking down the hall.

I brought the girl to the small table, led her to sit in one of the chairs.

"Calm down now," I said. "It's all going to be okay."

She made a sound, her mouth still pursed, and I knew more was wrong with her. Her face had shrunken in on itself. She opened her mouth to show me short brown teeth repelling her gums, a scarred stump where her tongue was supposed to be.

"Did he do this to you?"

She shook her head fast, eyes closed, and brought her hands up to her nose. She smoothed the creases of her face, just for a moment, running her hands back to her ears.

"Mmh mmh." She sounded out a wordless negative.

"We need to get her some help," I called to the hall.

"EMTs on the way," Bennett said in the door.

"Finish the search for our guy. Keep checking the chapel." To the girl I said, "Father Michael? Is he here?"

She stood, shook her head again. Spread her hands out in front of her and brought them wide, indicating the whole place.

"Not here?"

She nodded.

I eased her back into the chair, fearing what he might've done to her in this little room. I wanted to ask Father Kevin how she had gotten inside, how our man could keep a woman down here without anybody knowing.

Maybe she was what Father Kevin had been afraid to let us see. I couldn't imagine how a person could stay hidden down here in the church quarters without raising concerns.

"What did he do to you?"

She shook her head, made a few noises. Her breathing had calmed, and she no longer cried.

"Let's get her upstairs," Hendricks said, taking the girl's hand. "You check the room, okay?"

As soon as she felt Hendricks tug her hand, realized the direction he was leading her, she pulled away, tried going back to the bed.

I blocked her off with my body. "What's wrong?"

She shook her head violently, trying to push past me as Hendricks wrapped her up around her shoulders from behind. He could be too much with his force at times, but it was clear that we didn't know what she'd do next.

"Leave her be," I said, and he eased off. "I'm good here."

He stood back, watched us, and soon walked out without another word. Witness or victim, we didn't know what we had, and it was best to handle her with as much caution as we could.

"Calm now, calm," I told her. I patted her hand until she seemed calm, then stepped out into the hall to make a plan.

On my handheld, I gave the word to the others that our man was not in his room, but that he could still be in the chapel. I told them to be on the utmost alert, to use extreme caution.

I radioed for Bruce and her partner to come inside and assist with the search, told Cope and his boys to tighten up the perimeter. I wanted two of them out front replacing Bruce and two inside helping in the search. In a building big as this, we'd have a lot of dark corners, suspicious nooks, and strange passages. I couldn't even begin to imagine all the hiding places.

I nodded at Coggins. "Search the other rooms on this floor. Doors should be unlocked. Don't mess the place up, but be sure you don't miss anything."

I went back inside Father Michael's room.

The girl stared down at the floor. I waved to Coggins and told him to radio for the EMTs, to send them down here.

"Are you okay?" I sat next to her, tried to meet her eyes.

She nodded.

"Can you tell me your name?"

She hummed a few sounds, then shook her head, pointing at her mouth. I didn't need to see the tongue again; I could imagine what it felt like to try talking through that.

Coggins gave me the thumbs-up from the hallway; the EMTs were on their way.

I touched the girl's knee, told her it would all be okay.

CHAPTER TWENTY-EIGHT

When the EMTs had taken the girl, I sat back down on the bed and snapped on my latex gloves to search the room.

It held a certain kind of quiet I wasn't used to: the absence of anything electronic, phones or computers or wires. No wireless. There was a bed, a small table, and a large, dark wardrobe. Cool, thick stone walls, an earthy smell.

Off to my side a knee-high refrigerator clicked on and hummed. A hot plate sat on top of it next to a Mr. Coffee. I noticed a small sink.

I stood, paced around on the floor in my socks. This was *his* room. I knew it. Hendricks was somewhere else in the church, searching for a man we wouldn't find. He wasn't here—another hunch I knew was certain.

Taking a deep breath, I tried to smell him, get a scent, but there was nothing there. Maybe the place had no smell, or it smelled enough like me that I couldn't discern it.

Coggins poked his head in. "All okay?"

"Yeah. I'm good."

I crossed to the wardrobe. When I opened it, I saw two black suits next to a couple of plain white shirts on thin metal hangers. On a shelf above these was a small Bible and a pocketknife. I checked the knife for any traces of blood or signs of use, folding it open to find its blade as clean as you'd expect a priest's pocketknife to be. It had never been used for anything involving human flesh. Still, it'd need more checking later. I put it back on the shelf for the techs to bag later.

I lifted out the Bible and opened its cover. When I did, a Polaroid picture fell out onto the ground. I looked down, saw that it was a picture of her.

Her.

I picked it up: definitely a match for the others from Jay Piper's apartment. And it was a picture of her, the small blonde girl the EMTs had just taken upstairs.

In it, her face was full, skin clear and free of creases or pocks. In a word, she looked healthy. Healthy enough I could tell she was young. She couldn't be more than seventeen, eighteen maybe.

She was blonde like the others, her hair brighter in the picture than now, more done up, pretty enough to attract johns.

Her mouth was the biggest difference: full and not shrunken, cheeks broad. She had a whole tongue then.

I slipped the picture inside my jacket.

In the Bible, I found two more. The first was of a young blonde in Farrow's apartment. Not the girl who'd just left. I didn't recognize her, but his rumpled bed and stained wall behind it were unmistakable. I noticed a foot in the corner of the picture, a thin white one, possibly Farrow's, but I had no way to know. The picture from Dub's was here, the one Debbie Shine had described of the pimp and a few of his girls. The girl we'd found was there, sure enough: second from the left, scowling at the camera, a plastic cup of wine in her hand. The other girls looked older, drunker, as if they were having more fun. She didn't fit in. That much was clear.

I thumbed through the Bible's pages, looking for marks or key passages underlined—anything that would help me make sense of the man. I stopped when I saw more markings than I knew what to do with. It didn't take long. I was no Biblical scholar. I'd get someone else to do more checking into this later on.

I left the Bible with the pictures and his knife on the shelf to have the techs catalog them for evidence.

In the hallway, Coggins was making his way through the other rooms on the floor. I radioed to ask the others how their sweep was coming and heard back that they were moving through the chapel and the rectory's three floors with help from the priests. No sign of Father Michael.

I had that strange premonition again that he was gone. Call it the genius of lack of sleep, investigator's hunch, or a church-inspired call down from a god I didn't believe in, but I knew in my bones we'd missed him.

But the case would go on.

I radioed to Hendricks, "Give me your status. I'm coming up to talk to Father Kevin."

CHAPTER TWENTY-NINE

When I found him, Father Kevin looked like he'd receded inside himself, shut up tight like the church when we arrived. He sat at the end of a pew, near the back of the chapel. The smell of pungent bodies still hung in the air from the day's shift of homeless crashing out on the long wooden pews.

I watched a few of the officers move about in their search. More beat police in uniforms had arrived, no doubt from the Tenderloin station but also from the Hall, close as it was. The case was moving forward, even without our big sit-down with Bowen. I was driving it.

I stopped to lean against the end of a pew, feeling the aftereffects of the adrenaline from entering Father Michael's room. This, too much coffee, two full days on, and not enough sleep—I felt jittery, unhinged. I needed caffeine or a strong drink. One or the other at this stage, if I was to keep going.

When I sat down with Father Kevin, his face changed; his eyes cleared, and he looked through me. I hoped it meant something good.

"Father, what can you tell me about the man we're looking for?"

He shuddered. "That woman. Where did she come from? How long has she been here?"

"I thought maybe you could tell me."

His body sort of slumped, like he felt the blow of realizing we were not here to help. Maybe I'd been wrong about what he knew.

He said, "I have no idea."

"What kind of a man is he? How long has he been here with you?"

"Father Michael have own ways. He came from streets. After hard times."

I moved a hymnal off the pew to rest my leg on it, making it easier to turn around and face him. "Yes?"

"He was here before he priest." He held up his hands, gestured to the chapel and its pews. "Used to sleep here. Was one of them." That was when I noticed he was tearing up. He produced a handkerchief from a pocket, used it to wipe his eyes. "I sorry. I care for him very much."

"I understand. You two must be close."

"Father Michael is not open man. Closed off. But I can tell you one thing: he very sure of relationship with God."

I had three murder scenes that might contradict that, but I wanted to know more. "Go on."

"Father Michael walk own path. Since he came here, became priest, he have intense belief in Bible. More than usual. Even more, Father Michael *believe*. He tell me. Tell me he have directions from God."

"From God?" Something about the way I said it made the priest pinch his brows. I couldn't help myself. "He told you he talks to God?"

If we were trying this case, this testimony might justify an insanity plea. In the church, it meant something very different. Here, priests made careers out of talking to God.

But I wasn't comfortable going down that road; I'd never been good with religion.

If we caught this bastard, and the system let him skate? No. I'd sworn after Terranella that I'd never let that happen again, but I'd also sworn to Hendricks that I'd never tilt things myself again.

I didn't like either way.

"And what does God tell him?"

He frowned. "That I cannot say. Maybe you tell me? What has he done?"

There it was: not what did we think he'd done, but what *had* he done. This priest knew something else was going on. But I couldn't say what we thought it was. Not to this man, his friend.

The priest didn't wait. He said, "You cannot tell me. I understand. But"—he put his finger on the back of my pew, pressed the wood—"what he has done, whatever it is, Father Michael thinks he has done it in the name of the Lord."

He meant what he said. One hundred percent.

What was worse, he'd just articulated my biggest fear.

CHAPTER THIRTY
MICHAEL

I looped around the block to keep away from Gus, made my way down to McAllister and around to come up Leavenworth from its other side. It was here, between Golden Gate and Turk, that I slipped into the locked alley using my key and went around to St. Anthony's rear entrance. Here, where the deliveries came, the food stores, medicine for the clinic, books for tutoring. So much good happened here, and now He guided me inside. I slipped my passkey over the sensor and opened the door. No one greeted me but a small camera and the elevator. Perhaps this was the moment when Jermaine watched his monitor and he would see me, but perhaps he wouldn't.

I called the elevator, and the doors opened almost immediately. I pushed the button for floor five and the doors closed. No other stops; the car took me right to the top, to St. Anthony's storage rooms. The doors opened onto a series of shelves and boxes, and I exited to the left, slid along a few rows of boxes stacked high, and worked my way to the front of the building and the tall, arched windows that overlooked Golden Gate Avenue.

Below me I saw St. Boniface from above, across the street: its spires and bell tower, the roofs of the rectory and the chapel. I saw the closed front doors. Now it was all quiet, the police officer long gone. An occasional passerby labored up the block.

He told me to wait.

At the corner, a man called Rapier stood and ran his mouth, peddling his wares to anyone who passed. He had watches and DVDs but also the drugs that brought in his money. I noticed the occasional junkie come to him for a fix.

In time, the patterns of the block revealed themselves and made sense in their own logic until a set of four police cruisers pulled up in front of the church. This was His purpose, I was sure—why He told me to leave.

Someone had told them something. Immediately I knew it was the whore. Here I had done everything I could to free her, help her, let her run without concern of being followed by that pimp, set her on the path of righteousness, and she didn't take the chance to start over. She allowed herself to be guided by her fears.

I ground my molars in frustration, knowing it would always be the same: that the sinners would go on choosing the wrong paths. What was more, the police, these servants of the law, would not understand my work and what I had done for this city, freeing its heathens in His name.

None of them would understand the work I did for Him.

I shook my head, watched as Gus came from the front of St. Anthony's to greet the lead detective, who was a woman with brown hair. She told the others what to do. Looked to be more than ten years older than Emily, with a guarded hunch to her shoulders when she walked. I saw her face as she talked with Gus, and then he left, perhaps to call Father Kevin to open the gate.

Surely Gus and the priests would cooperate, do their best to assist the city's police. They wouldn't understand if or when they were presented with any details of what I've done. I risked condemnation in their eyes to be saved in His. In His name I would be saved.

As I watched, I found my interest drawn again and again to her, the woman with the brown hair. It was her, the head detective. She held a presence and authority as she told others what to do, pointed them in various directions. She told the men where to go and what to do. They respected her, I could see. There was something of an aura about her, possibly the glow of God.

She reached up to her hair, pulled it back tight to her skull, trapped it with a band. This streamlined her features and her approach to the world. She was ready to slice into the day.

A kinship rose up inside me as I watched her at work.

Father Kevin came out and greeted her clumsily. She was uncomfortable on the grounds of the Lord. She made an awkward gesture as he led her inside the gate. Her shoulders slumped, her carriage changed. Kevin stopped, and she showed him a picture. His face dropped.

I saw disappointment in his expression, a repeat of how he had looked earlier when he'd asked if I was all right. This picture, it was of me.

Kevin knew something. Perhaps he would give it to them, but perhaps he wouldn't. After all, he had saved me once before.

CHAPTER THIRTY-ONE
DONNER

After talking with Father Kevin, I made my way around the rest of the church, checking on the search. The other officers had found very little else, beyond the girl and what was in Father Michael's room. No other signs. The best we had was his Bible and the few other items in his wardrobe. The pictures from Piper's, Farrow's, and Dub's.

Beyond that, the man was a ghost.

What worried me more was that Father Kevin's testimony made sense to me, almost fell into line with what I'd expected.

I found Hendricks waiting for me by our car. "Nice work, partner."

"What?" He'd caught me by surprise.

"We got a suspect on the strength of your hard work. A priest in the wind, but still. You did good. Looks like our man. A triple homicide. At least."

"He might be. Yeah."

"So tell me what's next."

"Partner, I could use a ride home. A shower. I'm beat."

"You got it."

When we were both in the car, I asked about the girl. "Where is she?"

"I had the EMTs take her to General. Give her the full work."

"She say anything else before they left?"

"Say?" He shook his head. "She sure didn't. Not with that tongue."

"She's a fighter though. What do you make of it?"

"Don't know. Maybe she actually liked our man. Liked the safety of that little room underneath the church."

"Yeah," I said, "that's another thing I'm afraid of. If she liked that so much, what else was out here she wanted away from?"

"Something else we'll have to find out. After the docs get her stabilized, we'll go have a talk. See what we can get."

"Tomorrow," I said. "Tomorrow."

Later, heading west on Division, under the 101, I said, "I might need some help with something."

"Name it."

"Religion. I feel like an elephant in a china shop, like I'm going to say things that will be horribly offensive to people."

"You mean like how you spoke in front of the priest?"

I bit my lip. "That? I was trying my hardest not to offend."

"And failing."

"I wanted to ask him if he thought it was ordinary for a person to hear directions from God or if he understood that it's certifiably crazy, especially as far as the state is concerned."

He shook his head. "Makes me wish we weren't going into this with the church, you know? If my mother knew what all was happening here? She wouldn't talk to me for weeks. That or what's worse, she'd make me go to services with her."

"Maybe she can help me sort through some of the protocols?"

"Oh no. That is definitely the last thing that would help you. She'd only make things worse, believe me."

"You just don't want to tell her what you're working on."

He cracked a smile. "Well, that too. Priests can do no wrong in her eyes."

I relaxed into my seat as Hendricks turned onto De Haro. I was glad to be going home. "How long have I been on? Since we came on last night to talk with Sunshine, that's twenty hours."

"Plus the few nights before that we got called in. So you deserve a rest. Take it."

"I could sleep for a week."

"Not likely, my dear. I've got a date with you and the evidence room plus some report writing bright and early. We should also go talk to our girl at SFGH and loop Bowen in on all this."

"Pick me up?"

He laughed, told me a time that was earlier than I wanted to imagine getting started, but I agreed.

"Maybe we should go back at some of those priests again, after we look over their statements."

"Only if you let me do the talking."

I said I would.

When Hendricks dropped me off, I shook his hand like a good partner, and we bumped fists.

"You broke this one, Donner," he said. "Without the work you did in these last twenty-four hours, this guy would still be walking the streets. We wouldn't have squat."

I had one leg out of the car already but stopped and turned back. "He *is* still walking the streets, Hendricks. Let's not forget that."

He sighed. "Okay, but still, the point is valid. We're a lot closer. Because of you, Donner."

He went to chuck my chin, and I blocked it. I'd told him once that my father did that, and since then he'd only wanted to do it all the more. My father, the hard-ass cop—even when he tried to tell me I'd done something right, he could make me feel bad. I could never make up for the fact that my mother hadn't given him the son he wanted.

"Then thank you very much." I winked.

Before I could close the door, he said, "I'm serious, Donner. Give yourself some credit for once."

I looked up at my apartment building. It was just after six o'clock, and the sky was already going dark, but I felt like the longest day of my life still wouldn't end.

We were close though. I'd held the priest's Bible in my own hands, talked to the woman he shared a room with. She was bound to have a lot more to tell us. I knew that much. I'd go at her tomorrow.

I told myself to feel good, if even just a little, and tried to smile, but I was too tired to make it real.

CHAPTER THIRTY-TWO

In my apartment, I peeled off my clothes and threw them onto the floor of the bathroom. I wanted to get in bed and fall asleep right away, but for the grease and stickiness, the smell of the Hall and the church—I had to wash it off.

I scrubbed my hair with a tea-tree-oil shampoo, lathered my face with it even though it stung, and touched suds to the inside of my nose. The smell was strong, overpowering; mineral menthol was all I could smell. My skin tingled. I turned away from the water and let the hot stream beat on my back. Steam pulled oil from my skin and the smell from my nose.

I felt more like a person as I toweled off and rubbed the water from my hair. I brushed my teeth, moisturized even, and was heading to the bedroom, but I couldn't resist the pull of my computer. Nothing good would come from checking for emails and messages at this hour, but I was addicted.

I sat down and flipped open my laptop, waited for it to recognize the wireless and download my emails. Sure enough, they started popping up, and there were more than a dozen: messages from guys on dating sites. This was exactly the reason not to check in, to stay clear of the mild techno-flirtations that passed for my social life, the e-winking, messaging, and anticipation that did nothing but waste my time.

None of the guys understood what dating a cop would be like; they thought it was a hot idea for a minute, something cool they could tell their friends about, and that I'd have lots of good, gruesome stories to share.

Problem with the online guys was they were mostly too San Francisco, too convinced of their own free-thinking avant-garde laissez-faire bullshit to understand a person working over sixty hours a week for the city, giving a shit about putting dirtbags behind bars, and feeling like it made a difference. Not wanting to head off to Tahoe for a long ski weekend, basically a deal breaker more often than not.

That and it was like they'd all read the same handbook on how to treat a woman: rule number one was to listen acutely, make the conversation all about her, and act like you gave a shit when you really didn't. Talk about wines and show some knowledge there. Boring. If I wanted to sit around and listen to myself talk, I'd go to therapy; it'd be easier all around.

But still I spent the time looking, probably to fend off any possibility of ending up like Hendricks, or *with* Hendricks, which was even worse. Ninety-five percent of cop-on-cop romances ended in regularly scheduled sexfests with nothing behind it. It sounded good, but I'd learned it wasn't for me.

I thought about Alan, the fact that he hadn't called. How long had it been? Barely a day, not even. That was all right. It wasn't like I'd had a lot of time to talk. *He'll call,* I thought.

I didn't bother to check my work email, assuming I'd see more false responses about my suspect from other districts.

I was fading fast. Everything else could wait.

CHAPTER THIRTY-THREE

MICHAEL

Finally she came out: the woman detective with brown hair.

She appeared older now. Dark circles stood out under her eyes. I almost felt sorry for her.

She walked to the man in the brown coat, her partner, he must be. They both walked toward a car, and he got in first. She stood by her door, waiting, and for just a brief moment, she looked up.

I had the sensation she could see me but didn't shy away or hide. So be it.

"You," I said, pointing to her with my finger, marking her for myself and for God. She could not see me; with the lights out and dusk coming, she would never see me where I was, but something caught her eye. She stared at me as if she *knew*, but it wasn't possible. Still, she looked.

"You, police woman," I said, "you have done this. Taken Emily from me. You have broken me from my purpose in His plan."

She was still watching, looking. Finally I realized she wasn't looking at me but at Him. Whatever she believed and imagined, she must recognize His power, for He is the Lord. He would never speak to her, but maybe she could see His presence.

I listened for Him.

He was quiet.

A lesser believer might have doubted His intentions, His love, but not me.

I knew His path and His intention and knew I was connected to her. He wanted this.

In time I would know more.

Finally she stepped into the car. Its exhaust puffed, and then she was gone. There were still other officers yet to leave.

Father Kevin would be somewhere inside, dealing with it all. Again I was most sorry for him.

I watched her car creep up Golden Gate toward Market, waited, watching until she passed completely from my view.

CHAPTER THIRTY-FOUR

I sat in the darkness of the storage room for what felt like a long time, waiting for direction or guidance from Him.

Soon the building emptied; its workers went home for the night. I got up and walked around, stretched my arms, wrung out my hands.

After a while, I felt better for the time inside myself, letting the events of the past few days play across my mind and settle in. The sight of Emily being taken away still drove me mad. I replayed it in my mind. Why would God let them do this? Then: Where were they taking her? The fact that they'd found her in my room meant they were looking for me. They'd entered my room. A violation of my space, such as it was.

Father Kevin would know about Emily now, that I had kept her with me. What would he think?

Perhaps they knew something already, had heard her crying in the night. It was hard to imagine that no one would recognize her presence. Perhaps they were quiet about it out of a kindness. God would thank them for this. Or maybe he had shielded them from knowing she was there.

No matter. Now she was gone. And to where? How would I get her back?

The police might take care of Emily and not harm her, I hoped. But what if they kept us from finishing our work? What would she say to Gabriel at the gates of heaven? What would He say?

That depended on what I could do to clean her past.

I had the list in my breast pocket: four names from the pimp. My calling beckoned.

Now that I couldn't go back to the church and was without Emily, my conviction was stronger, my path more starkly defined. He had broken me from my old role in the church and sent me exclusively into His. Perhaps it could only have turned out like this. He needed more of me than the church would allow. He needed me completely. This I could accept.

There was also something about the brown-haired detective. She was a part of this now.

Her.

He pushed us together under His wings, bound us toward some task. What it was, I could not tell, but I knew to contact her. She had a purpose in His plan.

I retreated through the storage rows, back to the elevator and the door to the stairs. Perhaps the cameras were still working. I had no knowledge of the security in St. Anthony's at night. Who would steal from a charity that helped the poor?

I took the stairs down two flights to the clinic level and worked my way around the cubicles, looking for a computer that was still on. I didn't have to look long; one desk still had its light on, its computer screen saver running like its user had just stepped out a minute before. I could see by the pictures on the desk that she had a family, kids in grammar school.

I called up the San Francisco police department website and started clicking through the various materials about the "Hall of Justice"—as if real *justice* was a concern there. No, His justice didn't matter, just man's inadequate laws. I found the homicide department and a list of its investigators. Most of them were men; of the three women, I found her picture on my second try.

Clara Donner.

I found her, along with her cell phone, email, and office number. There she was. In her picture, she smiled a forced smile, trying to look ready to help save the city. There was something else in her eyes though: loneliness and pain, the knowledge that this city could not be saved.

"Clara Donner," I said, touching the screen. "You have been chosen to serve the Lord. He has put you on His path."

I opened my email and started my first message to the good detective, Clara Donner.

PART THREE
THURSDAY

CHAPTER THIRTY-FIVE
DONNER

The next morning, Hendricks picked me up at seven—far too early.

I'd slept twelve hours, almost, but it felt like half what I needed. He greeted me with a large dark roast, its smell helping out as I opened the door and got in.

"Thanks, partner."

When we got to the Hall, I found a Bible wrapped in handcuffs on my keyboard.

"What is this?"

Lund and Peters laughed. "Taking on the clergy comes with costs, Donner."

"Isn't it pretty for you two knobs to be here early this morning, making jokes? Don't you have a bunch of Catholic schoolgirls to be ogling?"

Lund said, "We're more into the Episcopalians. Plus, *you're* the one on the hot seat this morning." He pointed to Bowen's office. "Big man been here since way early. He got the chew-out from above, and now he wants to put you in the mix."

"Gonna be fun." Peters slid his eyebrows up and down his long forehead.

"Me? I'm busting my butt trying to solve this triple homicide. Where's my credit for *that?*"

The others were quiet, even Hendricks.

I sat down at my desk, made my plea. "It's okay to just wait him out, right? I don't have to go straight in."

Hendricks straightened his tie. "Least you look good today, you know? And that stuff I was telling you last night about doing a good job? It still stands. In my book."

"Thanks, partner."

I fired up my computer, trying to keep my head low. I wanted to finish my coffee before I got called in.

"Donner!"

That wasn't in the cards. I was toast. He called my name again from the other side of the room. When I looked up, I saw him outside his door, glaring.

"My office, *now*."

I brought my coffee, hoping I could deflect some of the pain by trying to scald my tongue while he spoke, but he started in before I could even sit. "What did you say to me when you left yesterday?"

I shut the door. "I can't remember, sir. You were on the phone, so I put it to the—"

"You said you had a collar in the Tenderloin. You did *not* mention word one about a church or our friends the Catholics."

"I didn't—"

"Did you consider the shit storm this would get us into? Don't you think I would want to know? Were you seriously planning to apprehend a *priest*? A Franciscan father?"

"We didn't get him, but the evidence we found on scene—"

"What? Why are you even talking? What is wrong with you?"

"Sir?"

"Do you know what I've been doing this morning? Do you know how I woke up?"

"No, sir."

"The captain called my house, Donner. Brought me in for a six thirty sit-down. Oh-six-thirty. Do you know what gets the captain in that early? This city being on fire."

"On the upside, I didn't—"

"You didn't *what*?"

"Well, we didn't get him, sir."

"But the upside. You said there was a—What were you going to say?"

Now I felt like I was about to throw gasoline on the fire, but I was already committed. "The gun locker, sir. You said to take the Benellis. At least I didn't—"

"No, no. You most certainly did not. *That*, that stands for something you actually got right." He waved a finger. Gesturing at the futility and almost, maybe even just a little, breaking a smile. "You're right. There is something you did not colossally mess up in this investigation. Congratulations, Donner."

I hoped he might roll over to his good side and stay there. "Like I said, I—"

"Because I got reamed like you actually went out and shot up a cathedral."

"We have the right guy."

"Brought me in this morning for a six thirty sit-down upstairs." I could tell he was running out of steam now. "Do you know what time that means I got called at home?"

I looked at the edge of his desk. Since we'd started, it had been shaking enough to knock over the pile of papers closest to me. "No, sir." I leaned forward, hoping to just nudge it farther onto the desk.

"It means he called me at oh-five-hundred hours." He closed his eyes, reliving the memory. In the second it took him to do this, I pushed the stack of papers onto the desk.

"That means it wakes my wife up, which means I get it for this on the home front. It means he's pissed off, and now *she* is too, and—" Under his breath, he said, "She didn't take the Benellis." To me, he said, "You didn't take the Benellis. That's just great, Donner. No one took the Benellis. Wonderful decision making on your part. Great police work."

"I—"

"Don't talk." He sat still for a moment, and then his voice rose up to its highest volume. "This is *politics*! The priest you spoke to yesterday—" He looked at the papers in front of him. "After one Father Kenny got through with your little interrogation and search party, he made a phone call. Do you know who he called?"

"Kevin, sir. I think his name is Father—"

"He called the bishop! Do you know who the bishop is, Donner?"

"No, sir." I dared to take a sip of my coffee. He didn't seem to notice.

"The only bishop I want to know is on a chessboard. Do you understand?"

I nodded.

"It's the man with the red pointy hat! Do you know what these pointy-hat guys do in their spare time? Do you?"

"No."

"You don't?" He sighed. "Me either. But whatever it is, they do it with *politicians*." His shoulders finally fell away from his ears, which meant he would run out soon. All I had to do was hang on.

"So this bishop makes a call and city hall gets its panties in a bunch because it's an election year, and we're over here pissing off religious people. Do you know anything about religious people?"

I didn't even try to answer now; better to let him get it all out.

"They vote," he said. "That's all you need to know."

I nodded. "They vote."

Somehow he had run out of air. I dared another sip of my coffee. When Bowen didn't take my head off for that, I took a full gulp, hoping the caffeine would speed me up. There'd be a pot in the break room I could use to warm it up—that was something to look forward to.

He sighed. "It's idiotic, Donner. You should know that by now. Nice job not taking the Benellis."

"Thank you."

"From what I understand, the word I'm getting, you did a good job. We have a legit suspect. But keep it low profile, as much as you can, okay?"

I bit the inside of my cheek. "Yes, sir. Copy that."

"You need any additional details or backup—*within reason*—you've got my okay. Just be quiet about it." He turned to his computer. "Keep on it, Donner."

I slowly went for the door. As I opened it, I braced myself for more, then again on my way out. I closed the door. Heard the click.

Lund said, "Wait for it."

I tiptoed across the room to my desk, lightly set myself down in my chair.

A loud shout came from the inside of the lieutenant's office, a short burst of expletives and curses that was as much a part of Bowen's anger as the cement was of the walls.

"There it is," Lund said. We all exhaled.

Hendricks gave me a wink. "Now we can go back to normal."

I said, "Wasn't too bad. His anger management classes are coming along pretty well."

"Maybe he's finally getting some at home," Hendricks said.

Peters frowned. "He just lets you off easy because you're a hot chick."

Lund brought one fist to his cheek and pushed out the other with his tongue.

Peters raised his eyebrows. "A little late-night hoo-ha between you two?"

"You know what? Gross." I got up and stormed across the room, heading for more coffee.

Hendricks was reading the files as I passed him, doing his best not to laugh.

CHAPTER THIRTY-SIX

After writing the preliminary report on our church search, I checked in with Ibaka, wanting to get the full rundown of everything she'd found. It was after ten thirty, when she'd normally be in her lab or at her desk.

She answered on the third ring.

"Here," she said.

"What you got for me from the church?"

"And hello to you too, Sergeant Donner. How are you this fine morning?"

Hendricks sat at his desk across the way from me, smiling. He shook his head, knowing exactly what she'd said. This was a routine we'd been through before.

I said my niceties, did what I could to appease her and enrich her morning with the proper friendliness. Then I asked again what she had back from the church.

"This Bible's got a lot of markings in it. Passages of fire and brimstone, laying with your brother's wife, and the oldest profession in the world. Nice stuff. A lot to go on. This could really be our guy."

"You *think*?"

She laughed.

"When we collar this guy, we're going to need *a lot* of evidence to make it all right politically."

"Someone upset? Can't imagine why that would be. From raiding a church?"

"So you can see the predicament. What else you find?"

"The Polaroid you sent down is a match for the ones we found at Jay Piper's."

"I like that. I like that very much. What else?"

"Trying to pull prints off it, but all I'm seeing are partials, smudges, and Piper's own. Nothing we can use. One of the others matched up with a couple of the ones from Farrow's. So that's good too."

"How about the knife?"

"No prints. No blood. Hasn't been used for any rough stuff, though that doesn't surprise me. You start using sink fixtures to take people apart, you're not too particular about your choice of tool."

"Who among us," I said, "has not at one time been there."

Hendricks stood up at his desk. "Everybody watch out. Donner is feeling good."

I threw a pen at him.

"Always nice talking to you," Ibaka said. "How about the girl? You go at her yet?"

"Next stop. I'll let you know how it goes."

"Catch up later over a beer?"

"You got it."

We made a plan to meet that afternoon, and I stood to follow Hendricks toward the elevators. Thinking about Ibaka, I knew I could tell her about Alan. That thought led me to check my phone. No, he hadn't called. Still too early.

What would I do if he had called, anyway? Wasn't like I had a lot of time to talk.

"How about it, partner?" I asked Hendricks. "Ready for a trip to SFGH?"

CHAPTER THIRTY-SEVEN

Twenty minutes later, we were parked at San Francisco General Hospital and navigating our way into the building through never-ending construction.

One truth about police work is we spend more time in hospitals than you'd expect. More than anyone but the doctors and nurses, I often think. No matter what your beat, you see the inside of the hospital almost daily, whether delivering suspects, dropping in for interviews, or—worst-case scenario—visiting friends.

We get to know the staff and the nurses by name, get passage without having to badge anybody.

All that said, I will never get used to SF General's lobby. Just inside the doors was an ever-present line of the city's lowest common denominator waiting for pills or to pay bills or just waiting. They filled the cheap leather benches along the inside of the windows—windows that looked out on nothing more than wooden construction barriers six feet away—and congested the air with sad tales and bad-news smells.

We stepped lively to make it through the lobby as fast as possible, but that only got us to the roulette-wheel elevators that much faster.

I pushed the "Up" button and waited. These ancient cars operated with minds of their own, stopping on certain floors unnecessarily or changing direction, skipping floors sometimes for no reason at all. You never knew what you were getting on board for and felt lucky if you made it to your level without at least one detour.

I waited, ready to take a down car if it came. A short trip to the basement was often faster than waiting for another car to arrive.

The doors opened, advertising a ride up, and we got on with a few others, all of us crossing our fingers we'd get where we wanted to go.

Hendricks pushed our floor: we were headed to the seventh, the psych ward. This girl would get there if she couldn't explain herself, they found her noncommunicative, or they just looked her over and guessed psych. I wasn't sure she didn't belong there myself.

"Psych ward," Hendricks said, "your usual, Donner."

"Maybe we'll see Dr. Eddings. Always good to touch base with him."

"Not saying nothing." Hendricks held his hands up, quiet as a mouse. He thought I was sweet on the good doctor, and in point of fact, Dr. Eddings was far from a bad catch, but divorced with two kids was way more baggage than I wanted. Also, knowing I could take him easily in a fight was not only a major turnoff, it was a full-on deal breaker.

"What's your take on the girl?" I asked. "You want a go at her?"

I had no game plan, didn't know how to go at a mute, a potential victim of a serial killer who was likely strung out on meth. She might know things about our suspect we couldn't get from anyone else, but she might not give them up. I wanted any leads I could get.

"I'm thinking you try first. Give it the woman-to-woman dynamic."

"You think she's all there?"

Hendricks frowned. "Are any of us?"

The elevator doors opened on three, and a couple of doctors got out. On the other side of the car was an elderly black man in a wheelchair. A boy less than ten stood beside him.

"She's a tweaker. Long-term. So I have no idea what we'll get. Plus the tongue thing."

"Yeah. That."

I watched the floor indicator. This was the car that sometimes went express from three to seven, ignoring the other stops. But today it stopped on five, a cosmic act of mercy for the wheelchair-bound man and his boy. I pressed the "Door Open" button while they rolled out, and he thanked me.

"I just want to know what our priest did to her, which of the scars we put on his account."

Hendricks pursed his lips. "I don't think any, Donner. Not his MO. Not this guy. Remember, he's a man's man. A john killer."

"I want to hear it from her myself."

The doors opened on seven, and we stepped out.

We found the doctor in charge, not Eddings, but a Dr. Matal, and she took us toward the girl's room. She was a pert little woman with light-brown skin and straight black hair wearing a white lab coat, dry-cleaned slacks, and a pretty white blouse. "We were calling her Jane Doe," she said, leading us down the hall, "but she identified herself as Emily once we gave her a pad and pencil. No last name. So I don't know what you can do with that."

"She give you anything else to go on?"

"No. But that tongue injury isn't new. She's had that for maybe two weeks now, and definitely should have had it treated here by a doctor. I can only imagine how long that must've bled. She's lucky it stopped at all."

"Is she healthy otherwise?"

We were outside a series of patient rooms, situated across from a wall of windows that looked out onto a small courtyard. A few sculptures, a potted tree, and a row of chairs took up less than half the space. The rest was empty, spare, but it was a way out into the air. For the long-term wards of the floor, this offered more than a little promise.

Now, hands on her hips, Dr. Matal made ready to lecture us on her patient. "She's had long-term chronic drug use, methamphetamines and who knows what else. Heroin, I'm guessing. So she's not likely to be fully 'healthy' anytime soon. If you asked me whether she'd make a credible witness in court, I'd have to say no. But you're not asking that."

Hendricks and I both waited. With doctors that was often the best approach: just let them get it out, show their importance, preen around, and then we could go on about our business.

"Who knows what state this girl's brain is in. From what I can tell so far, it's like someone stuck a hot poker in there, smashed everything around, and then pulled it out. What's left now is anybody's guess. I'm speaking off the record, of course."

Hendricks said, "Of course."

Everyone was worried about malpractice these days, just like we worried about mistrials, contaminating evidence, and trumped-up assault charges.

"I can give a professional assessment, with prognosis, but it would take a few days, at least. That's what it would say though, in more technical terms. But if she's not willing to stay in, you know the longest we can hold her is seventy-two hours. And pushing that far is a stretch."

I said, "As we know."

She shrugged. "We'll do what we can about that. But beds are hard to keep open around here, as you also know.

"She can communicate using paper and pencil, but to really get a picture of what she's capable of here, we have to get a better sense of what she's been through. We won't get that out of her for a while. So far as I can tell now, it's *a lot*. A considerable amount. But that's a quantitative answer. I need better than that to make a full assessment."

Dr. Matal pointed us to the first door. "There's her room. All this to say, please go easy. We're dealing with a young woman who's mentally on some very unsteady ground. And whatever pieces might be dangling, we're not eager to start picking them up."

CHAPTER THIRTY-EIGHT
MICHAEL

At night, I walked with my jacket pulled close, heading north and away from the junkies and Tenderloin dregs. I pulled up my jacket to shield my face, wondered how long would it be before my face was posted across the city or hit the front of a newspaper. If they still did that. I bent to the wind, tried to put these thoughts out of my mind. In the movies I'd seen suspects' faces hit newspapers, but never in real life. *Not ever.*

I would not let these ideas affect how I acted.

Given Father Kevin's ties to the bishop, he would find out about the police coming to St. Boniface. Word would pass along, even to city hall. Someone would get upset. Since it wasn't in the church's best interest for this story to get too big, someone would tamp it down. Where He doesn't provide, city hall will.

I put my head down, just walked, listening to my feet hit the ground. The sound reassured me I was here, moving on His earth. Soon I was beyond the Tenderloin, away from those who would disturb me, and as I made my way up and down the city's hills, I slipped into a peace that one cannot find in the grime. This was the peace of the privileged, the fondness for life that came from beautiful surroundings. Not something I usually knew.

I didn't know where I would sleep, a fact that made me like many of the city's destitute, but I had more than they did: my list from the pimp and a name in Russian Hill.

David Heyes.

These men were all listed in the phone book—yes, we still had one—and this pervert lived at an address off of Broadway. His name was what guided my path.

I pushed the buzzer for apartment two and used my deepest voice. *"It's Dub."*

"What?"

"Got to see you."

There was a pause. I stood at the intercom, watching clean young people on the street. Some parts of this city seemed as though no one under thirty-five lived in them. I buzzed again.

"Piss off."

I buzzed again, a long one, channeling how a pimp would respond to being brushed off.

"Dub's dead," he said. "I'm calling the cops."

A jolt rushed through me: panic. A change in my plan; he knew about Dub. Then my rational side restored order and calm. But in this case, calm meant action, aggression, pushing through the outer door of the apartment building to the locked inner door, which I kicked at the point of its lock. It released inward, opening onto the hall, and I dashed up the stairs to the second floor, found apartment two, and banged on the door with my fist. But if Heyes felt he was in danger, he might follow through with his threat, even call faster.

I stepped back and kicked his door at its lock. It sprang open, slammed against the inside wall.

"What the hell?"

I shouted back, a nothing sound, more exhilaration than insult. I stomped in to find David Heyes standing in his living room wearing a white shirt and underwear, one hand holding a baseball bat and the other holding a cell phone.

"Put the phone down."

He looked at the phone, trying to figure out his next move. No one was on the other end. His status as a heathen made me sure.

"The cops are on their way." He said it like he wasn't even sure if he believed it himself.

I stepped toward him. He held the phone away, pushed the bat toward my face like he would jab at me, not swing. So I grabbed it out of his hands, then swung it at the hand with the phone.

I connected with his hand, sent the phone smacking off a wall and his fingers to his mouth. "What?"

As I swung again, he flinched. The sound of the wood hitting him was a dull, hollow thud.

He glanced down at a second phone, this one corded: an old push-button model like we had in the church. He was judging how fast he could pick it up now, if I would hit him before he could. I had to laugh; I could swing the bat before he picked up the phone, even bring it around to connect with his head when he bent down. If I wanted to, I could beat the life out of him before he could ever dial and get anyone at the police to hear him.

"Go ahead," I said. "Pick it up."

He faked with his hand, jabbing but not reaching, wanting to see what I would do. I stood still. Heyes had to be very high. I didn't smell anything, but with the prevalence of pot cards and clubs across the city, there were edibles all around. I kicked the phone, knocking it off the handset.

"Make my day."

He said, "If you call the police from a cell phone, it goes straight to highway patrol. If you call with a corded phone, you get a real cop. It's fast."

"What?"

"That's why I keep it. For if there's a major emergency."

"Next time, call then." I swung away, brought the bat down hard on the phone and broke its faceplate in half. I smashed the bat down on the handset.

He tried to block the bat with his arms—a mistake—and screamed when it hit his fingers.

He collapsed onto a recliner covered by an afghan, probably where he'd been sitting before I arrived. A pipe and an overflowing ashtray sat on a table beside it, unwrapped lozenges and jelly lollipops as well.

I stepped back and turned off his TV. In the absence of its sound, I could hear him whimper.

"Tell me about Emily," I said. "You remember her, right? You had a party and did something to her you never should have."

He winced, eyes closed like he was reviewing it and couldn't stomach what he'd done. At least there was that then: some level of remorse. This man wasn't all bad. Still, I was there to do God's will.

Heyes hadn't planned it. There was always a leader, someone who pushed the others beyond the pale. He was the one I wanted last.

Heyes was no leader. Within ten minutes he told me everything he knew about Emily, the group of them. In some places I had to get him to shut up.

At times, it got to be too much.

CHAPTER THIRTY-NINE
DONNER

The girl was awake when we walked into her room, sitting up in bed. She watched us with those eyes: small, dark, and receded, hardly blinking. She picked up the pad and pencil, wrote one word, and showed it to us: *Police.*

I reached out and touched her hand. She didn't offer to shake or move at all, so I just rested my fingers on hers, finally offering what I thought was a reassuring squeeze. "I'm Inspector Donner and this is Inspector Hendricks. You can call me Clara."

Her eyes showed what I thought was recognition.

She sat upright in the bed, blankets drawn tight around her legs. Her hair looked cleaner now, brushed back to reveal more of her face. The face told a story of where she'd been, what she'd endured. I looked into it to offer her my sympathies. I wanted her to feel I could relate.

Instead, her eyes were cold. Maybe she knew what we were doing there. Maybe she didn't care.

I pulled a chair over from the wall and sat down next to her bed. She wrote on the pad and showed us again:

Where is he?

"Who?"

Father Michael.

"Did he hurt you?" I had to ask it, even if she didn't seem scared or worried that he might come find her. No, that wasn't why she was asking about him. In the same way that she hadn't shown any relief when we took her out of his room.

She hugged her arms to her thin chest, tucking her fingers into her armpits as if she were cold. I would have tucked the blankets around her legs, but she was already well sealed in.

"Who is he to you?"

She glared at me, searching my face for something. For what? Then she looked at Hendricks and did the same. I could hear her breathing, a hollow sound with a small whistle to it. She could be thinking of her answer, or just sizing us up, deciding if we were worth trusting.

After a time, she held up the pad again, pointed to her first question: *Where is he?*

"We don't know. I was hoping you could tell us."

She pursed her lips, shook her head.

Hendricks said, "Got a plan here?"

"Let me try for a minute. Just us girls."

"I'll be outside."

When he left, he shut the door behind him with a click.

"Can you hear me?"

She nodded.

"The priest, do you know why we're looking for him?"

No response.

"Do you know why you're here?"

Shook her head.

"Okay." I touched her forearm, squeezed lightly. She pulled her arms in closer, a message I read loud and clear.

"Who is he to you? What is your relationship? Or how'd he get you into that church? How did you wind up with him? Find yourself in the rectory?"

She scribbled on the pad.

He saved me. Found me after they beat me up. Beat me bad.

"Who beat you up?"

She shrugged, mouthed the word *men*.

"And now he wants to hurt them back, is that right?"

She shook her head, stared me cold.

Her look was determined. When she finally picked up the pencil, she wrote one word on her pad. In capital letters:

SAVIOR.

"I don't understand."

She wrote:

Him

She pointed to the word and then *SAVIOR.*

"He saved you? How?"

She took the pad back and underlined the same word, twice, showed it to me again.

"Your savior," I said. "The priest? What's he doing now? To these men?"

She made a noise in the back of her throat and showed me her tongue. More noises. Then, on the pad,

He found me. Took me in.

"He took care of you?"

She nodded.

"And now what?" I asked.

She wrote in small letters,

Alone. Afraid.

"You're okay now. This is a safe place." I put my hand on her arm, and she recoiled, made a kind of closed-mouth scream.

I had no idea what to do with that, so when she started that mewling in the back of her throat again, put the pad down on her bedside table and closed her eyes, I stood up. The mewling got louder. She waved her hands at the door and at me, shooing me away. Grumpy, irritated noises came from her throat.

"Okay," I said, taking a step back.

Hendricks opened the door and poked his head in. "Everything okay in here?"

"Seems like she doesn't want to talk."

"Doesn't like you?" He chuckled. "Who can blame her?" He came inside. "Want me to try?"

I offered him a clear path to the bed. "Be my guest."

"Hi there. Hi, Emily." He crouched low as he moved toward her, doing his best not to be threatening. "Hi."

When he reached out toward her bed, she screamed. He pulled his hand back, pointed at the chair.

"Can I sit?"

She shook her head. She was quiet now, eyes open.

"Tell us, did he cut you?" Hendricks asked. "Did he hurt you?"

She shook her head—no.

"Do you know what he does when he goes out at night? When he's not with you?"

She glared at Hendricks hard, squinting. She turned to me with the same gaze. She ripped off the top page from her pad and crumpled it into a ball, dropped it to the floor. When she took up the pencil, she wrote fast, angrily.

She showed Hendricks the page where she'd written: *He saves their souls.* Then she wrote the word *Savior* and underlined it.

She threw the pad at his face. Screamed at us even louder now, mouth open, and Dr. Matal came running in with a large male nurse in tow.

"What did you do?" Dr. Matal asked, pushing us out of the way. She and the orderly held Emily down in the bed. Still she screamed, thrashing her head. The orderly pinned her, and Dr. Matal produced straps that she started fastening to the bed.

More screaming.

I stood watching this girl's anger, her sense of being wronged by us for taking her away from a killer. Her mouth wide open, I could see her scarred and shortened tongue in the back of her throat. It shook with her screams, and the sound took the air out of the room, made it hard to breathe. Hendricks was pulling me back, but I stayed put.

"Come on, Donner." Hendricks took hold of my arm, pulled me back toward the door.

The doctor told us to leave. "Haven't you done enough to her already?"

She had a syringe in her hands and was tapping it with her finger. "Hold her," she said to the nurse.

I watched as she put the needle to Emily's arm, punched down the plunger.

Emily glared but calmed right away. Suddenly the room went quiet. Hendricks had me in the doorway, almost to the hall.

I saw anger in Emily's little eyes and spittle on her mouth. She had come alive with her passion, and now it was passing back away into a daze, as if she had blinked and all her emotion was gone like someone wiping a blackboard clean.

"Come on, Donner," Hendricks said, standing in the hall, his hand still on my arm. He showed me the pad as he ripped off the top page for us to take with us. He had the page she'd crumpled up too. "There's nothing for us here now. And I don't want to be around when that doctor comes out."

CHAPTER FORTY

In the car with Hendricks, I studied both sheets of Emily's writing. The words stared me in the face, challenging me to figure out more of their meaning.

He saved me. Found me after they beat me up. Beat me bad.

SAVIOR.

He found me. Took me in.

Alone. Afraid.

He saves their souls.

Father Michael.

That's what we had. I smoothed out the pages against the dash.

"What do you think?" I asked.

Hendricks snickered. "That doctor's not gonna let us back in to see her. That's what I think."

"We'll get a court order. See how she handles that." I pointed at the pages. "What do you make of this? Anything?"

"I don't know what more we could've gotten from her. She's hardly a willing witness."

"Not willing, not coherent."

"Amen." He turned to me and winked. All this religion business was still funny to him. He liked my discomfort.

"What's going to happen to your soul? You believe in saving it?"

"No. Huh-uh. I been saved since my baptism as a kid. Now I'm just living on borrowed time, doing my best not to mess things up before I go back to Him." He crossed himself over his chest, pointed to the sky.

"Yeah, that," I said. "What's this really mean to her?"

"You want to really talk about this?" He pulled the car over to the side, got into the far right lane, and put on our blinkers. Then he stared me square in the face. "Let's figure this all out," he said.

"What do you make of this? Her words?" I pointed at the pages again.

He looked them over, taking his time. "I think we blew it, Donner. She was pissed. We might not get that chance again."

"What more could we have gotten? She's on his side. What's that tell us?"

"This," he said, tapping the dash. "She lived with him in there. Whatever he was doing, she knows. And those johns?" He waved his arm in no particular direction. "He wasn't about saving their souls."

"But he *was* every bit about sending them on to the next world. To damnation or wherever he believes they wind up."

"And not without some pain first."

"He's getting back at them. Back at them for her and all the other girls out there they've hurt." I didn't want to admit it, but this was the part I kept coming back to, the part I didn't want to admire.

"So what's his next move, partner? More of the same?"

I wasn't sure, so I thought it over. Watching the city outside—a homeless man with plastic bags for shoes. Then I gave him the best of what I could come up with. "Debbie Shine said she heard him getting names from Dub. That's what she thought, anyway."

"Who then? More guys who roughed her up? More johns? Who do we get them from? Dub's dead."

"Emily?" I asked. "Should we go back at her? Try to get her to tell us who beat her up last?"

He shook his head. "Even if we get past the doctor, she'll protect the priest."

"What's she have for him?"

"Love. Loyalty. She'll never give him up."

He was right, but I didn't want to admit it. What else did we have but her? And maybe we'd just lost that.

Hendricks went on, "Who knows what two people have for each other. Maybe he gave her God. That's what being a savior means to me."

"Maybe he saved her from Dub. Gave her a place to sleep. Helped her get clean. Tended her wounds."

He didn't say anything to that. We both thought it through. Then he put the car into drive and started us moving.

I thought about the girl, wondered what Father Michael meant to her. A lot, I was guessing. In his little room, she'd been so calm on the bed, seemingly at peace, not wanting for anything. Her bruises and cuts were healing.

How many times had she felt peace in her life? In the last year? Maybe he helped her kick the habit.

He was her savior, she had said. Wasn't that something we all wanted? To be saved.

Some got saved by God or work, living in the moment, meditation, whatever it took. Some were saved by the bottle or their relationships—for a time. It always came back to the same problems, eventually. At least, I thought so.

The scumbags of San Francisco kept me busy. Ridding the world of them was as noble a goal as any.

Exercise was supposed to save me. Exercise and physical activity. Basketball, running, a cardio boxing class. Hitting the heavy bag. Getting outside or going to the gym, moving my body, working up a sweat. Endorphins, adrenaline. Holding all the world at bay with a focus on something else. That was my freedom.

Still, I missed something and had known that for a while. It wasn't just a guy to cuddle up to either. Though Alan was kicking through my head enough that I knew there was something there I wanted. And I definitely spent more than enough time on the dating sites.

The girl, Emily, had a family somewhere, her people. She'd come to the big, bad city and wound up on the wrong side of, well, everything: hooking, drugs, tracks. She'd gone through the bad, met her priest, and he brought her into his church, took care of her without asking for anything in return. Who among us didn't need that sometimes? She definitely wasn't in any rush to leave.

Now we'd taken her away.

"Sooner or later," I said, "he's going to find out where she is. When that happens, he'll come for her."

"You know that?"

"I'm betting on it." I pounded my hand on the dash.

"Then we need to find him first. That and get a patrol watching her room."

CHAPTER FORTY-ONE

Back at the Hall, we ate lunch at our desks: grilled chicken on a simple green salad for me and a Reuben hoagie with extra stomach pain for Hendricks.

I took Bowen's green light for help and requested an officer stationed outside Emily's room. Doc Matal might like that or not, probably not, but it wasn't my concern. As long as she could see through to keep Emily for the full seventy-two hours. We needed at least that much time.

I started updating the Clip on Father Michael—the series of images and critical information that went out to the districts, telling officers on the street what to watch for. I put in the new data about his name and particulars, whatever we had, and uploaded more pictures from St. Boniface. The more we had, the better, the closer we would get to him. I hoped so, anyway. All we had to do was wait. That and work the case as hard as we could.

Hendricks belched loudly and pounded his chest. He would start complaining about his phantom angina next, if patterns held. I always told him to eat healthier, that just a small change could help, but he didn't listen.

"Oh, the angina." He winked at me. "Just kidding."

I started to laugh.

Then his cell started ringing, and he made a dour face when he saw who it was. Had to be his daughter's mom. He answered the phone and mouthed her name, but I could already hear her voice. It wasn't one you easily forgot.

As Hendricks's partner, I was responsible for watching his back in all things—even with his baby mama—but from a woman's viewpoint, she usually had him dead to rights.

Now I tried to avoid listening. I forked into my salad. Protein for energy, greens for roughage and vitamins. Trying to eat healthy was another facet of my belief system, yet to steer me wrong.

Hendricks and his daughter: he never came close to marrying her mother, but she still haunted him like they'd had a divorce to beat all others. If he didn't do what she asked, he'd hear it from her for a week. Of course, she was his least favorite topic, and the other officers joked that his manhood existed to be squeezed in her pocketbook.

From where I sat, he didn't get off too badly for all his daughter privileges with very little of the work. He was an absentee dad, only around for the fun times on odd weekends. So he was lucky, all in all.

Finally, exhausted and beaten down, Hendricks put away his phone. "I need to pick up Trina at school."

"How's her mom going to like it when you and I run off together?"

He smiled. "Seriously. Please take me away." He folded the rest of his sandwich in its white paper.

"Seriously?" I said, "You better hope nothing else comes in the rest of the day."

He laughed, but it was an uneasy chuckle, something like a recognition of the Murphy's law of police work: that we were now sure to get a call.

Sure enough, the phone on my desk starting to ring. I checked the caller ID: Lieutenant Bowen.

"It's Bowen."

Hendricks sighed. "Uh-oh, partner, better get ready for more reaming."

"Roger that." I looked over to the lieutenant's office, and it was dark, blinds drawn. "Where is he?"

"Guess you'll find out."

I answered the phone, holding it away from my ear, expecting to hear him yelling more about bishops, politicians, priests. Even the pope maybe. Instead, his voice came through calm and at a normal volume.

"We got another body already, Donner. Your suspect keeps busy. This time Russian Hill. Lund and Peters on the scene, say he looks to be the same sort of john as the others. This is turning into a killing spree. Neighbors say they heard noises but thought it was the TV. Anyway, the body's in pretty bad shape, like the others."

I stirred my finger in the air, giving Hendricks the sign to round 'em up. We were on our way.

"On it, sir. We'll be there soon." I put the top on my salad as I stood up.

When I told Hendricks the what and the where, he swore. There was no way he'd make a four o'clock pickup for his daughter without a lightning bolt of major-league luck.

CHAPTER FORTY-TWO

MICHAEL

I started to take David Heyes's apartment apart in pieces. I broke and crushed everything I could using the bat, then stomped whatever was left with my boots. He cried out at first, but after I warned him not to, he did a good job of keeping quiet—biting his tongue, so to speak. Finally, I found a towel in the bathroom and shoved it into his mouth, let him bite down on that.

This was when I started breaking fingers.

"Why are you doing this?" he asked when I let him speak.

"To rid you of your sins. To take Emily's sins and the ones who created them out of this world."

"For Emily?" he asked. "This is all about *her*?"

I hit him again.

"How could you do that to another person on His earth?"

"She was dirty," he said. "Just a druggy slut."

I held the bat still, willed him to speak, to say more. Though it burned me, I knew this was what I needed to hear. I needed this anger to carry out His acts.

I said, "Tell me."

"We did that. We did it." He shook his head, looked upset and sorry. "I don't know how it came to that. The others. Of course I'll say that, right? But really. I can't—part of me still can't believe we did that. But come on. What's she worth, really? Not all this."

"Why? Why did you?"

He shook his head. "I don't know. How much you want? You want money?"

I hit him with the bat, lost control for a few moments. Such was my own pain.

When I stopped, he told me he understood what I was doing and why I had to do it. He said he knew someone would come to administer punishment, even stopped crying as he said it.

But these were lies. The trickery of a sinner.

I saw his filth, signs of his meager, disgusting life. He had a job that paid him well for doing something of no value, a series of tasks that added nothing to the world but helped to provide more financial distribution among the country's wealthy. He did nothing for the poor, the ones with actual *needs*.

He talked more: "Drugs, girls, all that. I did it all. Didn't ever have any problem getting the money, so why not? Right? I'm supposed to enjoy myself, aren't I?"

I didn't answer.

"Right?" He waited. "Anyway, why not? I get the work done, do my job, make the dough. No one around seems at all bothered."

"God," I said, "what about your life in the eyes of God?"

He laughed. "Never stopped to think about that one, brother."

I fixed a stern gaze on him. "Getting right with the Lord is your sole duty on this earth, my son. My wayward son."

"Father?" he asked. "Should I call you father?"

I ground the end of the bat down onto one of his fingers.

"Because that's bull. Pure bullshit."

"Come on." I dragged him into the kitchen, propped him up in one of the chairs beside a small wood table.

"I mean, I never gave a crap about religion, you know? Why should I look at that as a way of life? Just do and get done, right? *That's* the American way." He looked hard at me like he was waiting for an answer. "You know I'm right."

I turned on a burner, started warming oil in a pan.

"What are you going to do with that?"

I spun toward him, flipped one of the chairs around, and sat backward on it, right in front of his face. "Tell me again why nothing stopped you. Why you would do that to this poor girl?"

"It's just life, man. You should know. The things you can do in this city. Why shouldn't I? If there are items to be purchased here, why not try the wares, you know? See what I like to do for fun."

When I didn't answer, it made him uneasy.

"What are you going to do with that oil?"

I thought about cutting off his pant leg, one of them, and pouring the oil down his thigh once it was heated up. It seemed like this would make sense, what I should do to him next. Something in the old ways of religion led me to this desire.

"But what do *you* get out of this?" he asked.

He saw things clearly now, the pain having pushed away his high.

"This is for Him."

"Him? *God?* Are you serious? You're going to say something crazy like he talks to you now, right? Get serious."

"Get serious?"

"You're a man of the cloth? Swore an oath or something? Why don't you—"

I squeezed the top of his jawbone just in front of his ears until his mouth opened and pushed a wooden spoon in, all the way back until he gagged. He looked at me like he wanted to get something out, like I was interrupting some major revelation, the most important question he could ever ask. In all likelihood, it would be one of his last. Maybe he knew that right then.

He was begging with his eyes, whining in the back of his throat as I took the pan off the stove and held it over his leg. I hadn't cut off any part of his pants; they weren't going to do him any good. First, I started to drizzle. I could see the smoke or steam coming off his leg, the hot oil burning through his pants, and he started to go a bit wild from the pain, screaming around the spoon. I pushed it in harder.

"This okay for you?" I asked. He shook his head violently. "Oh, no?" More head shaking. "Guess not, then. Let me just see if—" I poured more along his leg. The skin melted a little, blending together with the fabric as it burned away, changed shape under the weight and heat of the pour.

"No, that's not good," I said. "That has really got to hurt."

After a time, he calmed. The oil had run off, and I took the spoon out. "Now, what were you asking?"

"You're sick," he said. "That's it. Just simple. You're sick. You get off on this."

"I'm not like you. This? I don't enjoy this. I do this for *Him. He has shown me my path, and I follow only where He leads.* This is not something I choose."

His head slumped against his chest. "What's the difference?"

"For one, you enjoyed what you did to her. For two, I have a stated path. A purpose. That's what makes us different. That's why God is punishing you."

I pushed the spoon back in, continued to pour.

CHAPTER FORTY-THREE

DONNER

We got to Glover Street in Russian Hill just after two. Neither Hendricks nor I had finished our lunch. Based on what we'd seen at the other crime scenes, we didn't want a lot of food on our stomachs, anyway.

Lund and Peters had left their notes with one of the duty officers from the Central. They left before we arrived, claiming they'd gotten a call in the time it took us to come over.

"If we're lucky, they'll actually hold on to this one," I said.

"Yeah." Hendricks was reading through the sheet.

"This has to be an all-time string of bad luck."

"Just one major case, partner." He looked up at me. "We really caught one. A killer on a spree."

"So we agree on something."

"Yeah. Maybe I should get myself checked out by a doctor."

I smiled. "That, or they're just yanking our chains and went out to lunch."

Hendricks got a sly look in his eyes. "Let's call and find out."

"Come on, partner. We should get to this if you want to have any chance of picking up your girl."

He nodded. Even if being a cop basically precluded any semblance of having a life, we had to try to be normal people once in a while. At least that's what I was thinking when my phone started buzzing inside my jacket.

I pulled it out, checked the screen. Sure enough, it was Alan with some of the worst timing: right after I'd told Hendricks we should get to it. But it gave me something to smile about. Maybe he'd leave a voicemail for me to look forward to. I silenced the ring and tucked the phone back into my jacket, then followed Hendricks inside.

This place was another one-bedroom, one-man apartment. Not so nice, initially, and left in much worse shape by the killer of its lone inhabitant.

There were no pictures of girls inside, but judging from the collection of porn on this guy's shelves—most notably of the bondage and S&M varieties—it wasn't much of a leap to assume he'd been with some of the same girls as Jay Piper and Doug Farrow. For Lund and Peters, it was enough to go on, and they weren't likely to be wrong.

We walked into the living room of one David A. Heyes to see a smashed flat-screen TV. One of the big ones. Hendricks read from his notes. "Baseball bat," he said.

"Looks like." There were shards of glass and pieces of plastic all over the floor.

He pointed with his chin toward the kitchen. "Our guy's in there."

"Where's Ibaka?" I asked.

He shrugged.

We wrote up our own report on the scene after examining the body of David Heyes: black male adult, dead, tortured with what appeared to be hot oil. Of course a priest knew more about the physical history of punishing sinners than your standard perp, had studied the history of practices dating back centuries. Punishment for breaking moral laws had been the purview of the church for so long that only in our most recent awareness did we think this wasn't normal. Just the past couple hundred years—basically nothing.

Go back before that and maybe this kind of sinner-salvation spree would be heroic. But there was no time machine anywhere near, no way these practices could be condoned.

What stuck out the most from the whole scene was Heyes's mouth. His tongue had been removed. We couldn't find it anywhere on the scene.

Hendricks put up his hands. "Maybe our priest took it with him."

"Just like with Emily. This is adding up. Maybe too well. We got him."

Hendricks looked around. "That's funny, Donner. Because I don't see anybody. Looks to me like we don't have zip."

"We're getting closer. He's on the run."

He puckered to spit, then choked it down. "He's killing a man a day. This is a killing spree."

"Maybe we'll get a promotion. Become celebrities."

"I'm not in the mood to laugh, Donner. Aren't you tired?"

"Don't even," I said. "You didn't have Bowen blast you this morning. You're in a good place."

"Let me go this afternoon? Will you do the reports on this so I can get Trina?"

Tough as Hendricks came off, he was no match for his baby mama. "Let me think about it."

"What'd I miss?" Ibaka walked into the apartment, dropped her kit onto the table.

I turned around, genuinely happy to see her, and tipped my pad to acknowledge it. "She arrives. Finally. What you got?"

"I'm the one should be asking that question. What's here? A whole body? A kill scene? How'd I get so lucky?"

In his grumpy voice, Hendricks said, "More from our priest."

He went out into the hallway.

"What's wrong with him?"

"Baby mama troubles."

Ibaka flipped through her kit, getting out the tools she'd need. "Don't see why people aren't getting married anymore. You want a kid, you get married. You make somebody pregnant, you get married. Simple. Lock yourself down and take away the happy. It's worked for centuries. The tried and true."

"You're asking me? I'm the girl can't even get a dude on the Internet."

"Right. Robocop online dating. That still not working out?"

Ibaka had become the closest thing I had to a true girlfriend. I was half tempted to pull up one of Heyes's chairs and sit down and vent.

"We still having that beer later?"

"As soon as I get done here." She winked.

I pulled my phone out and showed her the screen: "Alan—Voicemail and Missed Call."

"And who is *that*?"

"Exactly what I want to tell you about *later*."

"Deal." We bumped fists. Maybe the voicemail would be nothing, no big deal, but I liked knowing that he'd called, at least.

I followed Hendricks out into the hall, ready to let him go. Clara Donner, softie at heart. I wanted to listen to Alan's voicemail, but I couldn't. Didn't have time.

I found Hendricks hunched over the railing, looking down the stairs. I clapped him on the back. "Know what, partner? Go get Trina. You drive me back to the Hall, I'll cover the rest of the afternoon."

He perked up. "Yeah? You'd do that?"

"Absolutely. I got to keep *someone* in my life happy, don't I?"

"And I'm that person?" He moved in like he wanted to kiss me, but I pushed him off.

"No sugar?"

"No. Gross."

He turned as if to go. "Thanks."

"Don't mention it. Just remember sometime that I did this for you."

His brow furrowed. "Wait. What's *up*?"

"Nothing."

He angled his head down and toward my face, trying to meet my eyes. "Don*ner*?"

I avoided his gaze, sure by now I was blushing. He'd get it out of me sooner or later, I knew. So I showed him my phone, the call and voice-mail from Alan. It was all he knew and all he needed to. He laughed but was smiling genuinely.

"Come on," he said, "let's go."

Back at the Hall, I pulled out my chair, dropped into it, and slumped in front of the computer. Coffee wasn't helping anymore. Beer would, but I still had two hours to go until meeting Ibaka at the Mars Bar.

I checked my email and felt my jaw drop as I opened one with a St. Boniface SF address.

The subject was "Detective Donner."

The body of the email read,

> I saw you today. You entered my church. My home. The house of the Lord. You have no business there.
>
> Now, because of you, Emily is gone.
>
> Where did you take her? What have you done? You and your partner will not be

forgiven by the Lord. If you want to be saved, bring her to me.

Has God brought you onto His path?

Do you hear His words?

I am watching.

If God has chosen you, I will know it. He has chosen to reveal YOU to me, and now I see YOU. God knows your name.

I am watching.

"Holy smokes!" I said, pushing my chair back. "Sound the lunatic alarm. We got a live one."

No one responded. I looked around to see empty desks. It was the middle of the afternoon, just before shift change, and everyone seemed to be out on calls. A uniformed officer walked across the floor, but I didn't know him well enough to say anything. Bowen sat in his office, talking on the phone, his door closed.

I was alone with the investigation.

I sat back in my chair. The email was unsigned. The address was fr.michael@stbonifacesf.org. He'd been watching from somewhere as I came out of the church.

He had seen me, us. *He'd been there, and we'd missed him.*

I swore and stood up, slapped the side of my chair. I wanted to call Ibaka; I knew she had my back on this one, might even have some news to report. It was five o'clock: late enough in the day that I could go have a beer. I sent Ibaka a text letting her know where to find me.

CHAPTER FORTY-FOUR

The Mars Bar was the kind of place only cops and regulars went, unless it was nice out. Unfortunately for me, today had been one of the nicer days in the last few weeks. The sun was still out, no fog had come in to greet us from its ocean breeding ground, and it was warm enough to keep your coat off. People stood outside in the courtyard enjoying themselves, talking it up over happy hour's cheap drinks. I took a seat inside at the bar. I'd have considered leaving if I wasn't so used to coming here.

One thing I liked about the Mars was that most of the folks from the Hall didn't come in. They mostly preferred Teddy's Sports Bar both because it was closer and because it favored the old boys' club atmosphere. Teddy's was so close to being an extension of the Hall's locker rooms that some of the guys joked about putting showers in there so they could start drinking before getting out of their blues.

I'd tried to fit in there my first few years on the force but eventually gave up. Better to be alone and unbothered than feel the need to try hard and wind up as the butt of too many jokes anyway.

I was finishing my first beer when Ibaka showed up. She sat down next to me and said, "Still fighting off scurvy?"

I tipped my glass up: a Blue Moon that Ibaka thought I ordered for the orange slice that came on its rim. She said I did it for the vitamin C, which I liked because it might help me fight off colds. She said it was scurvy that would ultimately do me in. I'd looked it up once, a disease rampant on old sailing ships. One of its symptoms was the opening of previously healed wounds. I didn't know if she meant this as part of the joke, but it fit me a little too well, I thought. Vitamin C had cured the sailors way back when, but I wasn't sure what could cure my wounds.

"So what's the matter?" She nodded to the bartender, and he started drawing her a beer. I nodded for another. "What about the guy with the voicemail? I thought we were here to talk about that."

"He sent me an email. The priest. He was watching us at the church. He knows my name."

"This isn't about dating? Damn, I thought this would be about dating." Her beer arrived, and she took a big sip, leaving a foam mustache that she licked off. "Damn, that's good."

"Did you hear me? *He* emailed me. Our suspect."

She turned to me, but I just stared at the fresh beer as it arrived. I didn't want her to see my face—I was worried she'd be able to see that this was affecting me.

"So what'd you do? You tell Hendricks? Bowen?"

I shook my head, biting the inside of my cheek. It was a habit I'd started as a girl, something I did when I was nervous. Truth was, it never helped.

"No. Neither."

"What? Why not, girl?"

I took another drink, put the pint glass down maybe a little too hard on the bar.

She said, "How much catching up do I have?" I told her what beer I was on, and she nodded, drank off half of hers in one long swallow. When she set it on the bar, I turned to face her.

"What's the cause of death on Heyes?"

"Broken neck." She took another drink, signaled to the bartender for another.

"And his tongue?"

She shook her head. "Done after. But most all of the other damage was done before."

"This guy is cold. Stone cold. So why do that after?"

"Search me. I can't believe it at all. But I gather he's sending a message. What'd he say in the email?"

I bit my upper lip. "Said he's watching me. Wanted to know if I heard God's words."

Now she straightened. "What's that even mean?"

"Means our priestly serial killer is psychotic, possibly schizophrenic, and/or just takes his religion very seriously."

"Franciscans. All that gloom and doom and sin business."

I drank my beer, starting to feel the effects. "He was there watching us when we went in and out of the church."

"Spooky. Guy's not where he's supposed to be when you get there, instead he's somewhere you can't see him but he can see *you*. Kind of makes you wonder."

"Wonder what?"

"Nothing."

She didn't say it, but I knew what she thought: that he might be watching at other times, sneaking up when I didn't expect it. That or maybe he really got warnings from God. Or somebody had tipped him off.

I said, "Yeah. It worries me."

"Damn right. That's why I stay in the ME's office. Keep my interactions to the bad guys who're already dead."

"Amen to that." We clinked classes, toasting to her common sense and my lack thereof. It wasn't much to get excited about; on the other hand, given my situation, I might just as well laugh or drink.

"And what's new in the world of cyber dating?"

"Robocop's on a bit of a dry spell. That's the online world. Just this email from our suspect. But . . ." I raised my eyebrows. "But in the world of real people, I kind of met a guy at the basketball courts."

"Basketball?"

I nodded, feeling my cheeks warm. "He's hot."

She laughed, slapped my knee. "Girl! You go. What's he like?"

I told her. And then I took out my phone. It was time to hear his voicemail.

In the back of the bar, by the bathrooms and an actual working pay phone, I put the phone to my ear to listen to Alan's message. I was still freaked out about the priest, his email, and wasn't in a mood to go out and paint the town, but I had held out long enough. Now was the time.

"Hi," Alan said. "Clara. Hey. I was wondering if you were going to hit the court tonight. Figured maybe we could play. I'll tell the guys to let you stay on this time, no matter if you're too good for them."

I laughed. He was hitting my right spots.

"Maybe you're still working on your case though. If so, are you free this weekend? Maybe we could get dinner. I don't know. Okay. Anyway. Call me back when you can. Bye."

He ended like that, nervous and trailing off, and I admit I liked it. That he babbled a little actually felt right. This wasn't easy for him either. Maybe he was thinking about me during the day. I wondered about his job, what he did—I hadn't asked—and if he had time to talk usually or not.

I checked my watch. He was probably on the court now or getting close to it. I wouldn't be the girl to dial drunk or even after just a few beers. Likely not on the same day either. And he'd said weekend. It was . . . Thursday. I had to think to remember. Too many days on. Much as I didn't want to acknowledge it, there was no way I could go out and date with this case still on. Not with this guy on the loose, knowing my name, possibly watching.

I swore out loud and headed back to Ibaka. She had another beer lined up on the bar for each of us, ready to go, and I knew I wouldn't be getting home anytime soon.

CHAPTER FORTY-FIVE
MICHAEL

After finishing with David Heyes, I broke into an empty apartment and holed up. A small studio. Nothing special. I waited there a full day, twenty-four long hours, for His word. All my waiting and listening led to nothing. Emptiness.

Since the detective had entered St. Boniface, I had not heard from Him. Two days without His instructions, His word.

Days of quiet and cold.

Without God's guidance, I could only plan, plot to carry out my own goals: finding the last men, the ones who had left Emily beaten and bloody. I would find them, and then I would find the detective. *She* would bring back Emily.

My Emily.

Together we would return to the church and to heaven. When all was done, God would take us both. Bring us home.

I sat and waited without food or sleep for Him. Left alone to forge my own path with no certainty. I had been here before, a path that led to drugs, addiction, my own sins. Within the church, I had guidance all along. First from my brothers and more recently from Him. I had not known the fear of indecision or directionless uncertainty. Both fears that scared me more than hell.

Without Him I was left to forge my own path, take action without assurance. Nothing to rely on but my own volition.

Perhaps He had spoken to the detective and she knew what came next. I waited to hear from her too. Waiting for the response to my email, checking on a laptop I had appropriated from David Heyes.

As I waited, I wondered how He could test me in my final steps, even though I knew this to be His way. All the way back to Job, Abraham, and Moses, He has tested His best men. And now I would pass through the crucible and be made stronger.

He may have abandoned me, but I had not abandoned Him. I would do what needed to be done.

PART FOUR

FRIDAY

CHAPTER FORTY-SIX

I walked to North Beach in the morning, looking for the home of my next john, hoping to find God.

My volition led me now; after waiting in prayer, I knew to act of my own will. Even as I yearned to hear from Him.

Across the city, I walked along the Bay Trail. Across the Marina, I passed women in slight clothing, men watching hungrily, all in the name of exercise and what they considered to be good health. Their hearts were not well in the name of the Lord. Not these sinners.

With their hair bobbed, they bounced with every step, their minds oblivious, earbuds in. These women who sweat in front of anyone, breathing hard, skin slick and brown in the sun. Tempting all. He would have none of it. A pious soul, a considered and repentant heart—these were the path to heaven.

These sinners were all for *this* world: the present, sins of the body, the profane.

And they would reap what they sowed.

As I walked, the sun warmed my face; He told me with its touch that He was still above us, watching, following. He approved.

The grassy open spaces along the Bay, the trees and scattered flowers, all His creations smiled and shined out on the world. Walking across Fort Mason, Great Meadow, I blocked out the sound of cars. I could pretend they weren't there, but they were.

This was still the middle of the city, where man's filth abounded in the air. Two homeless men huddled in their dirt on a bench. There they were, mumbling to themselves. Their lives of pain.

If He asked me to wipe them away, to clean the streets in a flood, I would do so.

I stopped to watch. One man picked threads out of his pants with dirty fingernails. The other's mouth wouldn't stop running; he babbled to himself about flies. He picked at his face, fingers stained.

Sinners. Addicts. I saw it in their eyes, knew it because I'd been them once before, long ago.

What would have helped me then? Salvation.

I'd taken a knife from David Heyes's apartment. I wanted to send them on to heaven with it. Wondered if I sent these men on, who would notice? Would anyone care? Perhaps only the person who found them, who had to clean the blood and remove the bodies.

I approached their bench, got within five feet of them, and one said, "I know you?"

He eyed me closely, tilting his head for a different view. The other stopped picking his pants. Now they both watched my movements.

"I come from God," I said, waiting to hear what they would say next, wondering if I would hear their earthly words or God's answer.

"Who you?"

Then, "Why don't you keep walking?"

These weren't His words. He would not speak through them.

I showed them my hands, drew the knife. "I'm here to offer you salvation. A path up to heaven."

They both stood at that, started toward the back of the bench.

"Now, now, man. Don't do nothing crazy. Hear?"

I stepped closer.

"Go!" one said to the other. They ran, tore off in the direction of the Bay Bridge. I didn't follow. They left their disgusting bags, piles of dirty things on the grass. Garbage bags, a torn backpack, a suitcase with a broken zipper and no wheels—these held all their worldly possessions. I wanted to destroy it all. But it meant nothing to me.

I walked away, pressed on toward Columbus and Bay Street. I would stop at a church before finding the next apartment, one of a man named James Weber.

CHAPTER FORTY-SEVEN
DONNER

In the morning, I found Hendricks waiting at his desk. We had paperwork to process, work to do to begin documenting the case, and we needed to bring this all to Bowen. Time had come and gone where we should've been assigned to this case alone. These murders involved a big mess, one we'd need real help with. Help *and* a clean plate so we could focus.

I didn't bother trying to bring Hendricks up to speed on my night. Ibaka would do the honors, unless I got lucky. I wasn't betting on my luck holding up, but neither did I expect the phone to ring right then, for Hendricks to pick it up and say, "Well, *hello there*, Dr. Ibaka. How are you this fine morning?

"Yes?" He nodded, playing it up. She would be calling to check up on me, making sure I got home all right, as she had done on more than one occasion before.

"She *is* here. As a matter of fact, she just walked in." He waited as she spoke, looked me up and down to confirm that I was presentable. This kind of inspection was not out of the norm for a hangover morning, and I had done the right thing to make sure my appearance was as sharp as I could make it.

"She looks pretty clean overall, actually," he said. "Touch of makeup, hair brushed. Yes. It's a bona fide investigator we have here." He acted surprised and happy for me, but it was all to get my back up, get me to start the day on a razor edge, which I wouldn't. Regardless.

"Ask her if she'd like to talk to me or if your services have been enough," I said, sitting down into my chair. My computer was still on from yesterday, a series of lines bouncing around as the screen saver.

"Ibaka says she's good," Hendricks repeated. "And she can hear you. She just wanted to check in."

"Well, she has now. And I will call her back later."

"Oh." Hendricks looked taken aback by my response. "Guess we have some work to do here. She has arrived and means to do it. This seems serious."

He hung up. I'd call Ibaka later. The last thing I wanted was her mentioning the email from the priest to Hendricks before I had a chance to show him myself.

"You got to see something, partner."

"Edify me."

I waved him over to my side of the desks, and he came around. When he did, I had the email from Father Michael pulled up.

"What's this?"

"Read it."

He crouched down, hands on his knees, his tie hanging. "Shit, Jesus," he said, then kept reading. "He was *watching* us?"

"Keep going. It gets better."

"I can see that." He tapped the screen. "This means we have to take this sucker down, *pronto*." He read the rest of the email out loud, inserting "yadda, yadda" as he pleased. "This guy is crocked."

"He's something."

"This just went up another notch," he said. "He comes *down*."

"I'm all ears." I pushed back my chair, turning toward Hendricks as he stood and fixed his tie. "What's our plan?"

"First we up the APB on the Clip for this fool. Get cops across the city on tight lookout. Plaster that picture of him across walls, make sure it's at lineups, get people to know. This guy has a target on his back, starting now."

"Yes, sir!" I saluted him and handed over a picture of Father Michael that I'd printed from the St. Boniface website.

Hendricks picked up his phone and made a few calls. I watched Bowen's office for a break in his phone calls so we could approach. When he hung up from one call and didn't start another right away, I waved to Hendricks to speed up his talking and stood up to head in.

I thought about staying outside to keep my doghouse status and its taint off the meeting but couldn't send Hendricks in alone. This was *my* case.

"You ready?" Hendricks stood beside me, off the phone and all set to go in.

"Let's do this."

We walked over to Bowen's office, knocked lightly on the side of the doorframe, and he waved us in. We sat down across the desk from him, waited to have his full attention.

"Been meaning to circle the wagons with you two. Bring me up to date on this string you're working."

Hendricks started: "We've got four connected murders that we know of. Three johns and a pimp from a confined segment of S&M prostitution, all connected to a single girl. We think all done by the same man."

"That's one hell of a week there. What are Lund and Peters catching?"

"Not much. Not that we know of."

Bowen nodded, checked something on his computer. Clicked his mouse.

Hendricks gave him more details on the individual murders, Emily's status at SFGH, and what we knew about the priest. Bowen listened intently all the way. I was new enough to homicide that I wasn't sure how he'd react to it all. The word on Bowen was he had our backs, mostly, but he could be too straight at times, following protocols that didn't make practical sense.

I leaned forward to make my pitch. "We need to go beyond the unofficial support you gave me before. Where this sits now requires the attention of a task force. I think it's clear that we should be the leads."

"I can see that," he said. "Sounds like the right move. Who do you want on support?"

"Coggins and Bennett." Hendricks answered before I could even consider it. I'm not sure I'd have made the same call, but Hendricks knew them better than I.

Bowen nodded. "Lund and Peters will finish off the week on call, then. I'll give them a secondary as well. And tell Coggins and Bennet to circle up with you two." He made a few notes, wrote something on his blotter. "What else do you need?"

I said, "We put a uniform outside our girl's room at SFGH. Might need more manpower if we get any decent leads. If calls start coming in off the Clip, we'll need support to follow up."

"You got it. What else?"

Hendricks said, "I made a couple calls to the Northern and Central. If you follow up and put word out with some pull, maybe we can get this profile as a top priority at pre-shift lineups across the city."

"Done."

"And then we work it the best we can."

"Damn right you do." Bowen scanned over his notes and our file. "This is strong work—Hendricks, Donner." He made eye contact with each of us as he said it, then pushed the file back across his desk and stood up. He shook my hand and then Hendricks's. "I like what I see here. Do what you can and be sure to check back with me before the weekend. Anything goes down, I've got your back."

We thanked him and moved to leave. Just as I got to the door, he asked Hendricks to stay a moment. I walked back out into the squad room alone, waited for my partner in the middle of the floor. This case was becoming news around homicide, as was the work that I'd done on it. I could feel eyes watching me from around the room, but no one made eye contact. Just like that I'd been given some rope, enough to work the case with a wide berth, even a little political pull. Hendricks and I were now leads on a task force. A small one, but still. As a relative newbie in the department, this was big.

In his office, Lieutenant Bowen barked at Hendricks to "stay away from the churches," and I knew it was meant just as much for me. But what could we do? We had to go after this guy wherever he might be.

The rope had been granted. Now I could do one of two things: haul in our killer or hang myself. I would never let it be the second. So it had to be the first.

We would get Father Michael. Without a doubt.

CHAPTER FORTY-EIGHT

MICHAEL

At Washington Square, people with days free lay out on the grass. Drug dealers dealt their drugs. Others consumed them.

So much happened here in the name of sin, all under the shadow of Saints Peter and Paul Church. I walked right up to the stairs from the lawn and looked at the grand entrance under the inscription *"Per L'Universo."* The message: for everyone. Universal, for all.

The church welcomed all. Sinners. Just enter the house of the Lord to be saved. A daily offer, yet so few came inside.

So be it.

As soon as I passed through the door, I felt the silence. The silence of the space—its vaulted ceiling, arches, the wood of the pews. All this absorbed sound, changed the nature of the space. A peace descended on me, one I had not felt since I left St. Boniface on Wednesday. This was the peace that I needed to restore.

At this time of day, the pews were mostly empty—a few tourists and a believer or two. Midday mass ended, now the church simply waited. Welcoming.

I sat in one of the middle pews, removed my jacket, and laid it gently beside me. I knelt and began my prayers, begged His forgiveness for bringing this trouble to my church, outsiders into it, and asked His protection for Emily while she was in their hands. For myself, I listened.

I whispered, "Please, Lord. I am Your servant. Restore Your guidance to me."

Even as He failed to respond, I felt peace. Eyes closed, I knew the presence of all that was holy in His name, the eyes of His son looking down on me from the altar.

I prayed.

After a time, I sat back in the pew and pondered the beauty of His church. I had never been there before, but I still felt welcome. I was and would always be safe in the house of the Lord.

Safe under Him.

Then I noticed a man in odd dress, too formal, someone with the aura of a policeman trying to appear undercover. He walked along the far side of the pews, tried to avoid drawing attention. But in His house, he stood out like a man-size fire.

Believers, tourists, and *him*. Three different sets. I bowed my head, hoping he didn't see me.

But he was heading closer.

Slowly, carefully, trying to act as if he wasn't, he started toward me, walking across a pew. This, all wrong, something no believer would do.

I stood, pulled myself together, and moved away, headed for the far corner. And as I moved, I felt His peace, knew He watched over and protected me from harm.

CHAPTER FORTY-NINE

Sliding out of my pew, I reached the far side of the church and turned toward the altar, heading toward the sacristy.

The officer was no more than ten steps behind me, but it may as well have been miles given what I knew about His ways and His protection.

A friar left the sacristy, and I slipped in behind him unseen. The door closed with a dignified, resonant click.

"Yes? Can I help you?" I heard from the door's other side.

Inside I was alone. A chasuble and stole lay out on the sacristy credens, waiting to be put away. I moved quickly, stopping only for a moment at the piscina to make the sign of the cross. I heard the officer outside raise his voice, then I passed into a hallway and down a set of stairs. There, I found a solid exit door to the outside. To my left was another hall that would take me farther into the church's inner sanctums. I pushed through the wide release of the door and stepped out into the cold. I found myself in a narrow walkway alongside the church.

The door fell shut behind me as I made my way beyond the remainder of the church's length and then around a corner to a wide alleyway between a row of houses and the church's lot. This led me west then north to Greenwich Street.

I came out on the sidewalk. To my right I saw a wide driveway across the street. Back down the alley behind me, no one was there.

I jogged across the street and up the driveway toward a house set back from the street. Its beige backside stood against a white staircase that led up to apartments. A low gate lay opened for me, unlatched, and took me behind another house, then through a yard and to a back alley to the next street north of Greenwich, Lombard, where I was certain no one could have followed my route.

I slipped into a shop for a few moments to browse the day's newspapers, making sure my features didn't grace the covers. They didn't. Likely it was just the police who had my picture and instructions to watch for me around any church. Fair enough.

I crossed myself quickly, thanking Him for leading me from harm.

No one in the shop noticed me. High shelves protected us all.

From there, I made my way west in the direction of James Weber's apartment, where I would follow my desires.

Without Him, I still knew what to do, who my next victim would be. I knew where to find him and exactly what I would do when I did.

CHAPTER FIFTY
DONNER

We worked the phones and computers from our desks for the rest of the morning. After the meeting with Bowen, my hangover was long gone. Call it adrenaline or the honest clearheadedness that the job required, I didn't care. I took it light on the coffee and drank water to rehydrate my brain.

Then that afternoon we got a call from a beat officer in North Beach named Duncan Comrie who said he'd seen Father Michael, followed him, and then lost him in SS. Peter and Paul Church.

Peter and Paul was one of the most well-known churches in the city, a tourist staple for its location at Washington Square and appearing in the original *Dirty Harry*. In the movie, the killer, Scorpio, had his shooting there stopped by a police helicopter scouring the city for him.

As if.

Bowen had given us room, but no way were we securing a chopper. More movie magic in the name of police work.

Officer Comrie had lost the priest when he slipped into the sacristy, then somehow out a back door of the church, then down an alley and out onto the streets. It was a sighting though and, being a church, sensitive enough for Hendricks and me to follow up personally.

"What's he doing up there? What's in that neighborhood?"

Hendricks shrugged. It didn't matter, really. The priest was on the run, could be after another john in any part of the city. North Beach had Larry Flynt's Hustler Club and plenty of others. It wasn't a hub for the S&M sex trade, like the 'Loin, but it had a lot to see, even more to buy.

"So now we wait?" I asked. "Not this girl." I pushed in my keyboard, stood up, then followed it with my chair. "Let's go take a walk around the neighborhood, partner. See if we can dig up any clues."

Washington Square was full of stoners, hippies, and college kids, some resident trustafarians with facial tattoos and dreads, living on the street, exploring homelessness to drive some one-percenter parent insane.

Even in the relative cold of a San Francisco January afternoon, they were all out doing their thing.

"Not a bad place, this city?" I asked Hendricks as we strolled across the grass.

"Yeah. In the daytime." He threw something he'd been playing with onto the ground. A blossom of some sort. "What's not to like?"

We'd both seen our share of the city's horrors, enough to change the way we saw the world, and neither of us started out with a short list of reasons to give up hope.

We walked into the church through a wide entranceway under a grand stone arch. Above the door, *"Per L'Universo"* was carved in stone, meaning universal—for everyone. Welcome to all, a nice sentiment if it was true.

We split up and peeked around, looking for who knows what, and when we didn't find anything strange, we showed our badges to a priest, one Father Benedict. Even this had the potential of getting back to Bowen and raising a stir, so we played it light, making sure to stay on the priest's good side as we asked about anyone who had passed through earlier.

I was tempted to call the priest Ben but didn't. Hendricks would've walked me out and carried on the investigation himself. This man definitely didn't look like a Ben.

He and his peers were not left happy by Officer Comrie's visit. He made that much immediately clear, put us right on thin ice politically. Apparently Comrie had lacked the requisite niceties, following a potential suspect and all, so we listened extra closely to Father Benedict's earful and did our best to bring him around to the greater civic cause.

Once the priest finished up on Comrie's lack of sensitivity, we asked him about the possibility of a suspect coming through the church. I almost mentioned that he was a priest himself, this suspect, but Hendricks wisely put his hand on my arm before I did. He had a good sense about him, from time to time.

In any case, I asked about the chance of a suspect coming through the church, going out a back way, and whether they thought there might be any truth to the officer's notion that he might still be somewhere behind the walls.

Father Benedict wasn't a man to lie, being a priest and all. When he said anyone passing through must've gone out a side door instead of going farther down into the rectory and the interior, we nodded and agreed. I felt sure there were rooms down there, residences and who knew what else a church contained—I didn't think it was any pagan craziness, but I honestly had no idea—that we weren't going to see. We'd gone way deep and through St. Boniface, and I supposed that would be all I would get of a church's inner sanctums.

This was the stuff you got into political trouble for, I was learning.

The priest took us into a room he called the sacristy. It was off to the side of the main altar at the front end of the church.

"Here is where your Officer Comrie thinks this suspect went," he said.

The main article in the room was a big book open on a table. Around that were closed cabinets and a series of racks holding robes.

"*If* he was here, your suspect proceeded into this foyer." The father led us into a stairway, onto a landing between two flights. He pointed down to a fire exit door and beyond that a hallway.

"Any outsider went through that door," he said. "If someone was here, he's now gone. Of course, Officer Comrie wanted to see through the rest of the hallways and cloisters, inside the rectory even. But that's not possible." He smiled like a sly civil servant, one not entirely unwise to the ways of the outside world. "At least without a warrant."

It was more than lucky that Father Kevin at St. Boniface hadn't been as stubborn or sly, though a judge denying us a warrant to enter a church would've kept some downtown brass happy—while totally sabotaging our case.

"Right you are," I said to the father. "I'm sure we don't need to see any farther. As long as you say you're not harboring a known fugitive." I put extra emphasis on this last line, almost wanted to add a wink in there too, but I didn't. If the church was really screwed up enough to protect a murderer from the police—even one of their brothers—then the world was in even worse shape than I had imagined, child-molestation cases notwithstanding.

In truth, there was something I appreciated about this "no"-first way of handling our presence in the church. I'd be happier to know where I couldn't go than to blindly just go there, tip over an apple cart of political bull like I had at St. Boniface, and get beat up for it later.

But maybe that was just me.

"Maybe we should take that door, see where it leads," Hendricks said. I took it as a good sign: both for us to leave the church without breaking any more eggshells and as a viable next direction to follow our case.

CHAPTER
FIFTY-ONE

That was how we found ourselves in the alley behind the church, looking out onto Greenwich Street and a neighborhood of houses.

"Maybe he's holed up, found a hiding place around here," I said. "Want to call in and check for any crime reports today from this area?"

Hendricks followed my advice for once, making the call into Central Station, which covered all of Chinatown and points north to the Bay, including North Beach. "Anything strange on the books today?" Hendricks asked the dispatch.

I didn't want to hear that someone had found a body, but something else to go on would've been helpful.

Then Hendricks was nodding, and I felt a spark. He took out his pad and pen. Crunching his phone between shoulder and ear, he wrote down an address. "Yeah," he said. "Yeah. Sounds useful. Thanks."

He scribbled as best he could. This was a problem with the newer, sleeker cell phones: you couldn't squeeze them beside your ear like old wall phones or our desk models down at the station—yes, we still have those.

When he hung up, he looked puzzled, tapped the address on his notebook with the pen. "It's not much to go on, but this is what we got."

He showed me an address on Montgomery Street at the corner of Alta, right by Coit Tower. We couldn't see the tower from where we were, but I knew it wasn't far.

"Looks like a break-in. The owner reported it but says nothing was taken. Just a broken doorframe and a wedding photo taken from one of his shelves."

"A photo?" I said. "That sounds like our man."

He raised an eyebrow. "Like I said, it isn't much."

"More than enough for me," I said. "Let's check it out."

CHAPTER FIFTY-TWO

MICHAEL

Weber's apartment was on the northern end of Montgomery, just below Pioneer Park and Coit Tower. I saw the Transamerica Pyramid from his corner, and on the backside of his building, I saw the same set of fire escapes that so many old buildings in San Francisco had. Why no one realized these created a major danger from intruders was laughable. Another of God's favors.

The back of the building had no windows, like a spare concrete block with metal doors at each landing.

I jumped up from street level to the lowest rung of the fire escape, confident that no one watched me, and pulled myself up to the first ladder from there. I climbed it to the metal landing for the first floor, then the next ladder and the next to get closest to Weber's apartment on the third floor.

Knocking lightly at the third-floor door brought back the ring of hollow metal, a door not heavy but well locked. I pulled on the knob a few times, turned it, tried my best to see if it would break, and it wouldn't.

So I climbed the final ladder to the roof. No one saw me come over the wall onto the rough gravel. Then there, in the middle of the building, was exactly what I had hoped: a wide skylight over the main stairs. Familiar wire-mesh safety glass. I tried to lift it, knowing already I'd find it open.

In God's name.

The cover came right up on its hinges, and I slid underneath, to the ladder down to the hall. Someone had been more interested in getting up to the roof than wary of making sure the skylight stayed locked. So be it. In this manner, I got inside.

In the third-floor hallway, I saw one apartment at either end. The north one was his: apartment six. I walked calmly to that end and knocked. Then again. Too easy, almost, I forced the door with my shoulder and broke the lock. A skill learned in a former life, one that seemed necessary at one time. Now a trick I used rarely.

I entered slowly, certain I'd hear beeps, the warning of an alarm, but did not. My first view was bright wood floors and light.

I noticed none of the familiar features of the other apartments I'd visited on my path: no dirty corners, dingy walls, no straps or clamps or dusty bed. No, this was something from a magazine. Beautiful, detailed, decorated. This apartment had a good woman's touch.

I walked around noticing rugs, framed artwork, even paintings. On the living room mantle, I saw their pictures: a man and a woman, very much married, posing in a series of pictures. At the center of the row was their wedding: she wore the traditional white dress, beautiful. He had a tuxedo. Black tie.

But it wasn't only the two of them in the photos I saw. There were a young boy and a girl. Two sets of baby pictures stood on the mantle with the rest. Pictures of the children with them.

I turned around, checked the floors again, noticed the toys—not a lot of them, but definitely the playthings of a child. Books for school. Homework.

This john who had touched Emily, who was a partner in the events that left her beaten on the streets, was a parent. The father of a boy and a girl.

God's word came then, rushed back to me, said my work here was done. This man was not the one responsible for Emily's sins.

Just like that and of a sudden, I heard Him again.

Then I felt the apartment closing in on me, its air constricting my neck. I checked the room for signs of my presence, anything other than the broken door, and nothing showed that I had entered their home, nothing but the still echoes of my feet.

I went to the mantle and took one picture. To leave James Weber a single sign. I wouldn't keep it, didn't want it, but someone would put together the pieces, tell James Weber that I had been there.

My message would get through.

CHAPTER FIFTY-THREE
DONNER

We got to the apartment on Montgomery as fast as we could find a semilegitimate place to park our car. Police don't have to worry about the street signs, but half of San Francisco sidewalks are driveways—ones you never know when people will need in or out of. It's not good PR to block people in or out. We want to avoid impeding the flow of traffic too, so we do our best to find a fire hydrant or some other semireasonable spot. On these tight streets in North Beach, that wasn't easy. But it wasn't as hard as finding civilian parking either.

We buzzed our way in the front door of a three-story unit with six apartments, one of many in the area. When we got up to the third floor, a man with a beard and curly pulled-back hair greeted us. He wore green khakis and a striped shirt tucked in with a tan leather belt.

"Jimmy Weber," he said, extending his hand.

I shook it and explained who we were, asked him if he wouldn't mind answering a few questions.

"The other officers were here already," he said. "I really just called this in to file a police report for insurance. Like I told them, nothing was taken."

"Don't you think that's odd?"

He twisted his face like I'd surprised him.

I kept on. "We know you already gave a statement, but we think it's possible this break-in might have a connection to another case we're working."

"I don't understand. You said you're homicide. Can somebody breaking in our door have to do with a murder? Is my family safe?"

I came up the last stairs. "Do you mind if we come in? We'd just like to ask you a few questions. This will only take a few minutes."

He stepped aside, showing us the open door, now hanging limp on its hinges. "There's the door. You see it?"

I gestured farther into the hall. "May we?"

"How does this connect to a murder? How could it? Do you think my children aren't safe?"

"Do you?" I asked. "Because I would hate for you to have that weighing on you. Believe me, we want to keep everyone in this community as safe as possible."

He sighed. "Okay. But I'm trying to feed my kids their after-school snack, so let's make it quick."

Inside his door, the hallway led us to white walls and bright spaces. Off to the left, a living room opened to reveal a large fireplace and painted mantle lined with photos in ornate frames. I saw pictures of Mr. and Mrs. Weber from their wedding, several pictures of their two kids, and a few family shots all together. In the middle of the row was an open space like a missing tooth.

"That's where the picture was that went missing?" I asked. "What was it of?"

"Daddy? Who's here?"

I turned and saw two small faces peeking out of a kitchen up the hall: a boy and a girl, somewhere in the vicinity of eight or ten.

"Go back to your homework, guys. Please?" He waved them away, and they went. His voice wasn't hard or harsh. He struck me as possibly a good dad.

"Is your wife home?"

"No. She'll be back later. I got home at three thirty with them, and that's when I found the door was broken."

Hendricks was fingering the splintered wood. "And nothing wrong with the outside door downstairs. That seem strange? You don't think one of your neighbors would—" He gestured at the frame. "Do you?"

Weber waved it off. "No. Nobody suspicious living here. We're all *good enough* friends."

Hendricks stepped back into the hall, pointed up at a skylight above the stairs. "Could be that," he said.

I walked out into the hallway, looked up to what he saw. There was an iron-mesh glass hatch that was shut but could've been opened from the roof.

"Looks like the latch isn't locked. You see?"

Weber checked it out. "Yeah, the other officers said the same thing. I'm going to latch it up as soon as we're done with dinner."

"Why don't you let me do that for you?" Hendricks said. "I'll check it out at the same time. See if I notice any signs of entry." He headed for the black metal ladder bolted into the wall.

I went inside, guiding Weber by his elbow. "He's good with these things. Don't worry about him."

In the living room, I went back to the mantle and ran a finger along it. No dust. "You have your place cleaned often?"

He talked about his cleaning lady, how weekly visits had become a necessity since having kids, while I checked out the rest of the room: more shelves, straight-backed chairs with arms and fine upholstery, a mahogany coffee table. These were the type of people who didn't have a TV in their living room, probably sent their kids to a special private school to learn problem-solving skills. I didn't see any connection to the rest of the johns, but enough time on the force had taught me never to judge a situation by its appearance.

Beyond the surface, that's where the truth lies. I started to scratch the veneer.

"Tell me about the missing picture."

"It was one of my wife. The only one we have of just her from the wedding. A gift from her father, actually."

"His little girl."

"And don't I forget it." He laughed like he knew the joke was on him.

I heard his kids call him from the kitchen.

"Do you mind?" he asked, heading for the hall. "I need to keep an eye on them."

He left with that, and I lingered for a moment. In the hallway, I could see Hendricks's legs, still on the ladder.

"I've just got a few more questions," I said, coming into the kitchen.

The son had a book open on the table, the daughter eating pasta while thumbing messages into her phone. Weber took the phone away and told his kids to sit up straight. "No texting before dinner, Frances." He smiled at me, an awkward grin.

A small television set on a shelf showed *Friends*, volume low. His daughter dutifully pulled out a thick math textbook and found her page. I almost wanted to leave him alone, let the family find its own harmony, but I had one more thing to do.

"May I?" I came around the counter to stand next to Weber, angled away from the kids so I could show him the pictures. They thought I was about as interesting as the paint on the walls.

"Have you ever seen this man?" I showed him a four-by-six of Father Michael I'd had the Hall's photo/ID section print up. "Does he look familiar?"

Weber shook his head. "Should he?"

"No. Not necessarily." I would have hoped for a smoother transition into my next set of images, but there wasn't much I could do. If we were down at the station, I'd have prepared sheets for the occasion with unknowns thrown in, but here it was straight to the meat.

I showed him a picture of Dub. In all his glory. "How about this man?"

Weber squeezed his forehead at the gold teeth and ratty dreadlocks, shook his head. "Definitely not."

"Her?" Going to Debbie Shine next was my way of easing him in, such as it was.

"I don't know where this is going, Officer."

"And how about her?" I showed him the picture of Emily I'd had Photo/ID print up: not a photocopy of the picture from the priest's room and Jay Piper's, but an intake picture of her taken at SFGH.

"You ever seen this face? Her first name is Emily. Sometimes people call her Silver."

Something changed in his face. I thought, *Bingo*.

"No. And I have no idea where you're going with this. Excuse me." Weber brushed past me to get to the stove, where a steaming colander of spiral noodles sat inside a pot. He picked up a wide ceramic bowl off the counter.

Hendricks appeared in the open doorway to the hall. "I latched that skylight for you. It's locked tight now." He brushed off his hands. "And I can't say it looks like it had been broken into." He turned his attention to the kids, who'd suddenly woken up at his entrance. Hendricks had a way with kids—kids and dogs. "You two don't ever go up that ladder to the roof, do you?"

He gave them a serious regard, and they both denied ever going up there.

I wanted to get back to Weber, more on the picture, and gave Hendricks our special nod, meaning there was more work to be done. He got my message, asked Weber to come with him into the living room for a moment.

"Then we'll be going right on our way," he said. "Right, partner?"

"Yeah, we've wasted enough of your family's time."

Weber put down the empty bowl. "Best news I've heard all day."

CHAPTER FIFTY-FOUR

I followed Hendricks and Weber into the hallway and to the living room. Hendricks said, "You really should check that thing more often. And not leave it unlocked."

Weber stood just inside the entrance. He shifted his weight. "We *never* leave that unlocked. I'm sure of it."

"Okay. Well, that's good to hear, then. I wouldn't."

"I hear you, Officer. Thanks for that."

"Investigator," I said, coming up behind them. "Or Sergeant, actually."

Weber spun like I'd surprised him. "Excuse me?"

"We're with homicide, like I said, so my rank is sergeant. Not officer."

"Okay, sorry." Weber tried giving Hendricks a look, something like *women*, but Hendricks stone-faced him.

"Let me try this again," I said. "I'm going to show you a picture of a girl." I wagged my finger at him. "I know you know her. And you're going to tell me how. Is that clear?"

"This sounds like maybe I should call my lawyer."

"Lawyering up now?" Hendricks hooted. "That is *definitely* not a good play." He settled a heavy hand onto Weber's shoulder. "Since you've done nothing wrong here. Right?"

"What are you implying, *Investigators?*"

I shook my head. "Let's all stay calm. We're just talking, us three, no lawyers involved, nobody goes down to the Hall." I watched his reaction, and his fight-or-flight instinct did not kick in. That was best.

"We keep this simple. Believe me, as a matter of consideration for your own safety and your family's, this is the best route. You haven't committed a crime." I gave him my hard, steady stare. "So you want to be completely honest with us right now."

"What my partner hasn't told you," Hendricks said, "is that a very bad man is out there and might have come into your house. If you can help us put him on the business side of a jail cell, that will keep you and your whole family a whole lot safer. But we need real help."

All of this landed with significant weight on Jimmy Weber's shoulders. He sat down on one of the high-backed chairs.

"Maybe I should offer you a drink," he said. Then he saw our all-business reactions and added, "Or make one for myself."

"Let's make this painless. We talk, then we get out of your hair." I pulled another one of his chairs up close and sat.

"This girl," I said, showing him the picture of Emily. "Where have you seen her?"

He wiped a hand over his face like the memory wasn't pleasant. "Listen," he said. "It wasn't my idea. None of it was."

CHAPTER
FIFTY-FIVE

The kids were still in the kitchen as the closing theme from *Friends* played on the TV. James Weber sat in a high-backed chair beside a cold fireplace. Above it, the single picture was missing from the mantle—a picture of his wife.

"This isn't about Diana," he said, almost pleading. "Please just tell me this isn't about Diana. I want her to be okay."

"Your wife is fine, Mr. Weber," Hendricks said. "As far as we know, she's at work. You can call her as soon as we're done."

I touched the man's knee. "Nothing would lead us to believe that she's in any danger. Please just focus on what I'm asking."

"Right," he said. "Right."

He looked at two pictures of Emily. In the newer one, her hair was cut short, her cheeks drawn in like they were hollow, her skin pocked. In the other, she looked younger, healthier by a few years. In reality it was barely ten months in between.

Life on the streets: the disease eating her alive.

"When I saw her, she looked more like this." He touched the earlier picture, the one our priest had taken from Jay Piper's, the one we found tucked into his Bible. "But a little like this too." He tapped the other. "She was heading in this direction."

He checked my face. "These are the same girl, right?"

I nodded.

"Her father—I can't imagine." That stopped him. His boy and girl were right in the next room.

I said, "Your daughter's going to be fine, Mr. Weber."

"Okay," he said. "Right." He nodded like he had just considered some bad options and come back to the present. "I want to help you. This isn't easy."

"Just tell us what happened."

"Okay. This guy. I don't even know him that well. He's a friend of a friend."

Hendricks and I exchanged a quick glance. We'd need their names, eventually.

"We got together a few times to party. Play some poker. We did some drugs. You know, nothing big, right?"

He waited for some confirmation, so I nodded. We were *not* here to bust him for using drugs.

"This one time he brought in a girl. Youngish, you know, but definitely legal." He looked back and forth between our faces. "I mean. Well, you know. So far as age is concerned. She took her clothes off."

Hendricks patted his back, man-to-man. "It's all right. Just tell us what you know. Nothing is going to happen. We're looking for information."

"I was on the side. Not my deal, right? But then it happens a few times, let's say. Couple of poker nights. I mean, shit. Diana and I were in therapy. She was telling me I had to get out more and find other ways to socialize. Make friends. That's all it was. What was I supposed to do?

"This girl." He tapped the picture again. "Sometimes it was her. They'd take her in the other room, this guy and one other. Sometimes I heard—"

He stopped, then leaned his head from shoulder to shoulder, equivocating, unable to get it out.

"They hurt her," I said.

He nodded. "I could hear screams. But then I'd see her after, and she didn't seem upset about it. I just figured—I thought it wasn't any of my business. But I didn't do anything to stop it either. That's something I still think about. I mean, she has a father somewhere. I know that."

He rolled that around in his mind while we waited.

"I stopped going." He stared at the rug, deep into the memory. "Just like that. I needed to find something else. Started going to the gym instead. Picked up spinning." He shrugged. "Who cares, right? Just something to get out of the house."

I knew exactly what he meant. *Exactly.*

"But I knew." He tapped the newer picture of Emily, the one with her hollow cheeks. "I know what they did. Dan told me."

Hendricks had written down the name. "You knew what?"

He nodded, touched the picture. "I had no idea they would get like that. Or how it happened. Dan just said it did." He swore, closed his eyes. "That's all I can tell you. I'm sure it was a lot of blood. I swear I wasn't there."

I said, "We're going to need their names. Dan and the others."

"Dan Steele," he said. "He was the one I knew from before. We worked together in Boston, before any of us came out here. The others I was just introduced to."

"Their names," I said. "Then we leave, and you can go back to your kids."

"Dave something. I didn't know him that well. Heyes, maybe. He was a friend of Eric's. That was another guy, Meaders. That's what everybody called him. Maybe once I heard him called Eric. But everyone always called him Meaders. He was the one who brought her. Him. Mainly it was those two guys, Meaders and Heyes. They were the ones."

I exchanged a meaningful look with my partner. This was pay dirt, these names. Weber was giving it all.

He looked at the picture of Emily again and his lips curled like he had something sour in his mouth, something he needed to spit out. "Maybe I need that drink."

Hendricks and I got up, and Hendricks patted Weber on the back. "That was good what you just did here. It'll help us a lot. It'll help us help these guys."

I was guessing Weber hadn't heard about the others' passing. This wasn't a tight-knit group, I supposed, and that was best. He had moved on, made the smart choice, but our priest wasn't going to let him forget. Not unless we could find him first.

Weber would need protection: an officer or two at his apartment and maybe someone to watch over his wife until she got home.

"Listen. How would you feel about going out of town for a few days? You have any family that's close?"

He scrunched up his face. "No way. I've got too much going on here. At work. The kids have school."

"What if I told you that David Heyes is now dead?"

"What?" He stopped still, holding a glass tumbler in one hand and a bottle in the other. Then he put the bottle back down. "He's *dead*?"

Hendricks said, "Earlier this week. We've got a spree of murders on our hands. And I think you'd better be real careful."

"I can put officers on you full-time, if you need to stay in town," I said. "But obviously . . . things would be much simpler if you could go away for a few days."

CHAPTER FIFTY-SIX

MICHAEL

At Dan Steele's modern house on South Van Ness, I pounded the door. Only just after five o'clock, and I knew he'd be home.

"Yeah?" he said in the hallway, already opening the door. His confidence kept him from worry. To his mind, he controlled this space and his life. I knocked it right out of him with a fast jab to the nose.

He stepped inside fast, backing away with hands to his nose, and I followed him inside, shut the door.

Leaning into his left side, he dropped down to some kind of fighting stance with his knees bent. All over the city, they practiced a form of fighting now as fitness. They thought they did, anyway. Kicking a pad, punching a bag. I stepped inside and slashed across his forearms with my blade, ripping through cloth and skin. At the sight of his own blood, he went white, clueless, defeated. He held his hands up.

"No. Please."

I hit him again in the nose. He cried out and covered it with his hands.

"Is that what the girl said before you cut her? Tried to remove her tongue?"

He fell to his knees, maybe finding religion, which would be a first. I kicked him in the stomach, and he fell back, working to catch his breath.

"Anything," he said. "Whatever you want."

Then I stood over him, looking down.

"How did you know that? About the girl?"

"The pimp and God. And now the pimp is dead."

"Did you—?"

"This is about you. Get on your feet."

Then I heard a woman's voice from farther inside the house. "Dan?" she said.

I froze. This wasn't what I'd planned. I put my finger to my lips for him to keep quiet.

"Dan?" she said again. I heard her moving upstairs.

His hallway floors were bright hardwood and led into a kitchen where white cabinets surrounded a wide white-topped island. All new appliances. Bright hardwood stairs led up along an exposed brick wall to the second level.

"Tell her not to come down."

He called to her to stay upstairs.

"Who is she?"

"My wife, Julia. Please don't hurt her. I'll give you anything."

I shook my head. The second sinner married. A day of surprises.

He posed as a person who fit in, was right with the world. He needed to be exposed.

"Call her down."

"What?" He slowly realized what I meant, how this might play out.

"Call her."

"No. Do what you want to. Hurt *me*."

"Julia!"

More movement upstairs. "Who is that?"

"Come down, dear," I told her, and she appeared at the top of the stairs wearing a white shirt, high-waist pants. Long brown hair to her shoulders.

"Who are you?" Then a scream. "Oh my God, Dan! What happened? I'm calling the police." She disappeared. I heard a door slam.

I kicked him in the side. "Get up." He scrambled, and I kicked him toward the stairs. Crawling on hands and feet, he hurried up the flight with me behind him. Calling the police in San Francisco was not a speedy proposition.

I took my time.

We reached the top of the stairs, and Steele fell forward onto the carpet. I said, "Wait here."

I curled around the banister, back toward the front of the house, and kicked open the door to her bedroom. She sat on the bed, iPhone to her ear, held up a fireplace poker with her right hand.

"No. No." I closed on her and pulled it away. "Put down the phone." She didn't. "This isn't about you. Put down the phone and come with me. I won't hurt you."

"Hello, police?" she said.

"Give me the phone," I said louder, holding out my hand.

"Police? Hello?"

I grabbed her arm, pulled the phone away from her.

Steele said from the door, "Just give it to him, honey. We don't want him to hurt us. I'll give him money. Whatever he wants." He dabbed his nose with a white towel now, collecting blood.

I listened on the phone, as a hold message repeated, then hung up.

"This man," I said, pointing at Steele with the poker, "has hurt women. Girls. Do you know what he does?"

His wife sat down hard on the bed.

"A girl," I said. "I know her. Emily is her name. He and his friends hurt her. They beat her. Cut her tongue."

She turned to him, confused, but I could see the questions in her eyes. She knew there were things she didn't know.

A phone in the bedroom started to ring.

"Dan?"

"It was before our talk," he said.

I said, "It was last week."

The phone rang again.

The look of pain on her. Her eyes closed. "Dan. Oh God, Dan. What is this about?"

The phone rang.

"I am here for God," I said. "This is all about Him."

CHAPTER FIFTY-SEVEN

DONNER

Five minutes later, we were in the car, patching into DMV records to find out what we could about Eric Meaders and Dan Steele. The sky was dark already, and I couldn't believe how fast the day had passed.

We could put a watch on Weber's apartment, at least until he decided to get out of town. I wondered what had saved him, them. Maybe seeing the wedding pictures on the mantle was enough to ease the priest away. Maybe pictures of the kids. If the names had come from Dub, then Emily couldn't have told him who did what to her, specifically. Maybe James Weber and his kids just got lucky. It wasn't a good feeling to process.

"What do you think, partner? What's our play?"

Hendricks was writing down Steele's particulars into his pad. He could've emailed them to his cell phone, but that wasn't his style.

"You mean with Weber?"

I nodded. "How you want to keep him safe in case the priest comes back?"

"We put men on the house. Use Bowen's blessing to call in extra troops. Tighten the web. Then we worry about the other two."

I said, "We catch this son of a bitch. Do it now. Fast."

Hendricks nodded like that was a novel solution, something I had just thought of. I suppose I deserved that or worse. He got on the phone with dispatch to start the work of getting a unit sent to watch the Webers' apartment. Next we could work on the others: Steele and Meaders. I pulled the laptop around to see the screen, saw all Daniel Steele's information, and called the first number on the list.

The phone rang and rang, then voicemail came on and said that Dan and Julia weren't home. Dan and Julia Steele, the perfect couple, I imagined. Except sometimes Dan went out to play poker and beat on a hooker or two. Nothing so much wrong with that.

Right?

The beep came, and I gave my name, told them to call me, that it was urgent.

No. There was plenty wrong with that. And what would his wife do if she found out?

Next I tried Steele's cell. Still no luck. His voicemail picked up right away this time and said he'd get right back to me after the beep. I left my info. Told him it was of the utmost importance.

Hendricks was off the phone with dispatch. He started punching Eric Meaders's name into the computer.

"Steeles aren't home," I told Hendricks. "I'll call a unit to go check their house."

"Try Meaders. I'll call for the unit to the Steeles'." He pushed the screen back toward me, showing all Eric Meaders's information. This time, I tried the cell first. Meaders's address was in Bernal Heights, along a quaint row of townhouses on a series of twisty roads.

He picked up on the first ring. "Meaders."

"This is Investigator Clara Donner with SFPD homicide. I need to meet with you."

"Oh, *homicide*," he said through the phone. I could hear a touch of excitement in his voice. "To what do I owe the honor?"

"My partner and I would like to talk with you about a case we're pursuing. It's important that we meet with you as soon as possible. We can come to you."

I heard him muffle the phone receiver with his hand, then he said something on his end. There was music in the background, something with a lot of bass. "I'm downtown. Can you come to the Thirsty Bear?"

"Ten minutes good?"

"You bet. See you there. Oh, and, Investigator?"

"Yes?"

"I'm looking forward to meeting one of San Francisco's few women in homicide. This will be a real honor."

"Yes, I—" But I didn't say anything else. I just hung up.

Hendricks said, "Unit's on their way to Dan Steele's place."

"Good. Meaders wants to meet us at the Thirsty Bear. He's also a little weird."

He laughed. "Happy hour, Donner. You probably caught him at the Gold Club."

It was one of the most popular strip clubs downtown, also right across from the Thirsty Bear. "Too bad we aren't meeting him there."

"Yeah. I hear they have a good buffet." Hendricks winked as he started the car.

CHAPTER FIFTY-EIGHT

As soon as we came into the Thirsty Bear, we saw Meaders standing at the bar, away from the crowd. If I hadn't just seen his driver's license photo on our laptop, I'd still have known him; he was the one who looked like he was waiting to meet with the police. He smiled like a real fanboy, one of those types who think police work is so damn cool. If only I could find a hot guy with this attitude about dating a cop.

My thoughts flashed to Alan, that I still hadn't called him back. Over twenty-four hours had gone by now. Maybe I'd gone beyond playing hard to get. Didn't matter. There wasn't time to think about it now.

Eric Meaders stepped toward us—no drink in hand, jacket still on. He was a white guy who looked like a polished tech type: bald head, cotton polo shirt, khakis.

He'd made us as cops the moment we came in. What else could we be? No one could mistake us for a date, even friends. But here we were, and Meaders was big into it.

"I'm glad to see you two, Investigators." He looked at each of us. "Is it Sergeant, or Inspector?"

It was enough to raise an eyebrow, at least. Hendricks gave me a wary look. The force had changed its designations for homicide cops to investigators with the rank of sergeant in 2009. Prior to that, homicide investigators ranked as inspectors, the only designation of its kind in the US. Now we were back "in the main": sergeants by rank, investigators by profession.

I was a sergeant, being that I'd come in after the switch. Hendricks was an inspector. Meaders seemed to know more than he should as a civilian, so I ignored the question.

"You like investigations?" I asked. "Sleuthing?"

He nodded. "Big reader. Love those Women's Murder Club books." A wink. "Bet you're something like Inspector Lindsay Boxer. Yeah?"

Patterson's books were known around the station as good paperweights and doorstops, if not much else. He had famously gotten the code for murder wrong in his first book of the series, and I had never forgiven him. Truth was, women made up a far bigger part of homicide in San Francisco than either TV or books made it out. A woman had actually led up homicide, served as lieutenant, for twenty years.

I didn't want to turn Meaders against us, but he was testing my nerves, setting off alarm bells like crazy. This was the guy who'd put a beating on Emily and started this whole chain of events. I was sure of it.

I said, "Do you want to interview us, or should we interview you?"

Meaders pursed his lips, pulled back a little.

Hendricks touched my forearm. "Easy, partner." He motioned to a table that was just clearing: two stools and a tall table of light-brown wood. "Talk here?"

We walked over. Meaders and Hendricks took the two chairs, and I stood. Hendricks started with the break-in at Weber's and asked Meaders if he knew him. He asked about Dan Steele just the same.

"We're not here to bust you for anything," he said, "but we're concerned there's a man who wants to do you harm for what you might've seen, what you might've been around."

I would have said he shouldn't have beaten on girls, that a renegade priest vigilante wanted to pay him back for it in kind, and that we might be willing to help. Or not.

That was why Hendricks did our talking.

I watched and listened, fingering the pictures of Emily in my pocket. I wanted to show them to Meaders, put the hard questions to him and see what he knew, but this wasn't the time or the place. So I listened as Hendricks built it up, asking him about his associations with Steele, Weber, and the others. He asked about the poker nights and what might've gone on there, and then, finally, he asked him about the girls.

"Have you ever brought prostitutes into any of these evenings? Maybe done one or two of them some harm?"

Meaders stepped away from us, looked taken aback. "What?"

"Listen." Hendricks tapped his wrist. "We're not here to do anything about it. From what I understand, this is basically legal at this point in our city. If not, that's someone else's concern. But—" And here he got very serious, waited for Meaders to meet his eyes. "We know someone is out there killing people who've done things to a girl named Emily. Silver, she's sometimes called. We're looking to track this killer. We have reason to believe he might be targeting you."

Meaders's eyebrows came together, and he bit his lower lip. "You're saying—"

Here's where I couldn't take it any longer. I slapped Emily's picture down on the table. "See this girl? You know her. We're not here to get you for what you did to her, but believe me I'd like to." I grabbed Meaders's wrist. "You're in danger. There's a guy coming after you and your friends, and we need to know everything about what you did and with whom.

"You want to get out of town? Fine. You want to run for your freaking life? Fine. Be my guest. But you tell us everything you know right now, got it?"

He stammered. Hendricks had badged the waitress earlier and asked her to bring us three waters, and now she finally delivered them. Meaders reached for his glass. I watched his Adam's apple bob as he drank.

"Tell me what you know about this girl. Now."

"She's a girl. One of. I seen her."

Now his confidence and inquisitiveness about homicide fell away—fast. He looked to Hendricks then back to me, and asked, "Who is he? This guy?"

Hendricks shook his head. "You don't want to know. Honestly. The things he's done to a few guys, Piper, Farrow, Heyes. You know them?" He tapped the table. "Never mind. You do or you don't. They're *nothing* you want to see now. Trust me."

I waited a beat before pouring it on. "Made plenty of good cops lose their lunch. The pictures we could show you. Man." I let it trail off.

"Something happened to them?" Meaders asked. "Why didn't I see it in the news?"

"I look like a reporter to you?"

Hendricks leveled his eyes at Meaders. "You beat her last, beat her bad. She lost a part of her tongue."

"I—No." He turned away for a moment, and I knew he was going to come back asking for a lawyer.

"You don't need a lawyer, Eric. You need us. You need protection."

He swore. Then nodded. "Yeah. Things got out of hand. We did more to her than I expected. Things they just, you know. I get excited sometimes. We'd been drinking, did a few lines."

Hendricks had been right about the Gold Club, and I knew it then. This guy was way worse than your average john or guy with a porn addiction. He was full-time, all kinds of obsessed, had a darkness inside him. He had no ring on his left hand, and that wouldn't change. It was going to be like this with him for a long time. Forever, maybe.

I wanted the priest to have him.

I wanted not to want that.

I sucked my teeth, trying to avoid saying what I felt. If we could catch the priest and stop this guy from getting hurt in the process, then fine. If we managed to catch him and there was some collateral damage—say Meaders got hurt? Well, I wasn't going to lose any sleep over it.

"Bait," I said, cutting them both off. I didn't even know what they'd been saying. Probably something about Emily we already knew, like how he didn't mean to hurt her, or sever her tongue, or that he just happened to punch her in the jaw when she had it out and . . . something I didn't need to hear.

"What?"

"We want to use you as bait. Set a trap for our guy. What do you say?"

I didn't listen to his answer. In truth, I didn't care what he wanted anymore.

CHAPTER FIFTY-NINE
MICHAEL

Julia Steele asked, "What did he do?"

"Do you want to tell her?" I caught Steele by his elbow, kept him in the room. "Tell her."

"This guy's crazy," he said. "Look at him. Are you going to trust some maniac who breaks into our house or me?"

She eyed me again, still afraid, but she didn't trust him, had her questions.

"Tell her." I brought my knife to his chest, pushed his loosened tie to the side, cut into his shirt. "Think carefully about the next thing you say."

"No!" she cried, but that was all she said. She dropped onto the bed.

"I'm here from God. To punish you. Because of *her*"—I pointed at his wife—"you will live. But I'll leave it to you two to sort out how." I pushed him out of the room, into the hall.

I had his wife's cell phone in my pocket, but I didn't care anymore if she called the police. If He wanted them to stop me, then His will would be done. I shoved Dan Steele into the bathroom.

"I can cut your shirt off, or you can take it off," I said. "Either way you're going to get cut."

He screamed, and I punched him in the face again. At that he sat down on the toilet lid. He called his wife's name.

"She won't want to see this."

"Those guys. We don't talk anymore. Not since that night." He shook his head, blood and tears dripping from his nose. "It was—I won't see them again."

"Tell me how it happened. Who caused it?"

He squeezed his face with a hand. "I still can't believe it. Wasn't my idea, that's for sure."

"But you took part. You helped them do this."

"Not me. Eric. It was Eric."

I slapped his face with the back of my hand. "To allow is to do." I punched him again; his head snapped back and then lolled forward. *"Bystander. Sinner."*

"But she was—"

"On meth. An addict. Druggie. What else did you want to say?"

"A whore. That and a whore. She *liked* it."

I slapped his face. Seethed, wondering why I had let him speak. "She is God's child under heaven. Was and is, then and now. You *don't* do that."

I grabbed his face with my left hand, squeezed his jaw open, and brought the knife in close. He squirmed, but I held tight.

"Please don't," the wife said behind me. She leaned in through the door, meeting my eyes in the mirror.

"You would save this man?" I asked her. "Do you know what he's done?"

"I don't care. He's a good man. I believe that. He's my husband." She touched her stomach. "Please."

I hadn't hurt her and wouldn't. In my hands, he whined his plea.

I wanted God to speak then, to say how I should mete out the pain that He desired. Again I was alone in my volition.

"Flesh," I said. I pushed his head back, let go of his face. "I want an inch of your flesh. You can choose where it comes from."

"You're crazy."

"Choose, or in a minute, I will choose."

The husband and wife exchanged a look. They knew I was telling the truth.

CHAPTER SIXTY
DONNER

"Don't worry, Meaders. You'll be safe." I said it with a straight face, had gotten used to acting the part. Hendricks stared at me hard, maybe not liking the plan, that we hadn't discussed it first, or that I was saying this without his approval. I didn't care.

"Our man is in contact. We can tell him where you are. *I'll* tell him. Then we watch you, keep you safe, catch him when he comes." I touched his hand with the least malice I could manage. "Don't worry about it."

His eyes, his face showed he believed every word.

Hendricks was another matter. "Yeah, Donner. He'll listen to you *because?*" Then he stood up, told Meaders we'd be just a minute.

Hendricks led me toward the back of the pub. When we were out of Meaders's earshot, he leaned down and spoke. "Are you crazy? What are you thinking about right now? What's the plan?"

"Just that," I said, showing him my hands. "Nothing up my sleeve. Based on the email, Father Michael thinks I'm some kind of parallel religious beacon who hears from God, and maybe we work that to our advantage. We put Meaders out like a goat on a leash and wait for him to come."

"A goat on a leash? How'd that work out for the goat?"

"When? In *Jurassic Park*?"

I thought of the bloody chain the T. rex left behind.

"This isn't a T. rex, Daniel. And otherwise, what are our choices? We keep chasing him? Wait and hope our thin manpower can be in the right place at the right time? No. We lost our shot at surprise with St. Boniface."

Hendricks stared hard. If thoughts were gears, I'd have heard them turning. I didn't want to give him a chance to argue, to put words to the problems with my plan. I just wanted him to come along.

That's when I slapped him.

I'd never slapped a man before, certainly not my partner or another good cop, never outside a bedroom, anyway, and I wasn't sure who was more surprised: him or me. We both froze.

Then I checked Meaders. He hadn't seen.

"We do this," I said. "That's it. Come back to the table, we convince goat boy, and then we go ahead. We'll be with him the whole time."

"What was *that*?"

"What?"

"You kidding?"

I offered to shake Hendricks's hand, held mine out in an offer of truce or friendship. I wanted to make a deal.

Hendricks smiled. He didn't accept my hand. Instead, he reached up and gently laid his palm against my cheek, not a caress and definitely not a slap. Just a touch. Then a second later, a light slap. I deserved worse, I knew.

"So we do this?"

"Yeah," he said, "we can try it. But Donner, we got to get you some rest."

Inside ten minutes, we had Meaders in our car and confused to the point where he was ready to go along with what we suggested. Hendricks kept on talking, while I checked my phone and thought about how I'd reply to what Father Michael had said. Sure, answer a nut with another nut. Fast and sweet, that was what we needed.

"Who lives with you?"

Meaders shook his wrist, loosing a gold Rolex down onto his hand. "I live alone," he said. "A condo on—"

"Elsie Street," I finished. "Come on, we're the police, Eric. Don't think we don't already know."

Hendricks said, "How's the rest of your Thursday night looking? I hope you didn't already have plans."

Meaders shook his head. His eyes were full Bambi.

"Where do we go? You're not thinking we let him come to my place, right?"

In the car, Hendricks explained the bulk of our problem: too little funding in the department, our balls being cut off by budgetary constrictions and bad management, and, specifically, not enough manpower, too many possible targets on this case for us to effectively watch where our guy would strike next. We needed to narrow the odds, and that's where Meaders came in. Hendricks was on board, driving us to Bernal Heights, talking Meaders blind.

I sat in the back, still figuring out the last parts of my email. So far, it went like this:

Dear Father,

Forgive me for I have sinned. I took the girl
away from your protection and now she is at
the mercy of the state. We both know she
was better off before. This will be rectified
soon.

First, I know there is a small number whom
you still pursue. I want to help you achieve
God's plan. He has spoken to me. I am delivering Eric Meaders to his home at 323 Elsie
within the next hour. Once there, he is yours.

I hope you take him, make him pay.

I didn't know if he'd believe me and act on this or how long it
would take for him to come if he did. All I knew was that this was our
play. That was my email. I read it over one last time and hit "Send."

That's when Hendricks's phone rang, and he picked it up.

"Hendricks."

He listened as dispatch spoke on the other end. I could tell it was
them from the official tones. Dispatch didn't talk long.

"Got it," Hendricks said. "Thanks for the update."

"What's up?"

"Unit just got to the Steeles' place. Father Michael has already been
there. He took a hunk of Steele's flesh out of his side. They're pretty
distraught."

Meaders's head went on swivel; he looked around like the bait he
was. "Dan Steele? This guy's already been to see him? What happened
to him? And what do you mean by *a hunk*?"

"A lot of questions," I said. "And for a guy you don't know."

Meaders grimaced, unhappy that I'd brought back his lie and was
basically rubbing his nose in it.

I leaned forward, between the front seats, so he could see how serious I was. "He was part of your poker night, asshole. He was there when
you beat up Emily, Silver."

"Easy, partner," Hendricks whispered.

"This guy we're after? He's into some real medieval pain, Meaders. You better hope he doesn't get to you without us around."

I relaxed back into the rear of the car.

Hendricks said, "Guy was bleeding pretty bad, wasn't going to a hospital. If you can believe that. Now we've got him on the way there."

I shrugged in agreement, and just then my phone buzzed. I checked it to find a text from Alan: *Everything all right?*

I nodded to myself. Here he was, breaking the standard Laws of Cool by following up on his own message in a day's time. I liked that. In truth, I wasn't cool and knew it, so I liked that he wasn't. He didn't apologize or act uncertain either; he just came out, got in touch, asked after me. It was enough to make a girl smile.

I texted back quickly as Hendricks drove: *Mess of a case. Will call when I come up for air. Am okay.*

Hendricks saw what I was doing. "What's that?"

I lied, told him I'd just emailed the priest.

CHAPTER SIXTY-ONE
MICHAEL

I walked north on Van Ness. Crossing Market, I dropped a bloody cloth with Steele's flesh inside into the gutter. I had held it for long enough, this man's flesh.

In the end, he couldn't decide where it should come from, so I chose. If I had given him longer, he might have settled on a place that seemed less painful, but it wouldn't have mattered. Anywhere on his body, I'd have made it hurt.

I took it from his side, fat along his stomach. People call them love handles, go to the gym and work out to lose them. He lost a bit of his left one; it was smaller now. His flesh and a lot of blood. That—the blood—was for her.

"Press this towel into it," I had told them. "Do this to make the bleeding stop, and you will heal. But hope that you never see me or do anything to any woman again."

The wife cried. The husband sniveled and dripped snot from his nose.

"Don't go to the hospital," I said. "If you call the police, I'll be back. You don't want that."

They didn't. Steele would go on living, maybe raise a son or daughter as best he could. As God's will.

And my cut would leave a mark, a scar to remind them.

CHAPTER SIXTY-TWO
DONNER

Eric Meaders's apartment was actually a small one-story house on a narrow street in Bernal Heights. We parked in the drive, left the back end of our sedan blocking the sidewalk, and took Meaders up the steps. There weren't many places on the block someone could have been watching from, but we checked around to be sure just the same. As for leaving our car in the driveway, it was about as inconspicuous as an unmarked police car could get and finding another place to park would've been near impossible in this neighborhood at night.

Before going in, Hendricks and I pulled our guns.

"You two stay out here," Hendricks said. He took Meaders's keys, opened the door, and slipped inside to case the interior.

"Watch out for my dog," Meaders said.

I heard yipping from inside, the unmistakable call of a small canine.

Meaders checked all around us, his forehead wrinkling to the top of his bald dome. It was cold outside, a strong wind blowing cold fog up the block, and he hunched his shoulders up to his ears, rubbed his hands.

After a little while, Hendricks came back, told us the place was safe. "It's empty. The priest's not here."

"Little girl," Meaders said, rushing in with his hands at his knees to greet the small dog. He made kissing sounds to her, and they went through some kind of an embrace. Guys and little dogs—not a turn-on for me.

"Come on, girl, let's go get your dinner."

Once the dog got calmer, Meaders seemed to relax as well. "I'm making coffee," he said, then stormed off toward the back.

We holstered our weapons and watched him go, dog following. We stood in an open central hallway that served as a living room, foyer, and, after another ten feet, dining room.

"Some place," Hendricks said. "A fancy fourteen hundred square feet."

"Welcome to the city."

Hendricks lived south of San Francisco in Daly City; he had a place with a yard and a patch of lawn for his kid when she came over. Sure, it was foggier than most of San Francisco, but he maintained that the extra space gave him a peace of mind he'd never be able to afford in the city. That and easy parking in his driveway. Maybe he was right, but I didn't need much more than my simple one-bedroom in Potrero Hill: I had a deck with a view, an attic apartment that was plenty tall, as long as I stayed in the middle of the floors, with room for chairs and a couch on the sides, and that was all the air or space I needed.

I was not a girl who would move to the suburbs; I rode my bicycle to the gym and the grocery store, caught the occasional Lyft ride if I needed it—despite the stupid pink mustache on their cars—and took BART as often as I could. Sure, running on concrete sidewalks wasn't my favorite and definitely played hell on my shins, but I could live with that. I rarely got to run outside anymore since making homicide, anyway, given the hours I worked.

"Probably cost a lot too, this place," Hendricks said.

"Yep. It definitely did." Such was our San Francisco. I wasn't there to sugarcoat.

"So how long do we wait?"

I checked my watch. "How long do you think? I hope he makes good coffee."

"We're ordering dinner in. Check your email to see if we heard from the priest."

I checked my phone, but there was nothing new from Father Michael. It didn't surprise me. Actually, I'd have been *more* surprised if he'd written back so fast. I didn't exactly expect to start up a correspondence. I did think he'd be coming for Meaders on his own soon enough though. At the rate he was chopping through his victims, Meaders didn't have long. I hoped we'd be able to wait him out.

There was an email from Dr. Matal with the subject line "Need for Beds."

I swore, then tapped on the screen and started to read. The short and quick was that things were getting crazy over at SFGH, and Dr. Matal wasn't sure how much longer she'd be able to hold on to Emily.

When I told Hendricks, he swore. "How long's she been in?"

"Just over forty-eight hours now. Looks like we'll be hard-pressed to get our seventy-two."

"Beds," he said, shaking his head. "Can't bring her here. See what the doctor sounds like, whether she can hang in another day. If not, we'll have to move her to the Hall."

"Definitely not letting her back into the population."

"Like I said. How long we going to sit on Meaders here?"

"We could call in Coggins and Bennett, get them to go babysit fair Emily. What about that?"

He grimaced like he wanted to spit on Meaders's wood floors, actually turned around and hawked something into a potted plant. "I'd rather have them sit on this tool. Call the doctor. See what she says."

"Aye-aye, sir." I moved to a white leather couch and dialed the doctor—this was not something to take standing up.

I got the mental health nurses' station first, asked for the doctor, and was put on hold. Somehow the doctors at General still wore old Blackberry flip-open pagers. It was a miracle of outdated technology, but that was our civic system in all its glory.

They'd be paging her on it now, telling her she had an urgent call from the police—all basic standard operations. Meaders came out of the kitchen, offering us cups of black coffee. I thanked him as he set them down on a wooden coffee table next to an artful array of design magazines. *Who was this guy?*

Finally, Dr. Matal came on the line. "Investigator Donner. I'm afraid we're going to need this bed. Can we release this woman, or do you want to come get her?"

"You're kidding me. We can't have her back out on the streets. Doesn't she need more treatment?"

"Frankly, we've done all we can for her. The tongue is going to heal on its own, she's through the worst of her withdrawal symptoms, and she doesn't want to be here. Without her consent, you know as well as I do we can't keep her indefinitely."

"Can you give us another twenty-four hours? It's still very dangerous for her out on the street."

"I'm sorry. Under normal conditions, in a perfect situation, I could give you seventy-two hours. The way things are now, and with this officer outside her room intimidating the other patients, I've done all I can."

Doctors: they were either throwing the whole book at you or they had no answers at all.

"He's intimidating the patients? How?"

Hendricks rolled his eyes. Meaders watched me with great interest, as if observing the workings of some great machine.

"Frankly, it's just the uniform. Most of our wards don't have a lot of good experiences with that, and it freaks them out."

"Freaks them out? We'll put a plainclothesman in. No one will know."

Hendricks stifled a laugh with his fist.

"We need her to leave. Can I release her to the care of the officer on duty, or do you want to take her into your own care?"

"So where, then? Where does she go next?"

"I imagine a drug treatment center might be helpful. We have several in the city where—"

"Where she'll walk right out on her own and disappear. We need to keep her under watch. She's our main lead in a highly unstable case."

Dr. Matal made me wait before she made her next comment. I'd just broken another rule: Don't interrupt the doctor.

"Well, Investigator, you'll have to arrest her then. Otherwise, we're letting her go. You have an hour. I'm sorry, but I have patients to tend to." Without another word, she hung up.

"Ouch." I moved the phone to see its screen. The call had in fact ended. "An hour or our girl goes into the wind."

"We can't have that."

"No. Not at all." I got up, tried the coffee, and found it wasn't bad. *Strong,* but this guy knew what he was brewing. "Call in Coggins and Bennett?"

Hendricks nodded, thought it over. He paced over to Meaders's television and back. The little dog came out of the kitchen licking its chops.

"Did you have a good dinner?" Meaders went back to the crouched hugging and rubbing.

"I can let the duty officer take her back to the Hall, keep her in an interrogation room for a while."

"No, no." Hendricks walked closer. "I want to ingratiate ourselves to her. If she's got things to say, I want her saying them to us."

"Ingratiate? Really?"

"You like that. I know you do."

I ignored him. "Maybe we watch her. Let her go and follow. See if she takes us to him."

"No. Not now. She's not going into the night. We—" He stopped himself. "He can't be back there, can he? At the church?"

"I wouldn't think so."

"She gonna go somewhere else for shelter?"

"Where? A drug treatment center? That's where Doc Matal said she'd send her."

He looked at Meaders with skepticism, thinking he'd rather we go with the closer lead to our killer: Emily. Waiting with Meaders was just that—waiting. Emily was a world of unknowns: what she might say, what we might get, where she might go.

"Yeah," he said. "We call Coggins and Bennett, set them up here with boy wonder, and we pick up the girl."

"That works for me."

CHAPTER SIXTY-THREE

MICHAEL

I was saved one cold afternoon on a Tenderloin street six years ago—
years I spent getting clean and becoming ordained. I found my path in
that time but didn't find Him. That came later.

The day I was saved, I waited for my meal with the other vagrants
at Glide Memorial Church. Ahead of me, a woman slept on a box, sitting up against the wall of a dirty building. I studied her, noticing her
thin, greasy hair. Blonde.

Rain soaked her thin jacket. She didn't mind. A dirty hood covered
most of her hair. She slept with her head back, her cheeks thin, even
thinner than the rest of ours—drug addicts all.

When the door opened at the head of the line—time for dinner
already at three thirty, so early and better to get a spot in the lines
for a bed at the shelters—she didn't move. In minutes, the line began

its grueling shuffle forward. Lost souls creeping toward our food. Eventually, the progress reached us, and someone woke her with the toe of his boot. She began screaming, shaking her hands and crying out that she wasn't ready. A volunteer of the church told us to walk around her.

"Leave me alone!" she called out in pain.

She was losing her place, someone muttered.

The volunteer repeated, "Keep the line moving."

I watched her put herself together, such as it was: she gathered herself to stand, jostling the separate pieces of her body onto her too-thin legs covered in tight, dirty jeans that had trailed down her heels for so long they'd worn through. She wore white sneakers, so dirty they told tales of where she had been, what ruin she'd traversed.

By the time I reached her, she pushed off the wall, then wobbled and fell against me. I caught her against my chest, but she pulled away.

When I steadied her with a hand on her elbow, she screamed, "Don't touch me."

Her head nodded, then popped back up to face forward. She was on the dose, still knocked out in the afternoon. They would never let her in. I followed when she stepped out of line and wandered onto Ellis Street in front of a honking car that barely stopped. She walked on, careening forward, carrying a purse that hung to her waist, its strap threatening to fall from her shoulder.

"Do you know where you're going?" I asked.

When she didn't hear, I asked again. Louder. But I *did* nothing. I was into my own brand of ruin then, my own destruction with pipes and needles, and I didn't have conviction or faith. Or Him.

"What?" she called out, not to me or to the dealer who answered, a man who spent his days on that particular corner.

I waved him off to leave her alone. She walked on, heading toward Market. This was when I knew something terrible would happen, that

I should stop her. I knew not to let her walk onto the Muni tracks, but I did nothing. I watched as she pushed her hood back and shook her thin blonde hair in the rain. Her cheeks were sunken; she didn't see the same world as the rest of us, and I couldn't imagine where she understood herself to be.

Then she turned her hood up again and walked forward, leaning into the strut so that I couldn't stop her if I'd wanted. She pushed her body down the hill past Golden Gate Avenue and followed Seventh as it jagged across McAllister. By the time she reached the bottom of the hill, she was running. I did my best to keep up, didn't want to scare her—a part of me feared that I had, that she ran from *me*, but she never knew I was there. She ran from her own demons, those that spoke only to her ears.

The Muni car never saw her coming. If the driver did, it wouldn't have mattered; she ran right in front, into it head-on. I'd never seen Him make such a mess of a human body, couldn't believe she had held all that inside of her until then—every inch of the red guts and tubes, every pint of the dark juice—inside of her from the moment she'd woken on the box.

He showed me. That was the first I'd seen of His acts.

She had held all the demons and torment, all that, inside her for as long as she could. Now it was revealed to me.

People screamed, and I didn't linger. It was my first moment of belief, a belief so pure that I had no sense where it had come from— almost as if the same strange bolt that caught her, caused her to throw herself into the train, had caught me too, made me bear witness to her end. Later I knew it to be one of His signs.

She was the first. The one I couldn't help.

I walked straight back to Golden Gate Avenue, turned into St. Boniface, and pounded on the wooden door, calling out to the priests to let me in. Father Kevin answered. He brought me inside through

God's grace, let me sit, listened until I told him why I had come, and then he let me sleep on the floor.

Only much later could I fully understand why he did this. Of course, it was Him.

In this manner, I was once saved. When I found Emily, I knew it was my purpose to save another.

That was when I first heard His words.

CHAPTER SIXTY-FOUR
DONNER

So we found ourselves on the seventh floor of General again, this time waiting for Dr. Matal to finalize paperwork and sign Emily out. We had called in Coggins and Bennett, used our task force chip to get them right over. I briefed them on the case as they drove to Bernal Heights. They knew most of the backstory on the priest, and I brought them up to date on the dirty poker circle, Emily's relationship to the priest, what we knew of it, and where things stood with Steele, Weber, and Meaders. They'd heard about Heyes already.

Meaders himself, I was happy to be rid of; my own idea or not, I was glad to be out of his apartment. Waiting around wouldn't cut it. A dead end is one thing, a slow-burn stakeout for an action addict, hopped up on caffeine and adrenaline, is another.

It all took less than an hour, transit included, and Matal greeted us as if she'd been counting the seconds.

As I poked my head into Emily's room, she was still sitting on the bed with that sour expression, hollow cheeks and stern eyes, arms crossed over her chest. She looked a little better for her few days of civic care. Her skin had a slightly healthier glow.

Dr. Matal came in to give her a final examination: felt her neck for her lymph nodes, listened to her chest and asked her to cough. I almost expected her to bang on Emily's knees to see if her feet popped up.

Matal waved us into a corner with her lips pursed. "She's yours now, Investigators. This woman isn't suffering from any known trauma and has basically a clean bill of health, all things considered. Given her past medical history, there's not much more we can do for her. She's stable." Then she turned back to her patient. "Good luck, dear. I really wish you all the best."

For her part, Emily wasn't interested; she gazed at the floor, doing everything she could to avoid acknowledging the doctor's interest. Even if the care had helped, she had yet to take a shine to Hendricks, the doctor, or myself.

"Okay," I said, "why don't you get dressed, and then we'll take you wherever you want?"

She still wore the standard hospital issue. The clothes she had worn were folded at the foot of the bed.

"I'll wait outside." Hendricks went out and shut the door.

"Go ahead." I bent over, patted the stack of clothes.

Emily slipped her feet down to the floor. She sat at the edge of the bed like that for almost a minute, breathing hard. I could hear a wheeze in her chest. Below her gown, her legs were basically bones with skin. Even seeing this drug-addled emaciation on the streets all the time, I found it hard to believe her condition given her age. Meth did terrible things.

She wiped her eyes with the back of her wrist, biting her top lip.

"These are your clothes," I said.

She tried saying something, asking a question I couldn't understand. Finally, she took the pad and pencil off the chair.

Him,

she wrote.

Where is the Father Michael?

I held out my hands. "We don't know. We need to talk to him. Where do you think we can find him?"

She didn't answer. Instead, she stood and dropped off her hospital gown. I couldn't believe what I saw: her legs were nothing compared to the hollows of her chest. I had never seen a person look like that, not at any age; the closest form her body compared to was an undernourished dog. I could see all her ribs, her collarbone, the balls of her shoulders. How Meaders and the others could do anything to her, I couldn't believe, wouldn't understand.

Her hips looked like I could circle them with my hands.

"How did you—What did he do to you?" I asked.

She turned to face me. I saw the scars on her arms. She had a better chance of having HIV than not.

"Don't you have a family?" I knew it was a stupid question, that my asking wouldn't resolve broken bonds. She glared back, pointed to the pad.

"Him," she said. "He is." I could understand the words. No mistaking them even from her mouth.

She slipped a red Chicago Bulls T-shirt over her head, pulled on a black zip-up hoodie.

I wondered where this would end, where she'd go once we caught him and what she would do. We would catch him; I was sure of that. Just a matter of time. I didn't know if she'd be better off then, or worse.

I had no idea how to help her. What did she have to look forward to? How would she not wind up dead? Maybe it was all a question of religion, the afterlife—two things I didn't understand.

"What do you want?" I asked. "Where can we take you?" If it would get her out of the city, out of this life, I would let her go. Put her on a bus and get her clear of it all.

"Him," she said again. She sat, unfolded a pair of worn, dirty jeans and guided her legs into them, first one, then the other. "He will—" The rest of the sentence was unclear; she'd either said that he would "tell me" or "kill me." I didn't know which, though the difference was an ocean.

"What makes a priest kill people?" I asked. My biggest question in the open. I tried to come at suspects from odd angles, not to let them know what I really wanted, but now I put it out, simply asked. All I could do was wait for her answer.

She gave it to me too.

"He's punishing sinners."

I was sure of her words and that she believed them.

"He's killed four men. We have to stop him. Help us."

She shook her head. "No. Help him. Help him give me salvation." She wriggled her thin shoes on. "He's absolving me."

"So what's that mean? Where do you end up when he's done?"

She shrugged. "He takes me."

I squinted at her, trying hard to read her face for the words' meaning. What did she want from him? What was she willing to let him do?

I wasn't sure I wanted to know.

"You ready to go?"

She stood up, held out her wrists as if I might cuff them or help her slice them open.

"Come on." I opened the door to find Hendricks leaning against a wall. When I barked at him, he moved aside. We turned and made our way back through the range of beds, curtains, doctors, nurses, and patients. I did my best to respect everyone's privacy, but there wasn't much of it. Everyone's worst problems were right out in the open here. Through windows in doors or gaping holes in the curtains, I could see it all: breakdowns, crying jags, and attempted suicides.

We walked Emily out through all of it, leading her, hoping she'd do nothing more than follow. We would take her out into the night with us: first to the Hall and then where? I wasn't sure.

But we were doing the right thing as much as I understood it, accepting responsibility, watching over our case as a priority to our lives. This was what honorable police work was supposed to be about.

Dr. Matal stood by the nurse's station as we got to the exit.

"Just need you to sign this, Investigators. Then she'll be released to your custody." She looked to Emily and said, "How's that sound?"

Emily could've done a lot worse, but all she did was shake her head. I was grateful she didn't cause a scene or start fighting. I took the pen from the doctor and signed the sheet on her clipboard.

We took the elevator down and walked out into the night then, Emily in her dirty clothes, skin-tight and shabby, Hendricks and myself—tired, worn out, on our own—heading to the parking lot of SFGH and bound for the Hall.

The first thing Emily did when we got outside was ask a guy in a gown, holding on to an IV pole, for a smoke. He got pissed off right away; he was down on his luck, clearly. Unshaven and wearing only bed slippers in the cold night, his greasy red hair hanging almost to his shoulders. He wouldn't have many in the pack, and the next could be hard to come by.

"Come on," I told her. "I'll buy you your own pack."

We stopped the car at a gas station on Potrero, the first place where I could buy the cigarettes. She wanted Marlboros, reds. What else?

When I came back with the pack, she tapped them down hard for a few blocks as we drove. As with any witness we couldn't predict, someone who rode with us but might not be all there, we put her in the backseat, behind Hendricks, and I sat sideways, watching her the whole time.

Hendricks rolled down her window, said, "You're not smoking where we're going, so you might as well get it done in the car."

When I asked how she was feeling, she didn't respond, just gestured at the car's lighter and waited with the cigarette hanging out of her mouth. Once I pushed it in, she looked out at the road, the lights of the city. That was when it started to rain.

I could smell the ash and dirt in the air first, then the oil from the asphalt, mixed with gas. Finally the lighter popped out. I held it as Emily lit up.

After that all I smelled was her smoke. It hung thick in the car, reminding me of my old habits, my own solitary smokes in the night. Luckily, reds were far enough from my palate that I had no urge to join.

"You hungry?" I asked.

She didn't answer that either, and I knew it would be a long night. I raised my eyebrows at Hendricks, and he returned the look. After a couple blocks, I turned on the radio, flipped to KCSM, and let jazz spread into the car, hoping it might help, knowing it wouldn't.

CHAPTER SIXTY-FIVE

After she had smoked the better part of two cigarettes, I decided to give it another try. I glanced at Hendricks, then back at Emily again. He'd been driving aimlessly, letting the wheels roll as she smoked, hoping the ride and the solidarity would help us make personal contact.

I asked her, "How much can you tell us about your priest, Father Michael?"

"He is *good*."

"She talks?" Hendricks asked.

"Best she can. Did you catch that?"

"No."

I clarified for him. Watching her mouth helped.

She told us he meant to save her, that by taking away the men who had caused her sins, he was "cleansing her," saving her soul.

"When he is done, my sins will be erased."

It sounded like a good deal, but I wondered about the endgame. "What do you want to happen when he's done?" I feared the answer.

"I will go to heaven," she said. There was no mistaking her words.

"How?"

"He takes me home. To Him."

That was the answer that worried me most.

"Not if I can help it," I said under my breath.

We had come to a dirty corner south of Market, were stopped at a red light. Emily peered out through the glass.

Outside, I saw a few kids about her age with tattooed faces. They were fighting similar addictions. One of them, a girl, sat on a refrigerator box against a wall. Her face and hands were dirty. She had no shoes, and her formerly white tube socks were gray, almost black. She swayed her head ear to ear like Stevie Wonder.

Emily pursed her lips, still staring out the window. Then the light changed, and Hendricks began to pull away. She reached for the door, but I grabbed her arm, stopped her before the handle. "You're not going to buy," I said.

She turned to meet my eyes with something like fear and disdain. Then those broke, and she nodded.

Hendricks said, "Jesus, don't tell me you still want to be out there."

Her expression turned to disgust.

"She's clean," I said.

Maybe I could win her over eventually. We'd be a new version of good cop, bad cop: insensitive cop, observant cop.

"Check your phone," Hendricks said. "See if he responded to your email."

I pulled up email, checked to see what had come in. More responses to the Clip, sightings real and imagined, cops from different districts chiming in to tell us what they'd seen, none of these an apprehend. Then the message from him. His reply: "Bring him to me." That was all.

"He wants us to bring him Meaders. Didn't say where."

"Write back. Tell him we will. Give him your number."

"Yeah? That's our plan now? You sound like me at the Thirsty Bear."

"We ride together, Donner. I listen to one of yours, you listen to one of mine. Turns out, we wind up sounding like one another."

It was almost meaningful enough to work.

He added, "And I don't slap you when I make a suggestion."

I laughed but not easily. "I don't know what came over me."

"Forget it. You're tired."

"Maybe the case. Maybe not enough sleep." I shrugged an apology. "He's going to want *her*," I said, "more than Meaders."

"That's the chip we don't use. Write him. Let him know we'll come with his man."

She sat in the back during all of this, watching us, listening to our back and forth.

"I want to go to him," she said. "*Let* me *go*."

"Time to head back to the Hall, partner. Circle our wagons."

I agreed. We could get Emily under control there, give her a place to stay safe for at least a little while. Hendricks made a wide U-turn at the next block, hitting the siren to clear the way, and took us north toward the Hall.

I wrote an email back to Father Michael, agreed to bring Meaders to him, asking him to call to set up the place.

We'd figure out the rest as we went. Coggins, Bennett, whatever or whomever else we needed, we'd make this work.

"It's sent," I said.

Emily asked from the backseat where we were going. Neither of us bothered to answer.

My phone vibrated in my hand: a text message coming through from Alan. It was an image: a picture of a clear backboard and the rim and net of a hoop. The rec center. At just after nine o'clock, they'd be finished and leaving the gym. I'd missed the games, though they seemed like a very distant part of my life now, an activity from a different place and time. I wondered if my world and Alan's would ever intersect.

Hendricks and I sped south through the night, with our bruised and battered passenger in the rear, headed for the Hall.

CHAPTER SIXTY-SIX

In the homicide squad room on the Hall's seventh floor, Hendricks showed Emily to the chair next to his desk and plopped down in his own. We'd picked up food along the way: burgers for us and a vegetable soup for Emily. I put the bags down on our desks. This, just a fast few bites in the middle of it all, was the best we could do for the night. Hopefully it would be enough to keep us going.

"Fire it up," I said. "Call Coggins and Bennett, see what's what over there."

Hendricks unwrapped his double cheeseburger, took a huge bite, and said through the mouthful, "We don't want him here."

"Oh, no. But get them ready to move if they need to."

"Roger that." He finished chewing, took another bite before putting the burger down to shove his phone under his ear and dial. When someone was on the other end, he said, "Yeah. How's our friend?"

He nodded, took another bite.

"Got it." He pushed the phone away from his mouth, told me they were already sick of Meaders. "He won't stop asking questions."

I unwrapped my own cheeseburger, a single with lettuce and tomato. "Shoot. Bring him down here. Let's scare him into submission. Throw him in a box, get her to make an ID, and charge him with solicitation. Then see what he has to say."

"I don't want to see any of those men. Please, no." Emily hadn't touched her food. The spoon sat on top of a covered Styrofoam container.

Hendricks waited, eyebrows raised, for my next thought. Something would have to break before too long; we couldn't keep Coggins and Bennett on Meaders all night. Neither could Hendricks and I babysit Emily in the Hall until morning—not if we were to come at it again functioning tomorrow. I fired up my old desktop computer.

"Yeah," Hendricks said into the phone, "keep sitting on him. We'll call you back."

When he hung up, he said, "They're restless. Can't blame 'em."

"I hate little dogs."

"Come on, partner. Lighten up." He turned to Emily. "She should lighten up, shouldn't she?"

Emily stared down at her spoon without responding.

"Meaders will want to walk that thing soon. They prepared for that?"

Hendricks shrugged, shoved more of the burger into his mouth. "Backyard?"

"Maybe." I wanted, needed to keep Meaders safe. He was our chip still, the goat on a leash that kept us from using Emily to lure the priest. I didn't want to involve Emily any further than we had to, not as long as it could be avoided.

As I ate, I clicked my email open. Nothing new. I checked my texts again and looked at Alan's picture. We had a few minutes, so I decided to make the call. I ate half the burger first to get my blood sugar headed in the right direction, then told Hendricks I'd be right back.

He got that familiar look like he'd give me hell for something, but I ignored him, took my cell, and walked over to the windows. Being new on the floor meant I had no seniority when I chose my desk. The best I could do was go along with where Hendricks had the clout to put us. I'd heard some rumors about him getting in trouble with Bowen over the years and that this accounted for our placement at the center of the twenty-by-thirty squad room, right under the harshest fluorescent lights.

At this time of night, the rows of desks by the windows had been abandoned. Everyone on the squad was either out on a case, on call, or at home. Against the black glass, I felt the cold radiating inward at me, looked out over the Bay in the direction of AT&T Park.

Alan picked up. "Clara? Hang on a second, all right?"

"Sure." He was in the car. "Where you headed?"

When he came back, he said, "Home. Just got done playing. You like my pic?"

"I miss it," I said, "playing tonight."

"There'll be other games. You'll be back."

How had it gotten this way: that we could simply talk? It all felt suddenly, inexplicably easy.

He said, "What do you say to dinner this weekend? Pick a night."

And then it didn't.

"You're not going to like my answer." I touched the cold glass, felt my finger pads press against it. Emily's head bowed, thin ribbons of muscle sticking out down the back of her neck. Hendricks's desk phone rang, and I turned to watch him answer. He waved his finger in a circle, telling me to hurry up. That was when the phone rang again, and I realized it was *mine*.

Hendricks pointed more dramatically now, waving me over. This call could be our priest.

I swore under my breath.

In my ear, Alan said, "Guess you're a hard woman to pin down."

"You don't know the half of it."

"I hope I get to find out."

"Yeah," I said, "let's talk again soon. I have to go."

He started to tell me to have a good night, maybe even to be safe, but I was already running across the room to my desk. I hung up before he got to finish. At my desk, I grabbed the phone receiver and rushed it to my ear.

"Donner here."

A deep male voice said, "Hello, Detective."

It was him.

CHAPTER SIXTY-SEVEN

"We've been looking for you."

"That I've gathered."

"Where do you want us to bring your guy?"

"Meaders."

Hendricks lifted an extension of the phone to his ear, listening in. This was how it worked in the real world: two cops in the Hall late at night, without any techs running phone taps, tracing the caller's location, using a landline. I had his number on my caller ID now, so I'd run it through the system and see what popped out, but that wasn't likely to yield much.

Emily had come out of her funk; she watched us intently, hanging on every word.

"Meaders. Yes. Tell us where to bring him." Part of me even hoped it could be that easy: that we'd just hand Meaders over and be done with it. But it wasn't. Never would be.

Emily said, "I want to go with him."

I waved at Hendricks to quiet her down. He got around the desk and put his hand over her mouth faster than I'd ever seen him move.

"Is that her? Emily is with you?"

I didn't know how he heard her through the line, though her voice was hard to mistake. I waited, not knowing what to say.

"Was that her?"

"It's not her," I said. "She isn't with us here. But she's safe."

I listened, waiting for what he'd say next. The sound of his breathing came through the line. Then he said, "Where is she?"

"In the hospital. They're seeing to her wounds. She's in very capable hands. Doing well."

Emily started squirming, struggling to get out of Hendricks's hands. Her mouth came free for a moment, and she screamed, *"Father!"* I saw her stump tongue flapping as she did.

Hendricks got his hand back over her mouth again, lifted her, and carried her off toward an interrogation booth at the back of the squad room.

The priest breathed loudly on the other end of the phone. If seething had a sound, this was it.

"So she's there. You lied to me."

"She's safe," I said. "We're taking care of her."

"Give her to me. Let me deliver her."

"*Deliver* her? Care to explain what that means?"

He did more seething. I waited.

"Give her to me."

"I can't do that. But I can help you with the other."

He said, "Tell me, Detective, has God spoken to you? Given you instructions?"

I waited for Hendricks to enter the booth before I answered. "He told me to lend assistance, that you deserve our help. These men are filth." I wondered what he'd do if I said God wanted him to surrender, if he'd believe me. "He said this will all be over soon, that you only have a few more acts."

The priest sighed. "He knows I grow weary. But I know too that He hasn't spoken to you. You aren't saved."

"I did—"

He cut me off before I could finish, though I didn't know what I wanted to say. "You can give me Meaders, but do not pretend to hear the words of our Lord."

Hendricks came back out of the booth, walking toward me.

"*Then* you will give me the girl. You must let us alone to finish this."

"I can't do that. You have to know I can't do that."

"I wouldn't expect you to understand, but I have done this out of love."

"What kind of love?"

"Love for her. God's eternal love. Let me ask you, Detective Donner, do you believe? In *anything*?"

I closed my eyes, wrapped the phone cord around my finger. I didn't know the answer or even how much I wanted to reveal about my own twisted logic about the world.

With Hendricks coming over, I was reluctant to say much. Somehow I was willing to tell this killer things about myself that I'd never tell my partner. The things I believed in, none of them simple or defined within the standard parameters, these were thoughts I felt more comfortable discussing with a madman or a priest. And Father Michael was both.

Hendricks tapped my shoulder, mouthed "You okay?" when I opened my eyes.

I nodded to him. "I believe in the law. That Eric Meaders did things he has to pay for and that you are an instrument of justice better than most. If God wants to punish this sinner, I don't have a problem with that."

With a furrowed brow, Hendricks nodded at my acting job. I assumed he'd take it as that. Maybe he couldn't see how close I was to convinced. But we needed the priest to believe, to trust that I was riding along with him, so I didn't question it. Neither did Hendricks; maybe he knew I wasn't acting and didn't care. We were both over the edge on this case, flying on our own, consequences be damned.

I said, "I'll bring him to you. Alone. You tell me where."

Hendricks's eyes widened; he wouldn't like that, me being alone, but we'd figure out the location and make it safe. The main thing now was that the priest believed, that he'd come.

He said through the phone, "Bring him to Mission Dolores. The old chapel. Where the Franciscans first prayed here in San Francisco. Bring him now."

I waited, expecting him to hang up. Hendricks made a churning motion with his hand, wanting me to keep the priest on the phone. I shrugged.

"I can do that." I didn't want to bring up Emily. He would want her, but that was a harder conversation. I waited, but then the priest didn't say more. I realized he had hung up.

I took the phone from my ear. "He's gone."

Hendricks frowned. He came around my desk and copied the number off the caller ID onto a scrap of paper.

"That's our guy." He crossed back to his computer, ready to punch in the number to see what came up. We could ask the phone company to triangulate the signal, trying to pinpoint his location, but that could take time, and its accuracy was debatable. The best we'd do was to confirm who'd registered the phone.

In a moment, he swore and hit his desk. "Comes back as a pay phone in North Beach," he said. "Nothing we can do with that. He'll be on the move before we can get there."

"So what now?" I was aware that I still stood next to my desk, hadn't sat down since I started the call. It was an odd position, I felt, but then a lot of this case had suddenly gotten odd—I had just told a murderer I would bring him his next victim. What's worse, I was seriously considering my own beliefs about life, wondering what I had if not religion, whether I had any form of faith. There was considerable risk to all this too—not just for myself and for Meaders, but for my job.

What did I have? I had my job, the law, justice, and truth. I had the trust of my partner, hope for maybe a boyfriend and some good times too, if I was lucky. I was a cop, here to serve the law. And I wanted my man.

Bowen was a matter we could work out later.

I was ready to do what I had to in order to get *him*.

"Your show, Donner. Tell me what's next."

"Call Coggins and Bennett. Tell them to get Meaders ready." I picked up my phone to call them myself.

Hendricks spun in his chair with his legs up, looking like a cowboy eager to get on a bull.

On my phone, Coggins picked up. I told him to get Meaders ready to roll.

"Where to?" he asked.

"Bring him to the Mission. Meet me on the south side of Dolores Park, at Twentieth Street." I knew the chapel stood at Sixteenth and Dolores. The park would be an easy place for us to stage out of sight, and Twentieth Street was its quietest side. Twentieth Street was a place we could talk things through.

I said, "Be there in ten."

CHAPTER SIXTY-EIGHT
MICHAEL

Waiting for the detective, I thought of my final morning at St. Boniface with Emily. After mass and giving out the Holy Sacrament, I heard confessions. The day's visitors were a few worshippers, run of the mill, those who might actually be saved by their attempts to find His path. I gave His forgiveness as a matter of course, blessed them, and asked for simple acts of penance.

Their presence in His house and willingness to confess assured me they were worthy of His love.

When I was done, I went down to my room to see her.

As I entered, Emily sat at the small table, held herself quietly in a chair, stirring a spoon through her tea.

"Did you sleep well?" I asked.

She nodded. I saw pleasure in her face now that I had returned but also concern and worry at where I might have been in the night.

If only she knew.

I started making oatmeal for us both on the hot plate, adding dried fruit and shaved coconut, as she liked it.

"Where were you?" Her words were soft, short bursts of breath from her lips. I knew them without hearing, could understand them from her eyes.

"Out for a walk." We met eyes, and I wasn't sure what she believed, what she would want to know. "I couldn't sleep."

"Was a long time."

"Not *too* long." I reached to touch her hand, but she moved it.

"Time?"

"I left around three," I said, "three thirty."

I turned my back, stirred our breakfast. The oats had soaked up water and risen to the right size. Steam rose. I turned off the hot plate and continued to stir.

Though my room was a small one, we made do. Emily didn't mind; it was better than where she had been.

In a minute, I scooped the oatmeal into bowls, added milk to my own, a touch of cold water to hers.

We sat in the silence, and I said a prayer for the gift of the food.

She said, "Gone for so long. I woke up. Worried. Where were you?"

"You don't need to worry. Don't fear. I protect us. He watches over us. Nothing will reach you in His house."

She was quiet again, for a time. I heard another priest enter the bathroom across the hall, shut the door, turn on the shower.

"How are your oats?"

She smiled.

I reached across the table and touched her arm, then her hand. Her fist stayed closed; there was something she was still keeping back. I touched her fingers, trying not to scratch her as I pushed her hand open.

"No," she said, turning away.

I wasn't sure what else to say then; I wanted to talk, tell her what I was doing for her. She knew I was taking back her sins but not the importance of the most recent names, that I'd found the four who had hurt her and left her on the street.

"Soon all of this will be over," I said. "Anyone who caused your pain and sins will be gone from His earth, and you will be absolved. Ready to enter heaven for true salvation."

"I want it," she said. "I do."

"You'll have it."

"My sins?"

I said, "He won't judge you. His love is pure. As is mine." After a time, I said, "I'll return you to His arms. I promise."

Her eyes probed my face, came to meet my own, and held them. She wanted what I offered. Knew the work I had to do.

"His love for you is pure."

She touched my chest, tapped at my heart with one finger.

I bit my lips between my teeth until I could answer. I turned to the table, concentrated on its wood: the grain ran sideways; every few inches a fresh board made a line where it connected to the next. Here and there scratches on its surface.

I said, "All is for Him. He guides my path."

I wanted to tell her I had found the four, that they were next.

My jaw tightened; I ground my teeth. I never spoke about what I did, would never tell her my own sins, where He led me. "You don't need to worry. I am right with Him and safe." I touched her hand—cold. "And I will make you the same."

After a time, I stood and carried our bowls to the sink, threw away what was left of our food. She didn't speak.

Before returning to the church, I bent to kiss her cheek. "You have love now," I said, "mine and His own."

CHAPTER SIXTY-NINE
DONNER

Hendricks's chair stopped spinning. He gave me his intense look. "What's going on here, Donner? Please tell me this isn't going to be another Terranella, that you have a plan and Meaders won't get hurt."

"I do have a plan. I bring Meaders to our man, make a handoff, and you guys pop out when the priest shows. Does that sound clear enough for you? You're practically the one who came up with it."

He rubbed his face. It was a long shift and a crazy week. He could use some sleep. We both could.

"We need someone here to watch her." He thumbed to where Emily was stashed. It occurred to me suddenly that Debbie Shine might be in danger as well. If the priest was true to his word, she'd wind up on his list and Dan Steele would be back on it, both for talking to us.

If we did this right though, did it fast, the end could justify the means. We'd get the priest before he got to anyone else. That was at least worth a roll of the dice. Despite the risks, it could cut off a lot of hard angles, bad outcomes if we acted now.

"Call it in. Get someone up here to watch her."

"But that's not all that bothers me about this." His level gaze hung on me. I'd only seen him like this once before.

"What else?"

"I don't want you going out on this alone. It's not safe."

I turned and looked behind me, making sure the room was clear. "Who else is there? I'm the one who has the connection with this perp. He asked for me. What's our other option?"

"Not to do this. We'll get him some other way."

I laughed at that straight out. "You're afraid I'm going to get hurt because I'm a woman. Admit that if you had a male partner, you wouldn't be worried in the least."

"That's not true." He got up, came around the desk to where I stood, then seemed to feel awkward standing tall over me, so he sat down on my desk. He looked uncomfortable but stuck with it. Finally, he said, "I'd be worried about any partner of mine going into this."

"Come on." I started toward the elevators, waving for him to follow. "Tell me the rest of this in the car."

Outside, driving southwest on Harrison, Hendricks made his case, and I made mine. His consisted of pulling back now, going in a new, better-planned direction with more backup, and mine was all about going in, having Coggins, Bennett, and Hendricks behind me, and getting this done before our priest had anything else flash across his mind, before he went back into the wind.

To Hendricks's credit, he was more worried about my safety than the protocols. That much I would have to thank him for—but not until later, when this all was done.

He said, "Give us an hour. At least let me call and get a few snipers on the roofs. We'll take him out."

I sat in the passenger seat, dreading the fact that soon I'd have to drive. Growing up in New York, I'd never learned to drive, chose to settle in San Francisco partly because you *could* live in this city without a car. And I did. I had my license, got it to make patrol and be a cop, but driving was definitely not my thing. I did my best to avoid it until now. It would only be a few blocks, I told myself. And at night. The traffic would be minimal.

Hendricks had other concerns. "What's Bowen going to say?"

"He'll commend us for moving so quickly and catching our suspect, for not letting snipers take shots at the city's oldest church or killing a priest in the process."

"What if this goes sideways and someone gets hurt? Then what's he say?"

"I don't know. Let's call him now."

Hendricks laughed. He looked over at me with his poker face blown, both of us knowing it was either worth a call in to Bowen at this stage or it wasn't. Here was the place where the rubber met the road: if we called Bowen, he could squelch the whole thing, pull us off the priest by a mile, get Meaders to a safe house, and send it all back to the Clip, a citywide search and days of inactivity. Or he could give us the green light for what we were doing, let us fly by the seat of our pants and take a risk that could pay big rewards, but it could also get us all in deep trouble, even risk him losing his job.

We both knew there was no way Bowen would green-light this plan if we called.

I said, "You got me there, partner. We do this by your book. How does it go down?"

We had reached Thirteenth Street, the freeway overpass where 101 ran east-west across the city. If Hendricks wanted to take us back to the

Hall, here's where he could turn left, bring us back up Bryant toward downtown. He didn't. Instead, he kept straight on, passed the Office Depot, and stopped at a stop sign across from Best Buy. A long taco truck served late-night patrons on the other side of the street. When we crossed Fourteenth, he put his blinker on, steered into the right lane, heading toward a right turn on Fifteenth, the best way to cross west to Dolores Street.

"We try this," he said, "but we do it according to *my* plan."

CHAPTER SEVENTY

At Fifteenth and Dolores, Hendricks took a right to go north. The chapel and the park were both behind us. In the middle of the block, he pulled over, shifted the car into park.

"Okay. This is how it's going to work." He turned to me, his voice dry and serious. "You drive. Take the car, meet Coggins and Bennett. Once you have Meaders, have them come around and find a low-key spot to set up by the church. We all watch the street. Tell them I'll be in touch.

"Watch for my texts, or I'll call you."

He turned for the handle, ready to open his door before I stopped him. "What are *you* going to do?"

"I'm going out there. I'm going to get our guy or find him when he comes up on you at the church."

"Get there early, get the drop," I said. It was a psalm from the Gospel of Hendricks, one he'd taught me in our first week together.

He nodded, added a wink. "Be careful."

Then he opened his door and was gone into the night.

Hendricks was a career cop in the SFPD, going on ten years of homicide, the furthest thing from a ninja with his ample belly and tweed jacket, but still, if our priest was out there and had some kind of a plan to hide from or play us, Hendricks would find him. I thought of the few ways this could go down, and none of them were good for the priest.

There was something else though too. A feeling I kept trying to shake. It felt like something was behind me, just out of my line of sight. I knew it was there, that it could do me harm, but if I stopped to turn around and look, it would be gone.

I slid over into the driver's seat and tested the gas and the brakes. Before I shifted the car into drive, I adjusted the seat forward, changed the angles of the mirrors. I wanted clear vision all around.

I went slow, driving to Fourteenth Street and making a U-turn. It felt quiet and lonely in the car with only the sound of the fan blowing heat. The other cars sped through this stretch of Dolores, all heading to other parts of the city, first from south to north and then, after I turned, the opposite direction. Dolores and Guerrero were the fastest routes through this section of town.

As I approached Fifteenth, I slowed even more, scanning the sidewalks for Hendricks all the way to Sixteenth then beyond. I passed the big church and then the smaller old chapel along my right side. Hendricks was somewhere out there, invisible; either hiding behind a tree or a car or some other long-term trick he'd come upon during his years. I didn't see the priest, didn't expect him to have any dramatic tricks or sleights of hand. Perhaps he thought God would grant him a miracle to help him on his path. I didn't know what to expect, only to be on my toes.

I picked up speed after the chapel, feeling some sense of comfort in driving. At Eighteenth I saw the park and got caught at the light. They'd been working on the whole north half of Dolores Park for over a year now, it seemed, and this after an epic period of redoing the playground at the southern end. But the clientele of the park never changed or seemed to mind; even in the cold of this January night, they'd found their benches and scored drugs. Every day in the sun or the fog, people were out having parties on the grass, carving up the territory with blankets, drum circles, towels, each section getting smaller and smaller on the weekends, when the crowds reached their max.

The light changed, and I drove on, climbed the hill, and took a right onto Twentieth, where I double-parked behind Coggins and Bennett. Bennett stood against the trunk, smoking. At the sight of me, he flipped his butt against a parked car. The cherry sparked, showed bright for a moment, and then went out.

I shifted into park and rolled down my window as Bennett came around.

"Where's your partner?"

"Out in the night," I said, "setting up to get the drop. You're supposed to do the same. You and Coggins. Park near Mission Dolores and see if you can spot Father Michael on his approach."

"That's the idea here? Turning this turd over to his maker?"

I shifted in my seat, tilted my head toward the door to see up into Bennett's eyes. "More or less. You don't like that?"

He smiled. "Listen, Donner. I got no love for that bald-headed bastard in there, but this goes wrong, it's all our asses. Where's our backup?"

I bit my lip, wondering how clearly he'd hit the nail on the head, called out my mysterious concern hiding out of my sight. Hendricks and I were stepping out of the mold, going far out on our own, and it was mainly my drive that was making it happen. In truth, if things shook down wrong, it would be my ass.

And I didn't want it any other way. This priest was going down tonight—by any means necessary—if it was my call to make.

As I'd seen my father and some of the key players around the Hall conclude before me, stepping out of bounds was a necessity once in a while. It was how crimes got solved. We had our pencil pushers like

Bowen and his bosses, the ones who posed as political saints and mainly served to cross t's and dot i's, and we had the blessed rest, the rank and file who got things done. That was how it had always worked.

Based on my father's experiences on the opposite coast, this went back one hell of a long way and across the nation.

I took it from my father, one of the best. It was the first thing he'd taught me—before anything else.

What else would a single father teach his daughter, his only child? I wasn't a son, but as my dad told me too many times growing up, "There's the world, and then there's its ways."

I searched Bennett's face for any signs.

"You with us?"

He nodded. "Let's get her done."

I exhaled a sigh. We'd pushed past our boundaries, Hendricks and I, and now we had our backup support out on the fringe too. But this killer was coming down. It was possible Meaders might get a little nicked up in the process. We were all aware of that, okay with it. A turd claiming a turd, so to speak.

The results? They'd come out in the wash.

I pushed back in my seat and opened the door. "Time to get Meaders and go catch our priest."

CHAPTER SEVENTY-ONE

MICHAEL

I found her on the street outside Glide—Emily—in almost the same position as the other.

This on one of my late-night walks before I found purpose, heard His word. I knew there was more to them than a simple diversion in the night, but I didn't know what until I saw her. She was passed out, in trouble, left for trash, and unwanted beyond His own love. I saw my path. Heard His words.

She was the first time I heard Him.

He spoke to me then, and everything changed. For six years I had been compliant in the church—compliant to man's ways. But then I began to follow His.

He told me to make her my own. To give her the love I had to offer, salvation beyond even what I'd had. He would accept her into heaven after I had cleansed her of her sins.

I went to her. Sleeping or passed out. Bloody. I covered her with my coat to keep her warm and carried her in my arms the five blocks back to my church. I snuck her down into the rectory. At that hour, it wasn't hard to reach my room unnoticed. There I laid her on the bed and cleaned her wounds, inspected her mouth. I feared she might never stop bleeding. God told me she would.

I knew then that God would see to all.

He told me she was all right there in my room, that He would protect her as I nursed her back to health and then worked to save her soul.

"In time," He told me. "In time, my son, you will avenge her sins. You will make her whole."

Finding and cleaning her scars then, that was how I came to know her damage. The first of her sins. The others, the secrets came out in time.

In time, she gave me the first two names: Piper, Farrow.

That was when I started. This was His real work, my true calling, my path. To cleanse her for His salvation, I carried out His word.

Now I had one more name to claim, and it would be over.

But that night when I first found her, it was enough to clean her wounds and give her warmth, offer her God's love. His love—and my own.

CHAPTER SEVENTY-TWO
DONNER

Coggins didn't say anything when I came up to the car. He nodded at me from the driver's seat but didn't open the door or put down the window. I could make my own decisions about what he was thinking, whether he liked our night game. Bennett would handle the rest.

If I could trust him, I could trust his partner.

All part of the code.

Bennett opened the back door, and Meaders slid out fast under his arm. He was all energy, hopped up on coffee or something else: adrenaline and fanboy excitement about being out at night with cops.

"What's our plan?" he said. "Fill me in, Donner."

Like the others, he had taken to calling me by just my last name. He was getting comfortable, like he was one of us.

I said, "My partner is drawing out our chief suspect in these murders. We're hoping you can make an ID at the scene."

"Sweet. I'm in it. But I never met the guy. Just saw the girls. Will that help?"

"She'll be with him. Hendricks drew our man out by posing as a john. If she's your girl, then we have him."

"So I'm not bait now?"

"No." I hit him on the arm. "Isn't that nice? Things really going your way."

He laughed, loosened the collar of his shirt around his neck. "Yeah, good." He got serious. "I still want to be in the middle of it."

"Oh, don't worry. You will be."

I led him to my car and let him sit in the front. He was on our side now, annoying fanboy or not, and we were all in this together. I had no idea how the lieutenant would see this all when it was over, but that was a matter for tomorrow morning, maybe the next day. This was the moment, the night.

We drove back to Sixteenth Street slowly and passed the churches. I knew the layout from experience, an early SF boyfriend who liked to show me the sights. First was a small graveyard, one of two remaining burial grounds within the city borders, full of headstones marking deaths over two hundred years old. Then the small original chapel dating back to the seventeen hundreds, and finally the newer, larger church, rebuilt after the great quake of 1906.

I parked across the street, half blocking the driveway of a building that was sure not to need it at this time of night, and watched the big wooden doors of the old Mission chapel. The wind whipped through the trees along Dolores; outside it looked cold. Somewhere Coggins and Bennett were setting up. I had to trust in that. I trusted in Hendricks to be there, even if I couldn't see him. The comfort I felt came from knowing that Father Michael did not want to hurt me, so far as I knew. I thought of my times on the basketball court, driving into the tall guys and finishing at the hoop. I would curl my limbs in between much bigger men to get my shot off. All it took was getting past my fear. Keeping my eyes open. This was the same. I thought about what I wanted, both for myself and for the city, and Meaders interrupted me by calling my attention to a guy on a bike.

"See him? Is that our guy?"

"No." A short Latino rode a rickety bike wearing a large backpack, likely coming back from a long shift of work. I couldn't remember how many hours I'd been on the job. "Come on. Time to get out."

I shut off the car and got out onto the street, pulled my jacket close. I went around to the trunk, watching Meaders's head surface from within the car. He slammed the door from a crouch, peering over the roof across the street. I stepped around next to him, along his right side and took his arm in my left hand. With my right I reached inside my coat to touch the handle of my gun. It was there, hard and warm and ready. I didn't need to check it, cock it, or chamber a round; I kept it ready at all times.

"Come on," I said, pulling Meaders foward. A van passed along the street in our direction and then was gone.

No one stopped us, called out, or did anything as we crossed the wide, grassy median and found our way to Dolores's west side. In front of the old chapel, the concrete sidewalk was broken by red bricks leading up to five brick stairs and two wooden doors that looked as if they had been there for centuries. And they had. They were mounted on great iron hinges, with patterns of squares and circles carved into the wood. No one did wood carving like this anymore. And they looked *thick*, these doors, like they could hold out a flood. They had been through an earthquake. Several.

We walked right up the stairs and turned our backs to the door, all the better to see the street.

"He's coming?" Meaders said. "Your partner is meeting the guy out here."

"On that corner." I pointed my nose at the far side of Dolores, at Sixteenth, about five yards in front of our car.

That was when I heard something creaking behind us, the whine of a large metal hinge and a rattling like a strand of old, heavy chains.

"What the—?"

I turned, but already felt a strong hand on my arm, someone pulling me inside the chapel, into complete darkness. I stumbled, got my bearings in time to see Meaders pulled in and the door slam. He barked out something unintelligible, and then I felt him bump into me, knocking me farther inside. I pulled my gun and swung it around, surprisingly not hitting anyone or anything, and fumbled with my other hand to reach my phone for some light. Anything to see what was happening.

When the wooden door slammed shut, any light from the street outside had disappeared. Now *everything* was black. I found my phone, pushed its button, and then thumbed up from the bottom of the screen to get more functions. In the lower-left corner, I saw the flashlight icon, pushed it with my thumb. The light came on. For a moment I looked up, trying to see what was around me. I registered more red bricks, long wooden pews and white walls. Then a hand slapped the phone out of my hand, and I heard it clatter to the floor.

It was swiftly kicked away; I watched it slide under what I assumed were pews.

I swore.

The smell of old wood registered to my nose and then something metallic, what I knew was blood but hoped wasn't.

"Meaders! Eric?"

I swung around with the gun again, not sure what direction to point or what, if anything, to shoot at. What dim light came in through the high stained-glass windows was minimal, murky, as if coming in filtered through muddy water. That Meaders was quiet couldn't mean anything good.

I felt for the door, moving toward the thin cracks of light around its edges. Then I heard Hendricks's voice and his fists pounding. My foot slipped on something slick underneath it. I caught myself. My next step bumped into something soft.

Meaders's body. Had to be.

CHAPTER SEVENTY-THREE

Hendricks pounded on the door outside. "Donner! Is everything all right?"

"No. Help me get out of here."

I pushed forward to try the door, but my hands landed on heavy chains. I tried the release, and it wouldn't budge; the lock was chained shut.

"I'm trapped," I said in a normal volume. "And Meaders is hurt."

Hendricks swore from the other side of the door again. "I'm coming around. I'll find a way in."

I turned back to the dark, crouching and feeling around on Meaders's body. I felt wet and knew it was blood. What my fingers got to first was leather, his jacket, and then his shirt. This is where it was especially wet. I felt upward from there and came to a knife handle sticking out of his throat. Blood still spurted around it and onto my hand; I felt the hot pumps coming, tried to cover the hole. It was no use. Pulling out the knife would make things worse. Meaders was gone. The priest had killed him before he could even make a sound.

But where was he? I hadn't heard any movement, hadn't heard him leave.

"Father Michael? You there?"

No sound came back but the weak echoes of my own voice against the tiled floor and the thick adobe walls.

I said, "I can help you."

Then I heard his voice, about ten or fifteen feet away toward the front. "Where is she?" he said. "I am ready for her. I'll make her whole."

I pointed my gun at the sound.

"As God's will." I don't know why I said it; I was trying for anything I could offer that might engender his trust.

"Perhaps." His voice came from a different location, off to my right now. My eyes were adjusting to the dim light of the church. I could just make out shapes though, the pews and a table to my left, nothing human.

"She needs you."

"We want the same things, you know. To clean up this city, even a small part of it. I've done that. Now I can give her what she desires."

"Which is what, exactly?"

"Absolution. God's love."

His voice kept moving, changing direction and location as well as height, as if he knew I might try to shoot if he stood still.

"Trust me," I said.

Then a door at the far end of the chapel opened and a band of light shone in. I pointed and aimed the gun, but the priest moved through it too fast. He passed outside into the night and the door slipped closed.

I started at a run down the center of the chapel between the pews, knowing there was a small chance that Hendricks or maybe Bennett would have gotten over the high wall into the cemetery next door, that I might not be the only one in pursuit. I couldn't risk waiting. I had to get to the door and outside after him. Luckily in the light of the priest's exit, I had seen the stairs up to the altar and the metal gate that ran in front of it. I ran up the short stairs, found the gate with my hands, and jumped over it.

I reached the altar just as a door at the back of the chapel opened. Hendricks stepped through it with his flashlight blasting, having come in through the gift shop. The first thing his beam hit was Meaders, his body, confirming everything I had felt in the dark: the knife at his neck, the blood. He was gone. We had lost him, and Bowen or our code or the ways of the PD would not be able to save us, or save me from another terrible turn to my career. My status as a cop hung in the balance all of a sudden, good ideas or thoughts behind it regardless, and all I could do was barrel forward after our man.

"He ran out into the graveyard," I called to Hendricks. "Get Meaders some help."

"What are you—?"

He'd ask the obvious question, but I didn't wait to hear. I hit the narrow wooden door off to the side of the altar and blew through it. What I came out to was the burial ground bathed in floodlights: shadows curled around centuries-old headstones and statues marking graves from long ago. In this light, the priest wouldn't stay; neither would he run back toward Dolores Street. I turned to my right, toward the back of the church property, seeing ten yards of assorted graves and then a high metal fence. The fence shook with movement; the priest had to have gone over the top and was coming down the other side.

"No! Stop!" I sprinted after him. This was where a game plan and knowing Coggins's and Bennett's locations would have helped; maybe I could've chased the priest into them, but I didn't have the chance to second-guess or do anything but give pursuit.

I dodged along the thin path through the cemetery to the back wall. He moved fast, this priest, and had to be a great climber or very blessed if he had already made it over the wall. But there was no place else for him to go. I hit the wall at a run and climbed it with my hands and feet, holding my gun in my right hand as I struggled to catch the chain links and stick my feet into the holes.

Up and up I went until my body was over my own height. I gave a quick look back and down, saw Bennett come out through the same door of the chapel that I just had. "Try that way," I said, pointing toward the new church with my right foot.

"You got it, Donner."

If there was another way around to the fence's other side, maybe he'd find it.

I scrambled up the rest of the fence and got one leg up over the top. Levering it, I got my waist and both legs over, and then I saw over into a huge open schoolyard absent of any light. With the moon covered by clouds and high vines or shrubs lining its perimeter fence on two sides, shadows kept large parts of the terrain in pitch black.

I slipped over the top and found myself suddenly clinging to a side covered in ivy. Below me were the white-painted lines of a tennis court, then darkness beyond. I started climbing down, through the ivy, and kept getting caught in it. It was slow going.

Too slow.

So I decided to get down the fastest way I knew: I let go and dropped.

CHAPTER SEVENTY-FOUR

In the dark courtyard, I landed on both feet and felt a sudden pain in my shins, bent my knees on the impact, and rolled over one shoulder, knowing that my flats wouldn't help any with my landing. I came up onto one knee and one foot with my gun in both hands, checking for movement, any sight of him.

Both knees and ankles felt fine. I was still young enough to pull off a stunt like this and run away.

Slowly, I turned from my left to my right, scanning the schoolyard for anything that moved. I saw nothing, started gathering myself to get up. I turned from the fence to run and try to catch him but saw nothing. Maybe Hendricks or the others had seen something. I started to radio them, when the priest jumped at me from out of the vines.

He tackled me, grabbing my forearms, holding the gun away from us both, aiming it into the night. We rolled forward and down to my right, falling to the asphalt, and I came down onto my side with his body on top of me. I tried to free my arms to throw an elbow, but he was heavy. He jerked my arms over my head and rolled me onto my chest, then he landed on top of me, smothered me with his weight. I was sprawled out, flattened underneath.

"Don't move," he said, "and I promise not to hurt you."

I struggled, tried to move my arms and legs, working to control the gun, point it at him, or get any parts of myself free. Nothing worked; he had me pinned.

I wanted to scream. "They're coming," I said through my teeth. "They'll be right here."

"For now it is just us. So listen to me."

"I can't help you. You should know that by now. You're better off running."

My breath raced, not only from his weight but from a sudden claustrophobia, a sense of being trapped that I'd only known one other time, when I'd tried spelunking as a child with my father, crawling through narrow caves half filled with water. I had screamed my head off until my father pulled me out. Now I couldn't even scream, couldn't gather enough air into my lungs to make a sound above a whisper, a low whine.

His face brushed my hair, his voice coming from way too close to my ear. "Take me to Emily," he said. "I must bring her home."

"No." I closed my eyes, rested my left cheek against the cold, rough ground, and tried to calm myself, regain my breathing. The last thing I could do was hyperventilate. I said, "Let me go."

"She needs me. You know this. I will help her pass through His gates into heaven. Guide her. The both of us. We are ready to go home."

"I know it."

I heard sirens coming, patrol cars and an ambulance. It would all be over soon. I let go of the gun, flattened both hands against the ground.

"Donner!" Hendricks's voice came through the fence. He rattled it, shaking the ivy and the vines. I hoped he was starting to climb. It sounded that way.

The priest moved his head, making room for me to push up, even just a little. I drew a big breath in through my nose, calmed my heart. It was only a second, two, but it made a difference. I brought myself back to my body, back from the brink of panic.

Lowering my cheek to the ground again, I made room for a move. "Father," I whispered.

"Yes, my child."

That was when he turned his attention back to me. I said, "I sin," right when I jerked my head up as hard as I could, knocking the hard part of my temple into his face.

I caught him flush on the nose, and he called out.

Suddenly I could push him off, his weight shifting from the pain and shock. I rolled, rolled him onto my side so he was next to me, then I bucked my legs to create space.

I tried to crawl away, but his strength returned fast. He regained control, caught my wrists, and held me there. Then he pushed me onto my back. We rolled, and this time I came up facing him from below. He held my wrists, crawled up until he sat on my chest, straddling my hips with his legs; I was pinned but had the breath and strength to fight. I tried raising a knee but couldn't connect. I tried another head butt; he was too far away.

"Why fight?" he asked. "Don't you see this is His way? Relax, my child. Let go." He leaned down close to me, close enough for me to see wrinkles at the corners of his eyes. I could smell his breath.

"I'm not your child."

"They were all sinners. Piper, Farrow, the others. Don't you know what I did was right?"

I gave up fighting with my arms and legs and stared into his face. The face of a murderer. This was the man who'd done things I might have wanted to do, hurt the men I dreamed about hurting. I saw only pain and fear in his eyes.

Nothing there rang familiar to me. His world was one of notions and thoughts unlike my own. Something in me would never let myself do these things—the actions he carried out. The two of us were nothing alike in the end. Seeing him like this, I had no doubt.

But there was something else too, something enviable in his expression, his eyes: I saw a calm there; he was at peace—whether granted by his religion or guidance from above or through his own acts. He believed. In his acts, in Him, in what he'd done. Emily or not, whether he saved her or didn't, he believed in heaven, believed he was going there, and that meant more to him than anything he could get on earth.

In that, he was saved in a way I would never be.

He had all he wanted, even if his work wasn't done.

"She'll figure it out," I said. "Emily. I'll help her get through."

"His salvation is what she needs. And to go home."

Up above and behind the priest, I saw Hendricks crest the fence and turn toward us with his gun in his hands. It was a tough shot, one he couldn't take without risk of hitting me. "Take your hands off her!" he called.

The priest didn't move. "I saved her. Cleansed her sins."

"Take your hands off her, or I'll shoot!"

Hendricks didn't wait. His eyes met mine, and I nodded.

"I'll take care of her," I said.

Hendricks took aim on the preacher from above.

I said, "I promise."

And then he fired.

CHAPTER
SEVENTY-FIVE

The sound rang out in the night, and I felt an immense pain roll through me, there on the asphalt courts behind Mission Dolores Church. I sighed, felt a new warmth spreading across my right side. In truth, it wasn't all that bad. I welcomed it.

The priest's face registered surprise at first. Then confusion. And then *he knew*.

He knew as well as I did that he had just been shot by my partner. And so had I.

"Hendricks!" I called out, even as the pain in my side doubled. I coughed. "Get him off me."

"Donner!" Behind the priest, Hendricks came all the way up over the fence and started down, hand over hand and foot over foot in the vines—his movements impossibly slow.

"Saved her," Father Michael whispered right above me, his face close enough to kiss. Metallic-smelling blood darkened his lips.

He said, "She has His absolution. Tell her she is saved."

I would tell her, but it wouldn't help any, not in the real world.

Emily's life wouldn't be easy, with or without "salvation" and "absolution." She had a lot of digging to do to crawl back to the surface. It wouldn't be easy, even if she committed to it. But she had more life ahead of her, its joys and its falls. I would do my best to ensure that.

"I'll take care of her." I tried pushing him off me, but he had gotten heavier, his body going slack, his left side growing wet.

I wanted him to stay with us, to have plenty of time in a concrete cell to find his own absolution or the opposite.

He said, "Listen for Him. He will guide you."

I knew who he meant, knew too, what world I walked in, the feel of the hard ground below me. I pushed him off, said, "I'll take care of her, but she isn't getting saved. None of us get saved in this life. Not a one."

The priest had his way, and I had mine. He groaned as he hit the hard ground by my side.

"I'm coming, partner," Hendricks said from above. He wasn't far away.

I felt my blood pumping, knew I'd get patched up and live. We'd invent a story to fit this all together in a way Lieutenant Bowen could swallow, get the brass to believe we did right.

They had to.

We had gotten our man.

Then Hendricks hit the ground, and I saw his face above me. I laughed. Cold air rushed into my side, and I breathed it in too. Down through my throat and nose, the air rushed in and woke me like new.

"Put the cuffs on him, Danny. We want this priest to live to see a cell."

CHAPTER SEVENTY-SIX

I rode to the hospital in a separate ambulance with Hendricks beside me, holding my hand. My partner, the man who shot me, and my friend—all rolled into one. "You're going to make it," he said.

I told him I knew it, reminded him that I'd just walked across the school yard and helped direct ambulances inside to the real target of his shot. I'd have sat up on the stretcher, but the EMTs insisted on strapping me down. One of them worked my side, doing what his profession advised him to do in these situations.

They said the bullet ricocheted off something inside the priest—his spine or another bone set—and from there it had passed through one or a couple of my ribs.

"You did the right thing, Danny."

He squeezed my hand. "It'll be okay, C."

"Get someone with Emily. Don't leave her all night in the box."

"Roger that," he said. "I'll take care of it."

"Call Ibaka if you have to. She can help."

"Okay."

"And no homeless shelters or drug rehabs. We need to keep her where we can. I want to help."

"Roger, partner." He stroked my forehead, sweeping the hair out of my eyes. "I'm on it. You get some rest now." He squeezed my hand. "Trust me."

The EMT said, "This will pinch for a second."

I felt a bump under the wheels, and then the ride went smooth. My arm got warm and fuzzy, sounds started to blur. Then I couldn't hear anymore. I just saw the solid white lights of the ambulance above me and the paramedic moving.

Hendricks would take care of Emily for the time being, but so would I. She was safe.

We could tell Bowen a story about Meaders acting on his own, running to the church to seek Father Michael himself. We'd get it cleared up.

We got our man, and that was what mattered.

He was in custody. We were coming home.

EPILOGUE, SATURDAY

Ibaka picked me up at the hospital the following day. Just after lunch. The doctors wanted me to taste one final sample of their cardboard-laced food before sending me back out into the world. This was their strategy for keeping cops safe, ensuring we wouldn't be back.

Ultimately, my medical needs and their work on me were minimal: just closing up the wound, making sure no metal was left inside, and wrapping my broken rib.

Hendricks had called that morning to tell me he had a briefing with Bowen at noon. The plan was to tell him that Meaders went rogue, tried to play vigilante, that we were never sure after interviewing him whether he might be a potential accomplice or a victim. He'd say we tracked him from his home to the chapel, with Coggins and Bennett assisting, and then rushed to pursue and contain the suspect once we saw Meaders slip inside the church with him.

We hoped Bowen would roll with this, figured the least we could do was get our stories straight and make sure Coggins and Bennett did the same. If it all fell apart, I told Hendricks to assure Bowen that he had *not* fired a shot on church property but rather the school's.

"Like that's any better," he had said.

And he was right. First, it wasn't better, and second—as he reminded me—the school was parochial and actually part of the church's property after all.

So we had neither of those things going for us and would rely strictly on the plausibility of our story and whether Bowen thought we'd done a good job on the case. It wasn't the most exemplary work SFPD homicide had ever done, but it was effective. We had gotten our man, and what else did they really want? As our fine government might point out, civilian casualties were minimal.

I wouldn't lose sleep over it, not that the painkillers would be leaving any doubt about that in the next weeks.

Ibaka and I rode down in the elevator together at UCSF, a straight shot from the fifth floor to the ground—none of the public-hospital elevator shenanigans like at SF General here at privately owned UCSF.

"You're going to have to rest up for a couple weeks," Ibaka said.

"I heard that when they told me upstairs."

"Yeah, well. Bears repeating so I know you understand."

The doors opened into a bright hallway full of people, and I braced myself for the pain of walking on my own. When I took three steps and had to rest against the wall, Ibaka held my arm.

"You see what I'm saying, right?"

I nodded. "Loud and clear."

"What about that guy?" she asked. "Maybe he can come make you chicken soup."

I laughed, but that hurt, sent me into a chain of coughs, and she apologized.

"Where's Hendricks?" I asked.

"Still meeting with Bowen and the others. Talking it all through in the debriefing. He said it'll all work out, told me to tell you you'll still have a job."

Now she laughed, didn't stop for coughing either.

"Enough," I said.

"Guess you two tied things up, didn't you? Maybe went a little rogue?"

I shrugged. If the rest of the department was an indication, this wasn't unusual.

I started to walk again, hoping the car would stop her from discussing the realities of my life. I was ready for some time in the ether of painkillers. Taking a long weekend or longer to rest and recuperate wasn't going to be a problem. Nothing would get me out of bed, not even exercise, for at least . . . two weeks. I decided it then and there, based on the simple formula of taking the doctor's prognosis for my recovery, four weeks, and cutting it in half.

Simply mind over matter.

Then I'd be out on the courts again, just shooting by myself, if nothing else.

Ibaka stared at me hard, making me realize she had been talking the whole time. She knew I wasn't listening.

"You thinking about exercise, basketball, or that guy?" She wouldn't break eye contact, held me in place until I answered.

"What guy?"

"Basketball then," she said. "Know that's going to affect your shooting arm, no matter what it did to your insides." She pointed at my chest. "You're not gonna move on that side as easy for a long time."

"I can run."

"Sure you will. Stay in shape, girl. Keep those young boobs perky."

She reached for my right one, and I pulled back. Some nurses walking the other way saw us and laughed.

Ibaka said, "Don't want her to lose them."

When they had passed, I said, "They're going to be just fine. And I will too." I saw the gift shop coming up in front of us, beyond that the family waiting room and the sliding doors out to the oval driveway.

I asked, "Where's a good spot to get coffee around here?" Ibaka was getting my ire up, likely by design. She had me feeling a little better already.

"We'll get to that. First some real food and getting you home to bed. I've got strict orders from HQ."

"What happened to Emily? Where'd she stay last night?"

"All under control. Hendricks got her into a drug rehab that will monitor her progress. She'll keep. We both know it's important to you."

"Thanks."

We walked out through the lobby, past the waiting room and a couple of beat cops who nodded at us, recognizing us for their sisters, even if only by the way we walked, met their eyes.

I was a homicide cop just like my father, recognizable by sight. I had stopped a spree killer with five murders behind him. Sure, I'd had help, but also made a few good moves of my own along the way. If I didn't have my partner's respect already, I was well on my way to getting it.

Ibaka reached into my coat pocket. "Where's that celly?"

I took it out and gave it up, but not before seeing the most recent texts from Hendricks, that all was good at the Hall. Bowen was buying in.

Hell of a job, Donner, the last text read. I wanted to text back my thanks—for that, for everything—but Ibaka pulled away the phone.

"Let me see that wrist ID." She pulled my arm out and snapped a photo of the ID with my phone. "Now where is he?" She started thumbing through my messages, looking for Alan's last text.

"Oh no," I said, pulling the phone back. "I'll handle it. Don't worry."

"Do it this weekend, all right? Hendricks and I don't want to be the only ones taking care of you." She winked.

I laughed, though it still hurt. "I got it. He'll hear from me. I think I just had a whole lot of dinner dates wiped clear in my schedule."

"Good." Then she put her arm around my shoulder and pulled me close. "I want you to be okay, Clara. You hear me? A lot of us do. You're our girl."

"Okay," I said. "Okay." It meant something to hear this, felt good to know I wasn't alone. Maybe Alan would join the picture, maybe not. But yes, maybe he would.

Even without him, I had more than just a job. I had friends. Ibaka kept her arm around my shoulder as she led me out toward her car.

"He better be good at ordering takeout too," she said, "because you ain't going nowhere for a while."

"I hear you. Rest and television. That's the doctor's orders."

"Not only television," she said. "Text him. Go ahead." She stopped walking and tapped the phone in my hand.

"*I will.*" I pulled her forward. "Let's get out of here and get some real food."

As we walked, I composed a quick text to Alan in my head: something like, *Just had some date nights open up. Still interested?*

I smiled, feeling some rare late-January sun on my face. Ibaka supported me, led the way with her arm.

I felt good about the case, my job, and the work I'd done: no regrets or fears. Everything had worked out all right.

And some things were even good in my world.

Though they'd clipped the locks and gotten the ambulance in through the school gates as fast as possible, loaded the priest onto a gurney, and given him medical treatment, by the time he reached the hospital, he was gone.

I would never know if he chose that route, got help from God, or if it was all just Hendricks's bullet doing the things that bullets do inside a human being. Maybe God let Father Michael leave this existence and ascend to heaven—or whatever happened when you died—or maybe the priest just gave up living, knowing that his work, as he considered it, was done.

Done or as close as he'd get to it before I stopped him.

Hendricks's bullet had hit a major artery, severed one of the main pathways to the heart. That was the scientific explanation for his death, the reason that made sense to the medical world.

But I would never know the extent of God's role. Maybe He had let the priest off the hook in the end, called him home, back up to heaven.

Maybe some part of me believed then. Believed in Him or had started to by then, if even just a little.

ACKNOWLEDGMENTS

I want to thank all the readers who have supported my work in the past: from the podcast faithful, the Palms Mommas and Palms Daddies, to the Kindle adopters of Jess Harding, to those I've had the pleasure to meet at various readings, events, and conferences over the years. Thanks for helping me continue to fulfill and live out my dream.

Thanks to everyone who provided insight into the life and procedures of a San Francisco homicide investigator. From those I could ping for a quick answer to those who took time out to tell me their experiences on the front lines: Brian Thiem, Meaghan McMilton, Drew Valderrama, and Lea Militello.

I had some great early readers along the way: Kimberly Ewertz, Connie Howard, Rich Ferri, Charity VanDeberg, and Dan Pope. Big thanks to you all, and to my wonderful research assistant, Amy Storer.

To the team at Thomas & Mercer: big ups Kjersti Egerdahl, Tiffany Pokorny, Alan Turkus, and the lovely Jacque Ben-Zekry. My excellent editors Alison Dasho and Gracie Doyle adopted this book as their own and helped improve it immensely. Thanks so much.

Thanks to my larger family for their love and encouragement: all the Harwoods, Vogels, Leshens, Faigels, Williamsons, Kalishers, and Cohens—sending all my love.

Finally, thanks to my wife and daughter for their love, patience, and support. You're my heart. My loves.

ABOUT THE AUTHOR

Photo © 2015 Sebastian Rene

Seth Harwood is the bestselling author of *In Broad Daylight*, *Jack Wakes Up*, and *Young Junius*, as well as two collections of short stories. He is a graduate of the Iowa Writers' Workshop and teaches creative writing for Stanford Continuing Studies, Harvard Extension School, and City College of San Francisco. His early novels can be found as free podcasts on iTunes. Originally from Boston, he lives in San Francisco and western Massachusetts.

For more information, visit www.sethharwood.com.